T. F. Thiselton (Thomas Firminger Thiselton) Dyer

English Folk-lore

T. F. Thiselton (Thomas Firminger Thiselton) Dyer

English Folk-lore

ISBN/EAN: 9783744768641

Printed in Europe, USA, Canada, Australia, Japan

Cover: Foto ©Andreas Hilbeck / pixelio.de

More available books at **www.hansebooks.com**

BOGUE'S HALF-HOUR VOLUMES.

ENGLISH FOLK-LORE.

BOGUE'S HALF-HOUR VOLUMES.

OTHER VOLUMES ARE IN PREPARATION.

ENGLISH FOLK-LORE.

BY THE REV.

T. F. THISELTON DYER, M.A. Oxon.,

AUTHOR OF 'BRITISH POPULAR CUSTOMS, PAST AND PRESENT.'

LONDON:

HARDWICKE & BOGUE, 192, PICCADILLY, W.

1878.

PREFACE.

Of late years there has been a growing interest in the study of Folk-lore; and the formation at the commencement of the present year of a Folk-lore Society, is a proof of the importance that is now attached to this portion of our social and domestic history.

The present volume is not by any means intended to be exhaustive, but has been written with a view of giving the reader information in a popular form about some of those superstitions that still linger on here and there throughout the country.

T. F. THISELTON DYER.

July, 1878.

LIST OF CONTENTS.

CHAPTER I.

CHAPTER II.

CHAPTER III.

CHAPTER IV.

CHAPTER V.

CHAPTER VI.

CHAPTER VII.

CHAPTER VIII.

CHAPTER IX.

CHAPTER X.

CHAPTER XI.

CHAPTER XII.

CHAPTER XIII.

ENGLISH FOLK LORE.

CHAPTER I.

PLANTS.

THE popular and universal love for plants and flowers has associated them in all ages and countries with the chief events in the social and domestic life of man. It may be said that flowers form an important part in the formation of character, for, to quote from the herbal of a quaint old writer, Gerard, "through their beauty and variety of colour and exquisite form they do bring to a liberal and gentle mind the remembrance of honesty, comeliness, and all kinds of virtues; for it would be an unseemly thing for him that doth look upon and handle fair and beautiful things, and who frequenteth and is conversant in fair and beautiful places, to have his mind not fair also;" and, as the author of 'Episodes of Insect Life' has remarked, flowers seem, as it were, to impart a portion of their own characteristics to all things that frequent them. Hence our forefathers adopted a language for these

B

loveliest productions of the vegetable kingdom, linking
certain of them, in poetic fancy, with whatever best
answered their description in human life. The purity
of childhood was symbolised by the early snowdrop,
from its exquisite and virgin whiteness ; and the hare-
bell, that fragile little inhabitant of our country heaths
and commons, was, on account of its delicate blue
colour, considered typical of truth. Browne, in his
' Pastorals' (book ii. song 3), says :—

> " The harebell, for her stainless azured hue,
> Claims to be worn of none but who are true."

It is not difficult, then, to understand that the same
idea in the human mind which originated a language
for flowers was equally instrumental also in attaching
to them certain superstitious and whimsical notions,
which, however, in course of time developed and
assumed a very different character. It is curious how
many of these superstitions arose from isolated and
trivial occurrences, the result of coincidence or chance,
but which were considered as infallible and unmis-
takable omens of good or bad luck. If, for instance,
a child fell sick after gathering a certain wild flower
on, we will say, a Thursday, it was regarded as almost
morally wrong for parents to allow their children
henceforth even so much as to touch this flower of ill
omen. It may surprise us that our ancestors could
have ever been credulous enough to believe that the
events of their daily life were influenced by such

childish fancies as are embodied in their folk-lore, worthy only of **nurserymaids** and other uneducated persons. Yet the fact remains, **and is** attested by the abundant information bearing on the subject that **has been transmitted to us in** old books and **miscellaneous** literature. Thus, Sir Thomas Browne, **in** his short treatise on **the** ' Properties of Plants,' wisely says : " We omit to recite the many virtues and endless faculties ascribed unto plants, which **sometimes** occur in grave and serious authors ; and we shall **make** a bad transaction **for** truth to concede a verity in half." Apart, however, from **such allusions as are to** be found in our own authors, **antiquity is by no means** destitute of references **to the same** subject. Plutarch **records how a few** mules laden with parsley threw into **a complete panic a Greek force on its march against the enemy. As this herb** was **very largely used in Greece to bestrew the tombs of the dead, it acquired** an ominous **significance, and** δεῖσθαι σελίνου (to be **in** need of **parsley) was a common phrase used to denote** those **on the** point **of death.** Curious to say, it is a **belief widely** spread in some parts of Devonshire, that to **transplant** parsley is to **commit a serious offence** against the guardian genius who presides over parsley-beds, certain to be punished either on the offender **himself or some member of his family** within **the course of the** year. **Many other** superstitions are con-**nected with this herb, one of which is prevalent in** South Hampshire, **where the peasants oftentimes** absolutely refuse to **give any away,** for fear of some misfortune befalling them ; **and in the** neighbourhood **of** Cobham, Suffolk, **it** is believed that if parsley seed **be sown on** any other day than Good Friday **it** will **not come** double.*

Again, **the** practice which formerly prevailed in this country **of** sprinkling **rivers** with flowers on Holy Thursday, alluded **to by Milton in** his 'Comus,'

> "The shepherds **at** their festivals
> Carol her good deeds loud in rustic lays,
> And throw sweet garland wreaths into her stream,
> **Of** pansies, pinks, and gaudy daffodils ;"

—a remnant of which still remains **in the** well-dressing of Tissington—was, no doubt, a relic of the Fontinalia **of the** Romans, ceremonies held **in** honour of the nymphs of fountains. **Seneca says,** " Where a spring **rises or a river flows,** there **should we** build altars and offer sacrifices."

It **might** be easy to enumerate further instances to show **how the** ancients had **their plant** folk-lore, by alluding **to the many** flowers **held to be** acceptable to the **dead.** For example, amaranthus **was first** used **by the** Thessalians to adorn the grave **of** Achilles ; and, **in** Euripides, **we find** Electra complaining that Agamemnon's tomb has **never** been adorned **with** myrtle :—

> " With **no** libations, **nor with** myrtle boughs,
> Were **my** dear father's manes gratified."

---

* See p. **27.**

Virgil, describing the grief of Anchises for Marcellus, makes him say :—

> " Full canisters of fragrant lilies bring,
>   Mix'd with the purple roses of the spring.
>   Let me with fun'ral flowers his body strew."

Among the Greeks the rose was very largely used for funereal purposes, and the tombs of the dead were frequently decorated with it, under a superstitious belief that it protected the remains of the deceased. Anacreon, in his pretty little ode upon this flower, says :—

> " When pain afflicts and sickness grieves,
>   Its juice the drooping heart relieves ;
>   And after death its odours shed
>   A pleasing fragrance o'er the dead.
>   And when its withering charms decay,
>   And sinking, fading, die away,
>   Triumphant o'er the rage of time,
>   It keeps the fragrance of its prime."

The Romans, too, were so fond of the rose that they left legacies in their wills so that their tombs might be decorated with this sweetest of flowers—a practice said to have been introduced by them into England. Camden and Aubrey both speak of the churchyards in their time as thickly planted with rose trees. Evelyn, who lived at Wotton Place, near Ockley, alludes to the custom for maidens yearly to plant and deck the graves of their defunct sweethearts with rose bushes. "The Romans," says Welby, "were much at Ockley: the Roman road (Stane Street) passes through the village to this day; so that we are inclined to agree with Mr. Manning, the historian of Surrey, that the rose-planting at Ockley is a relic of a Roman custom." In Wales, it is customary to plant the white rose on the grave of an unmarried female; and a red rose is appropriated to anyone distinguished for benevolence of character.

At the present day flowers are still largely used by us at funerals on account of their symbolical meaning. The bay is an emblem of the resurrection, for, according to Sir Thomas Browne, when seemingly dead, it will revive from the root, and its dry leaves resume their wonted vitality. The yew tree and cypress, often planted in churchyards, are symbolical of life from their perpetual verdure. The rosemary is still occasionally used at funerals, probably, says Nares, "from its odour, and as a token of remembrance of the deceased"—a practice thus touchingly alluded to by Gay :—

> " To shew their love, the neighbours far and near
> Followed, with wistful look, the damsel's bier :
> Sprigg'd rosemary the lads and lasses bore,
> While dismally the parson walked before."

In South Lancashire, we are informed, rosemary may, even now-a-days, be seen at many a funeral, the pleasing relic of an old and nearly obsolete custom. Mr. Brierley, in his 'Chronicles of Warwerlow,' in describing the funeral of the Old Huntsman, has the following remarks which bear on the subject :—" The old huntsmen gathered round the grave in a solid ring, each holding his dog by the slip, and when the final *ashes to ashes, dust to dust* was pronounced, the whole strew their sprigs of rosemary over the coffin, then raising their heads, gave a simultaneous 'yo-ho! tally-ho!' the sound of which became heightened by the dogs joining their voices, as they rung the last cry over their 'earthed' companion."

Pepys, in his 'Diary' (vol. i. p. 260), says : " Between Gosport and Southampton we observed a little church-yard where the graves are accustomed to be all sowed with sage." Our forefathers, it appears, had a great idea of the virtues of sage. The old monkish line[*] runs thus :—

" Cur morietur homo cui crescit *salvia* in horto ?"

In some parts of Wales it is customary for funerals to be preceded by a female carrying sprigs of bay, the leaves of which she sprinkles at intervals along the road which the corpse is to travel.

A pretty custom was practised by our ancestors of carrying garlands of sweet flowers at the funerals of beloved relatives and friends ; and not only strewing them on the coffin, but planting them permanently on the grave, as already alluded to, which gave the churchyards a pleasing and picturesque appearance.

This custom is said to owe its origin to an ancient belief that Paradise is planted with fragrant flowers.

[*] See Southey's 'Commonplace Book,' 1850, 3rd series, p. 785, *note.*

The description given in the legend of Sir Owain, of the celestial Paradise at which the blessed arrive after passing through purgatory, refers to this superstition :—

> "Fair were her erbers with floures ;
> Rose and lili divers colours,
> Primros and parvink,
> Mint, feverfoy, and eglenterre,
> Colombin and mother-wer,
> Than ani man may bithenke.
> It berth erbes of other maner,
> Than ani in erth groweth here,
> Though that is best of priis ;
> Evermore thai grene springeth,
> For winter no sooner it no clingeth,
> And sweeter than licorice."

In some cases flowers have an ominous significance. Thus, in Suffolk, to sleep in a room with the white thorn in bloom in it, during the month of May, will, to use the local phrase, " Surely be followed by some great misfortune," and according to an old proverb :—

> "If you sweep the house with blossomed broom in May,
> You're sure to sweep the head of the house away."

By the Northamptonshire peasantry the blooming of the apple tree, after the fruit is ripe, is regarded as a sure omen of death :—

> " A bloom upon the apple tree when the apples are ripe,
> Is a sure termination to somebody's life."

Even, too, the rose is not without its superstitions, for to scatter its leaves on the ground has been held to be most unlucky. As an illustration of this we

may quote the following from the 'Life and Correspondence of M. G. Lewis.' The lady to whom
the portent happened, was Miss Ray, or Reay,
who was murdered at the piazza entrance of Covent
Garden Theatre, by a man named Hackman (April 7,
1779) :—" When the carriage was announced and she
was adjusting her dress, Mrs. Lewis happened to
make some remark on a beautiful rose which Miss
Ray wore in her bosom. Just as the words were
uttered, the flower fell to the ground. She immediately stooped to regain it, but as she picked it up,
the red leaves scattered themselves on the carpet, and
the stalk alone remained in her hand. The poor girl,
who had been depressed in spirits before, was evidently affected by this incident, and said in a slightly
faltering voice, ' I trust I am not to consider this as
an evil omen!' But soon rallying, she expressed to
Mrs. Lewis, in a cheerful tone, her hope that they
would meet again after the theatre—a hope, alas!
which it was decreed should not be realised." A
note informs the reader that in certain districts of
Italy the red rose is considered as an emblem of an
early death; and it is an evil omen to scatter its
leaves on the ground.*

In Devonshire there is a curious superstition that it
is unlucky to plant a bed of lilies of the valley, as the
person doing so will probably die in the course of the
next twelve months; and in some parts it is believed

* See 'Gentleman's Magazine,' vol. xlix. p. 210.

that if in a row of beans, one should chance to come up white (instead of green), there will be a death in the family within the year.

In Scotland, says a correspondent of 'Notes and Queries,' boys prefer a herding stick of ash to any other wood, as in throwing it at their cattle, it is sure not to strike on a vital part, and so kill or injure the animal, which it is commonly supposed a stick of any other wood might, perhaps, do :—

> " Rowan, ash, and red thread,
>   Keep the devils frae their speed."

Lupton, in his third book of 'Notable Things' (1660), says :—" If a firr tree be touched, withered, or burned with lightning, it signifies that the master or mistresse thereof shall shortly dye ;" and according to Shakspeare (' Richard II.') the withering of the bay tree was a certain omen of death :—

> " 'Tis thought the king is dead ; we will not stay.
>   The bay trees in our country are all withered."

Formerly, too, it was a common idea that when roses and violets flourished in autumn, there would be some epidemic in the ensuing year ; whilst the falling of the leaves of a peach tree or elm tree was considered to predict a murrain. In some parts we are told, on the authority of Brand, there is a vulgar prejudice that if boys be beaten with an elder stick, their growth is sure to be checked.

The following allusion to divination by means of a daffodil we find mentioned in Herrick's ' Hesperides ' :

> " When a daffadill I see
> Hanging down her head t'wards me,
> Guess I may what I must be :
> First, I shall decline my head ;
> Secondly, I shall be dead ;
> Lastly, safely buried."

In Worcestershire we are informed that farmers were in the habit of taking their bough of mistletoe and giving it to the cow that first calved after New Year's Day, as this act was supposed to avert ill-luck from the whole dairy. In the same county it is regarded as most unlucky in spring-time to take less than a handful of violets or primroses into a farmer's house, as neglect of this rule is supposed to bring inevitable destruction on his brood of young ducks and chickens.

A notion prevails among the Norfolk farmers, that to bring into the house a bunch of the grass called "maiden-hair," or, as it is termed, "dudder grass," is most sure to bring with it ill-luck. In Dorsetshire * it is a common idea that if the plant "bergamot" be kept in a house, it will never be free from sickness.

A flowering myrtle is believed in Somersetshire to be a great acquisition to a house, and the saying connected with it is this :—" The myrtle is the luckiest plant to have in your window. Water it every morning, and be proud of it." In Surrey, and elsewhere,

---

* ' Notes and Queries,' 4th series, vol. viii. p. 58.

we are informed of the following superstition : *—" Cut a fern-root slantwise, and you'll see a picture of an oak tree ; the more perfect, the luckier chance for you."

In Wales it is considered highly lucky for the peasantry to have the roofs of their houses covered with the house-leek, as it is supposed to preserve and protect them from disease, and to insure prosperity. In some parts of Cornwall one may frequently hear the following charm made use of for invoking good luck :—

> " Even ash, I thee do pluck,
> Hoping thus to meet good luck.
> If no luck I get from thee,
> I shall wish thee on the tree."

Grose tells us, the elder is supposed to possess the virtue of protecting persons bearing a branch of it from the charms of witches. From this superstition no doubt originates the reason why so many of these trees are planted by the sides of our rural cottages.

According to a MS. on magic, preserved in the Chetham Library at Manchester, " the herb pimpernell is good to prevent witchcraft, as Mother Bumby doth affirme." The following lines may be used when it is gathered :—

> " Herbe pimpernell, I have thee found,
> Growing upon Christ Jesus' ground :
> The same guift the Lord Jesus gave unto thee,
> When He shed His blood on the tree.
> Arise up, pimpernell, and goe with me,
> And God blesse me,
> And all that shall were thee.   Amen.

---

* 'Notes and Queries,' 1st series, vol. vii. p. 152.

Saying this fifteen dayes together, twice a day, morning earlye fasting, and in the evening full."

The snapdragon, which is much cultivated in gardens on account of its showy flowers, is, in many places, said to have a supernatural influence, and to possess the power of destroying charms. Sometimes, in the North of England, one may see hung up in stables a branch of "wiggin," i. e. mountain ash, as it is considered a famous charm against witchcraft. Anciently, too, collars of mountain ash were put upon the necks of the cattle to keep off witches.* In Scotland a particular virtue is supposed to rest with the possessor of a piece of four-bladed clover, of knowing when anybody is practising witchcraft on him ; and Aubrey in his 'Miscellanies' has the following :

> " Vervain and dill
> Hinders witches from their will."

Good fortune is, in some places, supposed to accrue to the finder not only of four-bladed clover, but double-leaved ash, and green-topped seave,† as amusingly expressed in the following couplet :—

> " With a four-leav'd clover, double-topp'd ash, and green-topp'd seave,
> You may go before the queen's daughter without asking leave."

Rosemary worn about the body is said to strengthen the memory, and to add to the success of the wearer in anything he may undertake.

* See Scatherd's 'History of Morley,' 1830, p. 195.
† Seaves are the rushes of which rush-lights or rush-candles are made. 'Notes and Queries,' 3rd series, vol. i. p. 298.

Some plants are said to indicate the character of those in whose locality they grow. Thus Miss Plues, in her ' Rambles in Search of Wild Flowers,' tells us that there is a popular superstition that wherever the moonwort (the purple honesty, *Lunaria annua*) flourishes, the cultivators of the garden are exceedingly honest. In Leicestershire there is a saying to the following effect : " Sleep in a bean-field all night if you want to have awful dreams, or go crazy."

"Speaking to a lady," says a correspondent of the ' Athenæum' (Feb. 5th, 1848), " of the difficulty which I always had found in getting a slip of myrtle to grow, she directly accounted for my failure by observing that perhaps I had not spread the tail (or skirt) of my dress and looked proud during the time I was planting it. It is a popular belief in Somersetshire that unless a slip of myrtle is so planted, it will never take root."

Many, too, are the love divinations, still practised here and there throughout the country by means of plants. In Devonshire the following saying is very prevalent :—

> " An even-leaved ash,
>   And a four-leaved clover,
> You'll see your true love
> 'Fore the day is over."

In Derbyshire, when a young woman wishes to know who her future husband is to be, she must go into the churchyard at midnight on St. Valentine's Eve, and as the clock strikes twelve run round the

church repeating, without stopping, the following
lines :—

> "I sow hempseed, hempseed I sow ;
> He that loves me best
> Come and after me mow."

Presently the figure of her lover is supposed to appear
and follow her. A practice very similar to this was kept
up in some parts of the country on Midsummer Eve.

A curious divination is practised in Berwickshire by
means of "kemps," i.e. spikes of the ribwort plantain.
Two spikes—one representing the lad, the other the
lass—must be taken, Mr. Henderson* tells us, in full
bloom, and after being bereft of every appearance of
bloom, should be wrapped in a dock-leaf, and laid
beneath a stone. If, on the following morning, the
spikes appear in bloom, then, according to the popular
belief, there will be "Aye love between them twae."
This rite has been practised also in Northamptonshire. Thus Clare, in his 'Shepherd's Calendar,'
says :—

> " Or, trying simple charms and spells,
> Which rural superstition tells,
> They pull the little blossom threads
> From out the knotweed's button heads,
> And put the husk, with many a smile,
> In their white bosoms for a while.
> Then, if they guess aright the swain
> Their love's sweet fancies try to gain,
> 'Tis said that ere it lies an hour,
> 'Twill blossom with a second flower,
> And from the bosom's handkerchief
> Bloom as it ne'er had lost a leaf."

---

* ' Folk-Lore of the Northern Counties,' p. 77.

The same author informs us that a similar superstition is practised with the primrose. " Let a youth or maiden pull from its stalks the flower, and after cutting off the tops of the stamens with a pair of scissors, lay it in a secret place, where no human eye can see it. Let him think through the day, and dream through the night, of his sweetheart, and then, on looking at it the next day, if he find the stamens shot out to their former height, success will attend him in love ; if not, he can only expect disappointment."

Formerly, says Halliwell,* girls used to have a method of divination with a " St. Thomas's onion." They peeled the onion, wrapped it up in a clean handkerchief, and then placing it under their heads, said the following lines :—

> " Good St. Thomas, do me right,
> And see my true love come to-night,
> That I may see him in the face,
> And him in my kind arms embrace."

It was also, in days gone by, a not uncommon practice for girls, on retiring to rest at night, to place daisy-roots under their pillow, and to hang their shoes outside of the window, in order to dream of their lovers. In Devonshire, the young people pluck a rose on Midsummer Day and put it away, believing that if it is not looked at, it will be found as fresh on Christmas Day as when gathered. It is then worn at church, when their intended partner is supposed to come and

* 'Popular Rhymes,' 1849, p. 224.

take it.*   In many of the villages, too, of this county, girls are in the habit of plucking yarrow from a man's grave, believing that if they place it under their pillow, and repeat the following lines, their lovers will appear to them in their dreams:—

> "Yarrow, sweet yarrow, the first that I have found,
> And in the name of Jesus I pluck it from the ground.
> As Joseph loved sweet Mary, and took her for his dear,
> So in a dream this night, I hope, my true love will appear."

In Cambridgeshire† the following charm is used by young men and women who are anxious of ascertaining the names of their future husbands or wives :—

> "A clover, a clover of two,
> Put it on your right shoe ;
> The first young man (woman) you meet,
> In field, street, or lane,
> You'll have him (her) or one of his (her) name."

The "clover of two" means a piece of clover with only two leaves upon it.

It is a common notion that in Leap Year broad beans grow the wrong way—that is, the seed is set in the pods in quite the contrary way to what it is in other years. The reason of this is, "because it is the ladies' year ; they (the beans) always lay the wrong way in leap year"—the reference, of course, being to the privilege possessed by the fair sex of making love at this time. In a curious work, entitled 'Courtship, Love, and Matrimonie,' printed in the

* Whitcombe's 'Bygone Days in Devonshire and Cornwall.'
† Also in Norfolk and Suffolk.

C

year 1606, this practice is thus alluded to :—" Albeit
it is nowe become a part of the common lawe in
regard to social relations of life, that as often as every
bissextile year doth return, the ladyes have the sole
privilege, during the time it continueth, of making
love unto the men, which they doe either by words or
lookes, as to them it seemeth proper."

Herrick, in his ' Hesperides,' speaking of a bride,
says :—

> " She must no more a-maying ;
> Or, by rosebuds divine,
> Who'l be her valentine ?"

It was, too, an old custom among countrymen to
try whether they should succeed with their sweethearts by carrying bachelors' buttons (the flower of
Lychnis kind so called) in their pockets. They
judged of their good or bad success by their growing
or not.   Thus Shakspeare, in his ' Merry Wives of
Windsor ' (act iii. sc. 2), says :—

> " 'Tis in his buttons he will carry it."

Mr. Warter, in one of his notes in Southey's
Commonplace Book ' (1851, 4th S., p. 244), tells us
that in his time the custom was common in Shropshire and Staffordshire.

A practice called " peascod wooing " was formerly
very often to be met with.   The cook, when shelling
green peas, would, if she chanced to find a pod
having *nine,* lay it on the lintel of the kitchen door,

and the first man who **entered** was believed to be
her future husband. A Cumbrian girl, **says** Brand,
"when her lover proves unfaithful to her, is, by way
of consolation, rubbed with peas-straw by the neighbouring **lads.**" This explains a line in a beautiful
Scottish pastoral which runs thus :—

> " If you meet a bonnie lassie,
>   Gie her a kiss, and let her **gae** ;
> If you meet **a** dirty hussey,
>   Fie, gae **rub** her **o'er** wi' strae !"

The divination by **peascod** is alluded to by
Gay :—

> " As peascod once I pluck'd, **I** chanced **to see**
> One that was closely fill'd with three **times three** ;
> Which, when I cropp'd, I safely home convey'd,
> And o'er the door the spell in secret laid.
> The **latch** mov'd up, when who should first come **in,**
> **But in** his proper person—Lubberkin !"

It was an olden superstition, says Mr. **Coles, in his**
interesting work, 'Finger Ring Lore' (p. 169), **that
the bending of the leaves to the right or to** the left of
the **orpine plants, or** *Midsummer* **Men, as they were**
called (*Telephium*), would never **fail to tell whether a**
lover was **true** or false. **In an old poem, the 'Cottage**
Girl,' we find :—

> " Oft on a shrub she cast her eye,
>   That spoke her true love's secret sigh ;
>   Or else, **alas !** too plainly told
>   **Her true** love's faithless heart was cold."

In 1861 **a** small gold ring **was exhibited** at the
Society of Antiquaries (found in **a** ploughed field near

Cawood, in **Yorkshire**), **which had for a** device two orpine plants joined together **by a** true-love knot, with a motto above : "Ma fiance velt," **my** sweetheart wills, or is desirous. The stalks of the plants were bent to each other, **in** token, that the parties represented **by** them **were to** come together in marriage.

The custom of throwing the peel **of an** apple over **the head,** says **Mr. Conway,*** "marriage **or** single **blessedness being foretold by its** remaining entire or **breaking, and that of finding in a peel so** cast the **initial of the** coming sweetheart, **is well** known in **England and America."**

In Lancashire, in order to ascertain the abode of a **lover, the anxious inquirer moves round** in a circle, at **the same time squeezing an** apple pippin between the **finger and thumb. This, on** pressure being employed, **flies from the** rind, **in the** supposed direction of the **lover's residence. In the** meanwhile **the** following **rhyme is repeated :—**

> " Pippin, pippin, paradise.
>   Tell me where my true love lies !
>   East, west, north, or south,
>   Pilling brig or Cocker mouth."

We must not omit to mention some of the magic **influences ascribed to plants for curing** various **diseases.** Gerard tells **us that the** willow herb stops **bleeding, heals wounds, and drives away** snakes, **gnats, and flies. In some parts of Lincolnshire†** it is

believed that cork has the power of keeping off cramp.
It is placed between the bed and the mattresses, or
even between the sheets ; or cork garters are made by
sewing together a series of thin discs of cork between
two silk ribbons. A potato carried in the trousers
pocket is regarded by many as an infallible cure for
rheumatism. In various parts of England it is believed
that fuller's teazle (*Dipsacus fullonum*) is a certain
remedy for ague. In autumn, if the heads be opened
longitudinally, a little worm may often be discovered
buried in the very centre. Three, five, or seven of
these—always an odd number—must be taken,
sealed up in a quill, and worn every day as an amulet.
In some places, the following charm is used to prevent
a thorn from festering :—

> "Our Saviour was of a Virgin born ;
> His head was crowned with a crown of thorns ;
> It never canker'd nor fester'd at all,
> And I hope in Christ Jesus this never shaull (shall)."

In Cornwall the club-moss (*Lycopodium mun-
datum*) if properly gathered, is considered " good
against all diseases of the eyes." The gathering is
regarded, says Hunt, in his amusing book, ' Popular
Romances of the West of England ' (1871, p. 415), as
a mystery, and if any man ventures to write the secret,
the virtues of the moss avail him no more. In spite
of this, however, Mr. Hunt has boldly revealed to his
readers this wonderful secret, the mystery of which, to
quote his own words, consists as follows : " On the

third day of the moon, when the thin crescent is seen for the first time, show it the knife with which the moss is to be cut, and repeat :—

> " As Christ heal'd the issue of blood,
> Do thou cut what thou cuttest for good."

"At sun-down, having carefully washed the hands, the club-moss is to be cut kneeling. It is to be carefully wrapped in a white cloth, and subsequently boiled in some water taken from the spring nearest to its place of growth. This may be used as a fomentation. Or the club-moss may be made into an ointment, with butter made from the milk of a new cow."

A decoction of the nettle, often known as St. Fabian's nettle, is a favourable prescription among countrywomen for consumption ; and in Scotland there is a story related of a mermaid of the Firth of Clyde who, on seeing the funeral of a young girl who had died of consumption, exclaimed :—

> " If they wad drink nettles in March,
> And eat muggins* in May,
> Sae mony braw maidens
> Wad not go to clay."

Speaking of the ivy-plant, Gerard tells us that its " leaves laid in steepe in water for a day and a night's space, helpe sore and smarting waterish eyes, if they be bathed and washed with the water wherein they have been infused." In the county of Salop children affected with whooping cough are allowed to drink

* Mugwort.

all they require out of drinking cups made from the wood of the common **ivy,** this being considered an infallible remedy. "**I** once knew an old gentleman," says a correspondent **of** ' Notes and Queries,' "**who** being fond **of** turning as an amusement, was **accus**tomed to supply his neighbours with these drinking cups, and whose brother always supplied him with the wood, cut **from his own** plantation. It is necessary, in order to be effective, that the ivy from which the cups are made should be cut at some particular change of the moon, or hour of the night." In many parts of England we **find the** following piece of advice still carefully adopted :—

> " He that would live for aye,
> Must eat sage in May."

The passing **of children** through holes in the **earth,** rocks, or trees, once **an** established **rite, is still practised in** various parts **of** Cornwall and Devonshire. A correspondent **in the** ' Report and **Trans**actions ' of the Devonshire Association (1876, vol. viii. p. 54), **says :—**" Passing lately through a wood at Spitchwich, near Ashburton, a remark **on** some peculiarity **in** an ash sapling **led to** the explanation from **the** gamekeeper that the tree had been instrumental **in the cure of a** ruptured infant, and **he** afterwards pointed **out** four or five others **that had** served the same good purpose. With evidently perfect faith in the story, he related that **when a** young infant is afflicted with rupture a small maiden ash is split for a length of five or six feet down the middle, as it stands growing in the wood. The split halves being forced asunder, the naked infant, squalling as becomes him, is passed three times in the same direction through the opening, and henceforth the defect is cured. The tree is then restored to its natural shape, and as it thrives so the child thrives. My informant instanced several well-known young men of the neighbourhood who had been subjected to the process in their babyhood, and had grown up strong and healthy. In one case, in which the tree had evidently suffered from the experiment, he referred to the deformity and sickly growth of the youth who had been passed through it." White, in his 'Natural History of Selborne' (1853, p. 144), describes very fully this odd practice. He says :—" In a farmyard near the middle of this village stands, at this day, a row of pollard ashes, which, by the seams and long cicatrices down their sides, manifestly show that, in former times, they have been cleft asunder. These trees, when young and flexible, were severed and held open by wedges, while ruptured children, stripped naked, were pushed through the apertures, under a persuasion that, by such a process, the poor babes would be cured of their infirmity. As soon as the operation was over, the tree, in the suffering part, was plastered with loam, and carefully swathed up. If the parts coalesced and soldered together, as usually fell out, where the feat was performed with any adroitness at all, the party was cured; but where the cleft continued to gape, the operation, it was supposed, would prove ineffectual. Having occasion to enlarge my garden not long since, I cut down two or three such trees, one of which did not grow together." Reverting, however, to Cornwall, once more, there is in the parish of Madron a curious Druidical remain known as the " Mean-an-Tol," that is, " The Stone of the Hole." It is an upright circular block of granite, about eight inches in thickness, and in its centre has a circular hole, about eighteen inches in diameter. Formerly a curious custom prevailed of putting children through the hole a certain number of times, under the notion that this act would cure them of the complaint from which they might be suffering. The stone went by the name of the Creeping Stone.

Plants are, moreover, said to be good barometers; and many a country peasant places far more reliance in their appearance than in the various scientific contrivances of modern times for prognosticating what the coming weather is to be. Trefoil, or clover-grass, is said to seem rough to the touch when stormy and tempestuous weather is at hand; and its leaves, says Willsford (' Nature's Secrets '), " start and rise up, as if it were afraid of an assault." Heliotropes and marigolds, repeats the same writer, " do not only presage stormy weather by closing or contracting together their leaves, but turn towards the sun's rays all the day, and in the evening shut up shop." Coles, in his introduction to the 'Knowledge of Plants,' tells us that if the down flies off coltsfoot, dandelion, and thistles, when there is no wind, it is a certain sign of rain. The pimpernel, too, is a very favourite flower in weather-lore, and according to the proverb,—

" No heart can think, no tongue can tell,
The virtues of the pimpernel."

Gerard, in his 'Herbal' (1st ed. p. 494), informs us that country people prognosticated fine or wet weather by noticing in the morning whether the flowers of the pimpernel were open or closed. This practice is still, however, common nearly everywhere.

An opinion prevails in many quarters that an elder tree is safe from the effects of lightning, in allusion to which the 'Stamford Mercury' of July 19th, 1861, says :—" This notion, whether true or not, received confirmation a few days ago, when the electric fluid struck a thornbush in which an elder had grown up, and become intermixed ; but which escaped perfectly unscathed, though the thorn was completely destroyed." Sir Thomas Browne mentions, also, the bay as possessing the property of " protecting from the mischief of lightning and thunder, a quality common with the fig tree, eagle, and skin of a seal." He adds, however : —" against so famous a quality, Vicomercatus produceth experiment of a bay tree blasted in Italy."

In addition, also, to the curious weather predictions

connected with plants and flowers, we find credulous
farmers oftentimes divining the success of their crops
by means of them. In Gloucestershire, for instance,
it is a common saying that after the mulberry tree
has shown green leaf there will be no more frost ; and
"it ain't spring until you can plant your foot upon
twelve daisies," is a proverb still very prevalent.
Formerly, the leafing of the elm was made to regulate
operations both in the field and garden, and in the
'Field' of April 28th, 1866, occurs the following
rhyme :—

> " When the elmen leaf is as big as a mouse's ear,
> Then to sow barley never fear.
> When the elmen leaf is as big as an ox's eye,
> Then say I, ' Hie, boys, hie !' "

The Kentish people, when speaking, in spring time,
of the oak and ash coming into leaf, say :—

> " Oak, smoke ;
> Ash, squash : "

and believe that if the oak is the first to come out,
the summer will be hot ; if the ash, that it will be wet.

A belief was very prevalent, at one time, that
certain trees put forth their flowers on Christmas Day.
In the 'Gentleman's Magazine,' 1753, we are told that
at Quainton, in Buckinghamshire, above two thousand
people went with lanterns and candles to view a blackthorn in that neighbourhood—said to be a slip from
the famous Glastonbury thorn—as it was always supposed to bud on the 24th December, to be full-blown

the next day, and to die off that night. The people, however, finding no appearance of a bud, agreed that December 25th (new style) could not be the right Christmas Day, and accordingly refused either to go to church or to entertain their friends on that day as usual. At length the affair became so serious that the ministers of the neighbouring villages, in order to appease them, thought it prudent to give notice that Old Christmas Day should be observed as before. Collinson, in his 'History of Somersetshire' (1791), alludes to the miraculous walnut tree which grew in the abbey churchyard of Glastonbury, and never budded before the Feast of St. Barnabas, viz. 11th of June, but on that very day shot forth leaves and flourished. A similar sort of superstition is current at Oldenburg, where it is believed that the ash appears without its red buds on St. John's Day, because the witches eat them the night before, on their way to the orgies of Walpurgisnacht.* The roses of summer were said to fade away about St. Mary Magdalene's Day. The passion flower, too, was believed to blossom about Holy Rood Day, and allusions to this superstition are frequently to be met with in olden writers. The Shropshire peasantry say that the common brake only flowers once a year, viz. on Michaelmas Eve at midnight, when it puts forth a small *blue* flower, which disappears with the dawn of day.†

* See 'Fraser's Magazine,' 1870, vol. ii. p. 597.
† 'Notes and Queries,' 2nd series, vol. xii. p. 501.

In South-east Devon and the neighbourhood,* a curious legend is, we learn, current among the farmers respecting St. Dunstan and the apple trees. It is said that he bought up a quantity of barley and therewith made beer. The Devil, knowing that the Saint would naturally desire to get a good sale for his beer which he had just brewed, went to him, and said that if he would sell himself to him, then he (the Devil) would go and blight all the apple trees; so that there should be no cider, and consequently there would be a far greater demand for beer. St. Dunstan, naturally wishing to drive a brisk trade in his beer, accepted at once the offer; but stipulated that the trees should be blighted in three days, which days fell on the 17th, 18th, and 19th of May. In the almanacs the 19th is marked as St. Dunstan's Day, and as about this time the apple trees are in blossom, many anxious allusions are generally made to St. Dunstan; and should, as is sometimes the case, a sharp frost nip the apple blossoms, they believe they know who has been at the bottom of the mischief. There seem to be several versions of this legendary superstition. According to some, on a certain night in June, three powerful witches pass through the air, and if they drop certain charms on the blossoming orchards, the crops will be blighted.† In other parts of the county this is known as " Frankum's night," and

* 'Notes and Queries,' 2nd series, vol. xii. p. 303.
† 'Fraser's Magazine,' 1873, p. 778.

the story* is that "long ago, on this night, one Frankum made 'a sacrifice' in his orchard with the object of getting a specially fine crop. His spells were answered by a blight; and the night is thus regarded as most critical."

The following extract from the 'Tablet' of July 26th, 1856, is curious as being a specimen of the almost incredulous superstition of modern times: "Will it be credited that thousands of people have during the past week crowded a certain road in the neighbourhood of Melling, near Ormskirk, to inspect a sycamore tree which has burst its bark, and the sap protrudes in a shape resembling a man's head? Rumours spread abroad that it was the re-appearance of Palmer, who had come again, because he was buried without a coffin. Some inns in the neighbourhood of this sin- gular tree reaped a rich harvest."

It is a common persuasion, says Halliwell (' Popular Rhymes '), amongst country people that whipping a walnut tree tends to increase the produce and im- prove the flavour of the fruit. This belief is embodied in the following not very complimentary distich :—

> " A woman, a spaniel, and a walnut tree,
>   The more you whip them the better they be."

The mandrake, so called from the German *man- dragen*, resembling man, was formerly the source of much superstition throughout the south of England

* 'Fraser's Magazine,' 1873, p. 778.

—the belief being that it had a human heart at its root.* It was once believed† that the person who pulled the mandrake would instantaneously fall dead ; that the root shrieked or groaned when separated from the earth ; and that whoever heard the shriek died shortly after, or became afflicted with madness ; or to quote from Shakspeare ('Romeo and Juliet') :—

> " Torn out of the earth,
> That living mortals, hearing them, run mad."

Shakspeare also speaks of its power as an opiate. It is said, says Mr. Conway, "by popular superstitions in some places, to be perpetually watched over by Satan, and if it be pulled up at certain holy times, and with certain invocations, the Evil Spirit will appear to do the bidding of the practitioner."

The *Virgula Divinatoria,* or divining rod, is a forked branch in the form of a Y, cut off an hazel stick, by means of which people have pretended to discover mines, springs, &c., underground. It is much employed in our mining districts for the discovery of hidden treasure. In Cornwall, for instance, the miners place much confidence in its indications, and even educated intelligent men oftentimes rely on its supposed virtues. Pryce, in his 'Mineralogia Cornubiensis,' tells us that many mines have been discovered by the rod, and quotes several ; but after

---

* See 'Mystic Trees and Flowers,' by Mr. M. D. Conway. 'Fraser's Magazine,' 1870, vol. ii. p. 705.

† Timbs's 'Things not Generally Known,' 1856, p. 103.

a long account of the method of cutting, tying, and using it, rejects it, because "Cornwall is so plentifully stored with tin and copper lodes, that some accident every week discovers to us a fresh vein," and because "a grain of metal attracts the rod as strongly as a pound, for which reason it has been found to dip equally to a poor as to a rich lode." In Lancashire and Cumberland the power of the divining rod is much believed in, and also in other parts of England. The method of using it is this :—the small ends being crooked, are, says a writer in the 'Eclectic Review' (September, 1855), to be held in the hands, in a position flat or parallel to the horizon, and the upper part at an elevation having an angle to it of about seventy degrees. The rod must be grasped strongly and steadily, and then the operator walks over the ground ; when he crosses a lode, its bending is supposed to indicate the presence thereof. The position of the hands in holding the rod is a constrained one—it is not easy to describe it ; but the result is, that the hands, from weariness speedily induced in the muscles, grasp the end of the twig yet more rigidly, and thus is produced the mysterious bending. The phenomena of the divining rod and table-turning are of precisely the same character, and both are referable to an involuntary muscular action resulting from a fixedness of idea. These experiments with the divining rod are always made in a district known to be metalliferous, and the chances therefore are greatly in favour of its bending over or near a mineral lode. **From a** paper in Tilloch's ' Philosophical Magazine,' **by** William Philips (vol. xiii. 309), on the divining rod, **it** appears that it was advocated by De Thouvenel, in France, in the eighteenth **century,** and soon after, in our own country, by a philosopher of unimpeachable veracity, **Mr. Cookworthy,** of Plymouth.* In Sheppard's ' Epigrams ' **(1651) we find the following :—**

> " Some sorcerers do **boast they have rod,**
> Gather'd with vows and **sacrifice,**
> And (borne about) will **strangely nod**
> To hidden treasure **where it lies.**
> Mankind **is** (sure) that **rod** divine,
> For **to the wealthiest (ever)** they incline."

In the ' Gentleman's Magazine ' **(1752, vol. xxii.**
p. **77) there is told an** amusing anecdote about **M. Linnæus.** "When he was upon his voyage to **Scania, hearing his secretary** highly extol the virtues **of his divining wand, was** willing **to** convince him of **its insufficiency, and for** that **purpose** concealed a **purse of one hundred ducats under a ranunculus,** which **grew up by itself in a meadow, and bid the** secretary find **it if he could. The** wand **discovered** nothing, **and Linnæus's mark was soon** trampled down **by the company who were present, so** that when **Linnæus went to** finish **the experiment by** fetching **the gold himself, he was utterly at a loss** where to **find it.** The man **with the wand** assisted him, and

---

told him that it could not lie in the way they were going, but quite the contrary, so pursued the direction of the wand, and actually dug out the gold. Linnæus adds that such another experiment would be sufficient to make a proselyte of him."

There are many traditions connected with the wood of the cross on which our Lord was crucified.* The most common belief in England is, that it was made of aspen (*Populus tremula*), and that the leaves have trembled ever since at the recollection of their guilt. In the West of England there is a tradition that the cross was made of mistletoe, which until this time had been a fine forest tree, but was condemned henceforth to lead a parasitical existence. The gipsies believe that the cross was made of ash. Some again are of opinion that it was made of four kinds of wood, signifying the four quarters of the globe, or all mankind, and consisted of the palm, the cedar, the olive, and the cypress ; hence the line,—

"Ligna crucis palma, cedrus, cupressus, oliva."

In the place of the palm and the olive, some place the pine and the box ; whilst others again are of opinion that it was made entirely of oak. . A correspondent of 'Notes and Queries' says that according to another superstition, the cross was made of elder ; and that woodmen look carefully into the faggots

* See an interesting paper on this subject in ' Whitaker's Journal,' April 22nd, 1866.

before they burn them, in case there should be any of this wood in them. "Speaking to some little children," says a writer in the 'Book of Days,' "one day about the danger of taking shelter under trees during a thunderstorm, one of them said it was not so with all the trees, 'For,' said he, 'you will be quite safe under an *elder tree*, because the cross was made of that, and so the lightning never strikes it.'" The elder, too, has been supposed to be the tree on which Judas hanged himself :—

> " Judas, he japed
> With Jewen silver,
> And sithen *on an eller*
> Hanged hymselve." *

According to others it was a fig tree.

In Cheshire the *Arum maculatum* is called Gethsemane, because it is said to have been growing at the foot of the cross, and to have received on its leaves some drops of blood :—

> "Those deep unwrought marks,
> The villager will tell thee,
> Are the flower's portion from the atoning blood
> On Calvary shed. Beneath the Cross it grew."

In Scotland it was formerly believed that the dwarf birch is stunted in growth because the rods were formed of it with which our Lord was scourged.

* 'Piers Plowman's Vision,' 593-6.

CHAPTER II.

THE MOON.

FROM the very earliest times the moon has been an
object of popular superstition ; and, even still, to
quote the words of Dr. Johnson, "has great influence
in vulgar philosophy ;" many persons actually bowing
to it on its first appearance, in order by this act of
homage to insure good luck in the affairs of their
daily life ; thus, unconsciously on their part, keeping
up a remnant of the ancient idolatrous worship paid
to it. By some, on the other hand, it is considered
highly unlucky to see the new moon through glass,
and in Cornwall it is regarded as an omen that one
will break glass before that moon is out. "I have
known persons," says Hunt,* "whose attention has
been called to a clear new moon hesitate : 'Hey I
seed her out a' doors afore ?' If not, they will go into
the open air, and if possible show the moon 'a piece
of gold,' or, at all events, turn their money." Another superstitious practice, prevalent in many places,

---

* 'Popular Romances,' p. 429.

consists in looking at the first new moon of the year through a silk handkerchief which has never been washed. As many moons as the person sees through the handkerchief (the threads multiplying the vision), betoken the number of years he will remain unmarried.

In Devonshire it is considered lucky to see the new moon over the right shoulder; over the left shoulder is unlucky; and straight before, prognosticates good fortune to the end of the moon. In the same county many persons believe that if, on seeing the first new moon of the year, they take a stocking off one foot, and run across a field, on arriving there, they will find between the great toe and the next a hair which will be the colour of their lover's.

According to Vallancey, the Irish, on seeing the new moon, knelt down, repeated the Lord's Prayer, at the conclusion of which they cried, "May thou leave us as safe as thou hast found us!" And even still, they make the sign of the Cross on themselves,* and repeat the words of the blessing, "In the name of the Father, and of the Son, and of the Holy Ghost, Amen." On these occasions, they fancy that they will obtain anything they may wish for.

Aubrey, speaking of English manners in olden times, says that the women sit astride on a gate or stile the first evening the new moon appears, saying, "A fine

* 'Notes and Queries,' 5th series, vol. v. p. 364.

moon, God bless her!"*　In Norfolk there is a common proverb with respect to the new moon :—

> " Saturday new and Sunday full
> Never was good, and never wull :"

a superstition which may be found here and there in England as well as Scotland, varying, of course, according to the locality.　Thus, another version is :—

> " A Saturday moon,
> If it comes once in seven years,
> Comes once too soon."

A new moon, however, on a Monday is everywhere welcomed as being a certain sign not only of fair weather but good luck.　On the Continent we find, too, the same attention paid to the changes of the moon.　In the north of Italy † a change on a Wednesday is dreaded; and in the south of France a change on a Friday.

At Whitby, when the moon is surrounded by a halo with watery clouds, the seamen say there will be a change of weather, for the " moon dogs " are about.

The notion that the weather changes with the moon's quarters " is still held," says Tylor, in his most interesting book, 'Primitive Culture' (1871, vol. i. p. 118), " with great vigour in England.　The meteorologists, with all their eagerness to catch at any rule which at all answers to facts, quite repudiate this

---

* In Staffordshire, to see the new moon for the first time through trees is very unlucky.

† In some places it is said, " If the moon change on a Sunday, there will be a flood before the month is out."

one, which indeed appears to be simply a maxim belonging to popular astrology. Just as the growth and dwindling of plants became associated with the moon's wax and wane, so change of weather became associated with changes of the moon ; while, by astrologer's logic, it did not matter whether the moon's change were real, at new and full, or imaginary, at the intermediate quarters. That educated people, to whom exact weather-records are accessible, should still find satisfaction in the fanciful lunar rule, is an interesting case of intellectual survival."

The moon is said to be like a boat when its horns appear to point upwards, and in many parts there is a common notion that when it is thus situated there will be no rain ; a superstition alluded to in 'Adam Bede' : —

"It 'ud ha' been better luck if they'd ha' buried him i' the forenoon, when the rain was fallin' : there's no likelihood of a drop now. An' the moon lies like a boat there. That's a sure sign of fair weather."

Southey * also notices this odd piece of weather-lore, and assigns the following reason for it :—" Poor Littledale has this day explained the cause of our late rains, which have prevailed for the last five weeks, by a theory which will probably be as new to you as it is to me. 'I have observed,' he says, 'that when the moon is turned upwards, we have fine weather after it, but when it is turned down, then we have a wet season ; and the reason, I think, is, that when it is

* ' Life and Correspondence of R. Southey.'

turned down, it holds no water, like a bason, you
know, and then **down it comes.**'" According to
sailors, when the moon is like **a boat, it** betokens **fair**
weather, or, to use their phrase, "**You** might hang
your hat upon **it.**" **In** Liverpool, however, and other
parts, it **is** considered **a** sign of foul weather, as the
moon when in this position **is** considered to resemble
a basin full of water about **to** fall.   It is by no means
an uncommon occurrence **to** hear the villagers exclaim, **on** their seeing the **moon's** horns turned upwards, "**The new moon looks sharp,**" **an** expression
made use of in Dekker's '**Match Me** in London'
(**act** i.), where the King is made **to say**—"My Lord,
doe you see this change i' the moone ?   **Sharpe** hornes
doe threaten windy weather."*

> "The horny **moon is on her back ;**
> Mend your shoon and sort your thack,"

is a very common proverb in Scotland.

In Lincolnshire **it is** commonly believed by the
sailors and seafaring men that whenever a planet or
large star **is** seen near the moon,† or, **to** use their own
phrase, "a big star is dogging **the** moon," wild and
boisterous **weather** will soon set in.   **The** same idea is
current in Devonshire ; and, "some years ago," says a
correspondent of ' Notes **and** Queries,' " a fisherman of
Torquay told me, after **a** violent gale, that he had
foreseen the storm, **as** he had observed one star ahead

---

* Brand's ' Popular Antiquities,' 1849, **vol.** iii. p. **145.**
† **See** ' Notes and Queries,' 5th series, vol. i. p. 384.

of the moon towing her, **and** another astern chasing
her." In Cornwall it is a very general idea **that** :—

"A fog and a small moon
Bring an easterly wind soon."

In many places the following rhyme is found :—

"An old **moon** in a mist
Is worth **gold** in a kist (chest) ;
But a new moon's mist
Will never lack thirst."

"One of the **most** instructive astrological doctrines,"
says Tylor, "which has kept its place in modern
popular philosophy, **is that of the sympathy of grow-**
ing **and** declining nature **with** the waxing **and** waning
moon. Among classical **precepts are these** : **to set**
eggs **under** the hen **at** new **moon, but to root** up trees
when the **moon is on the** wane, and **after** midday.
The Lithuanian precept to wean boys on a waxing, but
girls on a waning moon, no doubt to make the **boys**
sturdy **and** the girls thin and delicate, **is a fair match**
for the Orkney Islander's objection **to** marrying
except with a growing moon, while some even wish
for a flowing tide." **In Cornwall, when a** child is born in
the interval between an **old** moon and the first appearance of **a** new one, **it is** said **that it will never live to**
reach the age of puberty. Hence the saying, "No moon,
no man." In the **same** county, **too,** when **a boy is**
born **in the wane of the moon,** it is believed **that the**
next **birth will be a** girl, **and** *vice versâ ;* and it is
also **commonly said that when a birth takes** place on

the "growing of the moon" the next child will be of
the same sex.   In Suffolk it is considered unlucky to
kill a pig on the waning moon, lest the pork should
waste in the boiling.   A correspondent of Chambers's
'Book of Days,' tells us that he has known the
shrinking of bacon in the pot attributed to the fact of
the pig having been killed in the moon's decrease,
and that within his own knowledge the death of a pig
has been delayed, or hastened, so as to happen during
its increase.   In Tusser's, ' Five hundred Points of
Husbandry,' under February, we read :—

> " Sow peas and beans in the wane of the moon ;
>   Who soweth them sooner, he soweth too soon ;
>   That they with the planet may rest and rise,
>   And flourish with bearing, most plentiful-wise."

In Devonshire it is commonly said that apples
"shrump up," if picked when the moon is waning.
In some parts it is a prevalent belief that the growth
of mushrooms is influenced by the changes of the
moon, and in Essex the subjoined rule is often
scrupulously adhered to :—

> " When the moon is at the full,
>   Mushrooms you may freely pull ;
> But when the moon is on the wane,
>   Wait ere you think to pluck again."

In Scotland it is an agricultural maxim that :—

> " If the moon shows like a silver shield,
>   You need not be afraid to reap your field ;
>   But if she rises haloed round,
>   Soon we'll tread on deluged ground."

Butler, in his Hudibras, asks the following question, which must certainly have occurred to many a student of the fine arts :—

> " Tell me but what's the nat'ral cause,
> Why on a sign no painter draws
> The full moon ever, but the half ?"

Numerous love charms are still practised by means of the moon. In Devonshire it is customary for young people as soon as they see the first new moon after Midsummer, to go to a stile, turn their back to it, and say :—

> " All hail, new moon, all hail to thee !
> I prithee, good moon, reveal to me
> This night who shall my true love be ;
> Who is he, and what he wears,
> And what he does all months and years."

A correspondent of ' Notes and Queries ' (1st series, vol. i. p. 177) tells us that being on a visit in Yorkshire, he was amused one evening to find the servants of the house excusing themselves for being out of the way when the bell rang, on the plea that they had been " hailing the first new moon of the new year." This mysterious salutation was effected by means of a looking-glass, in which the first sight of the moon was to be had, and the object to be gained was the important secret as to how many years would elapse before the marriage of the observers. If one moon was seen in the glass, one year, if two, two years ; and so on. In the case in question, the maid and the boy

only saw one moon a-piece. **In Ireland,** at the new
moon, it is not **an** uncommon practice for people to
point **with a** knife, **and after invoking the** Holy
Trinity, **to say :—**

> " New moon, **true** morrow, be true now **to me,**
> That I ere the morrow my true love may see."

The knife is then placed under the pillow, **and**
silence strictly **observed, lest the** charm should be
broken.

In Berkshire, **at the** first **appearance** of a new
moon, young women go into the fields, and while
they look at it, say :—

> " New moon, new moon, I hail thee !
> **By all** the virtue in thy body,
> **Grant this night that** I **may see**
> **He who my true love is to be."**

They **then return** home, firmly believing that
before morning their **future** husbands will appear to
them in their dreams.

Formerly, **it** was customary **to swear** by the moon,
as appears from Shakspeare, who makes Juliet reprove
her lover for testifying his affection by this **means :—**

> " O swear not by the moon, the inconstant moon,
> That monthly changes in her circled orb,
> Lest that thy love prove likewise variable."

In olden times, witches were supposed to have the
power of controlling the moon, a notion which dates
back to very great antiquity. . **The** earliest reference

we find is that in the " Clouds" of Aristophanes, where
Strepsiades proposes the hiring of a Thessalian witch
to bring down the moon and shut her up in a box
that he might thus evade paying his debts by a
month. Shakspeare alludes to this curious notion.
In the 'Tempest' (scene 1), he makes Prospero say :—

"His mother was a witch, and one so strong,
That could control the moon."

There is a very prevalent opinion among the lower
and uneducated classes that the harvest moon always
occurs at the time of harvest, let that happen when it
may. It is needless, however, to remark that such an
erroneous idea can only proceed from persons of an
entirely ignorant turn of mind—it being childish to
suppose that the change of moon could in any way
be influenced by such an occurrence. Olmsted, in his
' Mechanism of the Heavens' (p. 169), explains the
reason thus :—"About the time of the autumnal
equinox, the moon, when near her full, rises about
sunset a number of nights in succession. This occasions a remarkable number of brilliant moonlight
evenings, and as this in England is the period of
harvest, the phenomenon is called the harvest moon.
The sun being then in Libra, and the moon, when full,
being, of course opposite to the sun, or in Aries, and
moving eastwards in or near the ecliptic at the rate of
about 13° per day, would descend but a small distance below the horizon for four or six days in

succession—that is, for two or three days before, and
the same number of days after, the full; and would,
consequently, rise during all these evenings nearly at
the same time, namely, a little before or a little after
sunset, so as to afford a remarkable succession of fine
moonlight evenings."

A very singular divination practised at the period
of the harvest moon is thus described in an old chap-
book, quoted by Halliwell * in his amusing little book,
'Popular Rhymes.' When you go to bed, place
under your pillow a Prayer-book open at the part of
the matrimonial service, "with this ring I thee wed;"
place on it a key, a ring, a flower, and a sprig of
willow, a small heart-cake, a crust of bread, and the
following cards :—a ten of clubs, nine of hearts, ace
of spades, and the ace of diamonds. Wrap all these
in a thin handkerchief of gauze or muslin, and on
getting into bed, cross your hands, and say—

> "Luna, every woman's friend,
>   To me thy goodness condescend;
>   Let me this night in visions see
>   Emblems of my destiny."

If you dream of storms, trouble will betide you;
if the storms end in a fine calm, so will your fate;
if of a ring or the ace of diamonds, marriage; bread,
an industrious life; cake, a prosperous life; flowers,
joy; willow, treachery in love; spades, death;
diamonds, money; clubs, a foreign land; keys, that

* It is given also by Brand, 'Popular Antiquities,' 1849, vol. ii. p. 33.

you will rise to great trust and power, and never know want ; birds, that you will have many children ; and geese, that you will marry more than once.

The hunter's moon occurs just after the harvest moon, and is perhaps so called because about the time of this moon hunting begins. As the harvest moon is probably so called from occurring about harvest time, and being valuable to harvesters, so too it may be said with regard to the moon that succeeds it. Many of our readers are no doubt acquainted with the three children in the nursery rhyme, who went a hunting by night, for :—

> " One said it was the moon,
> Another said, Nay,
> A third said it was a cheese,
> And half o't cut away."

In the south-eastern part of England one may sometimes hear the expression, seedman's moon.

In many parts it is believed that the moon has a magic influence in healing certain maladies. Thus, in Staffordshire, it is commonly said if you want to cure chin-cough, take out the child, and let it look at the new moon ; lift up its clothes, and rub your right hand up and down its stomach, and repeat the following lines (looking steadfastly at the moon, and rubbing at the same time) :—

> " What I see, may it increase,
> What I feel, may it decrease ;
> In the name of the Father, Son, and Holy Ghost. Amen."

" For warts," says Sir Thomas Browne, "we rub our hands before the moon and commit any maculated part to the touch of the dead." In Devonshire it is said that the hair and nails should always be cut during the waning of the moon, as many beneficial consequences are supposed to result in consequence. Some say that if persons troubled with corns cut them after the moon has been at its full, they will gradually disappear. In the 'British Apollo' we have the following advice given to us on this subject :—

> " Pray tell your querist if he may
> Rely on what the vulgar say,
> That when the moon's in her increase,
> If corns be cut they'll grow apace ;
> But if you always do take care
> After the full your corns to pare,
> They do insensibly decay,
> And will in time wear quite away.
> If this be true, pray let me know,
> And give the reason why 'tis so."

Most persons are acquainted with the popular expression, "the man in the moon"—"a dusky resemblance to a human figure," says a correspondent of the 'Book of Days,' "which appears on the eastern side of the luminary when eight days old, being somewhat like a man carrying a thorn-bush on his head, and at the same time engaged in climbing, while a detached object in front looks like his dog going on before him." It has given rise to various superstitions, besides legends, one of which connects this remarkable personage with the man spoken of in the book of

Numbers (xv. 32 *et seq.*), who having been detected by the children of Israel in the wilderness while gathering sticks on the Sabbath day, was punished with death. Another legend refers the figure to Cain, to which Dante, in his 'Inferno' (xx.), makes reference :—

> " See next the wretches who the needle left,
> The shuttle and the spindle, and became
> Diviners : baneful witcheries they wrought,
> With images and herbs. But onward now :
> For now doth Cain with fork of thorns confine,
> On either hemisphere, touching the wave
> Beneath the towers of Seville. Yesternight
> The moon was round. Thou may'st remember well,
> For she good service did thee in the gloom
> Of the deep wood."

A third identifies it with the figure of Isaac in the act of carrying a bundle of sticks for his sacrifice. The German tale, says Baring-Gould, in his amusing book, 'Curious Myths of the Middle Ages' (1869, p. 191), is as follows :—" Ages ago there went one Sunday morning an old man into the wood to hew sticks. He cut a faggot and slung it on a stout staff, cast it over his shoulder, and began to trudge home with his burden. On his way he met a handsome man in Sunday suit, walking towards the church ; this man stopped and asked the faggot-bearer, 'Do you know that this is Sunday on earth, when all must rest from their labours ?' 'Sunday on earth, or Monday in heaven, it is all one to me !' laughed the wood-

E

cutter. 'Then bear your burden for ever,' answered
the stranger; 'and as you value not Sunday on earth,
yours shall be a perpetual moonday in heaven; and
you shall stand for eternity in the moon, a warning
to all Sabbath-breakers.' Thereupon the stranger
vanished, and the man was caught up with his stock
and his faggot into the moon, where he stands yet."
The Jews have some Talmudical story that Jacob is in
the moon, and they believe that his face is visible.
The natives of Ceylon, instead of a man, have placed
a hare in the moon, and it is reported, says Douce
('Illustrations of Shakspeare,' 1839, p. 10), to have
got there in the following manner : Their great deity
Buddha, when a hermit on earth, lost himself one day
in a forest.   After wandering about in great distress
he met a hare, who thus addressed him :—" It is in
my power to extricate you from your difficulty ; take
the path on your left hand, and it will lead you out of
the forest." "I am greatly obliged to you, Mr.
Hare," said Buddha, "but I am unfortunately very
poor and very hungry, and have nothing to offer you
in reward for your kindness." "If you are hungry,"
returned the hare, "I am again at your service ;
make a fire, kill me, roast me, and eat me." Buddha
made the fire, and the hare instantly jumped into it.
Buddha now exerted his miraculous powers, snatched
the animal from the flames, and threw him into the
moon, where he has been ever since. The New
Zealand version of this superstition, which deserves

praise for its originality, is in substance as follows:—*
Before the moon gave light, a New Zealander named
Rona went out in the night to fetch some water from
a well. Unfortunately he stumbled and sprained his
ankle, and was unable to return home. All at once,
as he cried out for very anguish, he discovered, to his
great alarm, that the moon, which had suddenly
become visible, was descending towards him. He
seized hold of a tree, and clung to it for safety, but it
gave way, and fell with Rona upon the moon, and
there he remains unto this very day. According to
another version, Rona had just escaped falling into
the well by laying. hold of a tree, when he was
together with the tree caught up to the moon, where
to this day he is visible. The Chinese represent the
moon by a rabbit pounding rice in a mortar. Their
mythological moon Jut-ho is figured by a beautiful
young woman with a double sphere behind her head,
and a rabbit at her feet. The period of this animal's
gestation is thirty days, and Douce† suggests whether
it may not typify the moon's revolution round the
earth.

Clemens Alexandrinus quotes Serapion for his
opinion that the face in the moon was the soul of a
sibyl. In Plutarch's *Morals* also Sibylla is placed in
the moon :—" And the dæmon said it was the voice of

* See 'Notes and Queries,' 1st series, vol. xi. p. 493, from whence
this is taken.
† 'Illustrations of Shakspeare,' 1839, p. 11.

Sibylle, for she, being carried about in the globe and the face of the moon, did foretell and see what was to come." According to fable, it is related by children, says Halliwell, that the man in the moon once favoured this earth with his presence, and "took a fancy to some pease-porridge," which he was in such a hurry to devour that he scalded his mouth :—

> " The man in the moon
> Came tumbling down,
> And asked his way to Norwich ;
> He went by the south,
> And burnt his mouth
> With sipping hot pease-porridge."

His chief beverage was claret :—

> " The man in the moon drinks claret ;
> But he is a dull jack-a-dandy ;
> Would he know a sheep's head from a carrot,
> He should learn to drink cyder and brandy."

In Scotland, in one of their popular ballads, we find the following allusion to the man in the moon :—

> " I sat upon my houtie-croutie,*
> I lookit owre my rumple routie,†
> And saw John Heezlum-Peezlum,
> Playing on Jerusalem pipes."

The allusion, says Chambers ('Popular Rhymes of Scotland,' p. 185), to Jerusalem pipes is often applied in Scottish popular fiction to things of a nature above this world. In Ritson's 'Ancient Songs' there is one extracted from a manuscript of the time of Edward I.

* Hams.   † The haunch.

on the man in the moon; the first verse of which
runs as follows :—

> " Man in the moon, stand and stit !
>   On his bot-fork his burden he beareth ;
>   It is much wonder that he do na doun stit ;
>   For doubt lest he fall he shudd'reth and shivereth.
>   When the frost freezes must chill he bide ;
>   The thorns he keen his attire so teareth;
>   Nis no wight in the world there wot when he syt,
>   Ne bote it by the hedge what weeds he weareth."

There is a curious seal appended to a deed preserved
in the Record Office, Mr. Baring-Gould* tells us, dated
the 9th year of Edward III. (1335), bearing the man
in the moon as its device. "The deed is one of con-
veyance of a messuage, barn, and four acres of
ground, in the parish of Kingston-on-Thames, from
Walter de Grendesse, clerk, to Margaret his mother.
On the seal we see the man carrying his sticks, and
the moon surrounds him. There are also a couple of
stars added, perhaps to show that he is in the sky.
The legend on the seal reads :—

> ' Te Waltere docebo
> Cur spinas phebo
>   gero.' "

Chaucer, in his 'Testament of Cresside,' alludes to
this legend. Speaking of the moon, he says :—

> " Her gite was gray and full of spottis blake,
>   And on her brest a chorle painted ful even,
>   Bering a bush of thornis on his backe,
>   Whiche for his theft might clime so ner the heaven."

---

* 'Myths of the Middle Ages,' p. 198.

In the ' Husbandman's Practice ' we are told, " when Christmas Day cometh while the moon waneth, it shall be a very good year, and the nearer it cometh to the new moon, the better shall that year be.   If it cometh when the moon decreaseth, it shall be a hard year, and the nearer the latter end thereof it cometh, the worse and harder shall the year be."

In Huntingdonshire it is a common saying that "a dark Christmas sends a fine harvest"—the dark Christmas meaning "no moon."   Another old proverb tells us that "so many days old the moon is on Michaelmas Day, so many floods after."

It is a common fallacy that the full moon increases the symptoms of madness.   This simply originates, however, from the fact that the insane are naturally more restless on light than on dark nights, and that in consequence loss of sleep aggravates all their symptoms.*   Shakspeare was not exempt from this vulgar error, for he tells us that the moon makes men insane when "she comes nearer to the earth than she was wont."   It is not improbable that in some degree we owe this superstition to the poet's fancy.

* 'Notes and Queries,' 2nd series, vol. xii. p. 492.

CHAPTER III.

BIRDS.

The **Cuckoo** — Robin — **Wren** — **Swallow** — Yellowhammer — Martin —Nightingale — **Lark** — **Kingfisher** — **Rook** — **Raven** — Crow — Magpie — Chaffinch — Owl — Woodpecker — **Peacock** — Cock — Hen — Chicken — Duck — Plover — Dotterel — **Swan** — Ringdove — Peewit —Seagull —Pigeon.

BIRDS have, at all times, been in most countries the subject of a very varied folk-lore, and the superstitious and credulous have generally discovered in their movements omens and prognostications of coming events. These, however, in many cases, must be looked upon as the result of mere caprice, since we find numerous birds with an extensive folk-lore, whereas to all outward appearance they seem to have no claim to such prominence. It is often extremely difficult to trace superstitions of any kind to their source, but those connected with birds, like all others, no doubt have frequently originated in isolated occurrences. Thus, in ancient times, if a certain bird was seen to fly over a city just before a calamity of any kind, it was ever after regarded as a bird of ill-omen, and shunned as such.

The North American Indians have a beautiful

myth, says Hugh Macmillan, in his charming book,
'The Sabbath of the Fields,' concerning a mystical
bird, that, coming in the summer evenings when the
moon is full, sings in the pine groves, beside their
wigwams, ethereal songs of the spirit land, bringing
tidings of departed friends. "May we not," he adds,
"look upon the cuckoo as our mystical bird, which
comes to us when the year is at its full, greatest in
beauty and brightest in bloom, to speak to us of that
land which is very far off, and of the lost and loved
ones who dwell in it? But a brief season it stays
with us. It vanishes with the bloom of the year ;
and its last note in departure gives expression, as it
were, to what the fading of the spring flowers and the
soberer green of the woodlands silently proclaim."
According to the Gloucestershire peasant :—

> " The cuckoo comes in April,
>   Sings a song in May ;
>   Then in June another tune,
>   And then she flies away."

It is, indeed, no doubt, because this strange mysterious little harbinger of spring comes amongst us to
announce its joyous heaven-sent message—telling
how the dreary winter is past and the bright sunny
days of summer nigh at hand—that he has been so
gladly welcomed at all times, and even acquired a
superstitious reverence.

The cry of cuckoo is the note of the male only, that of
the female being a "harsh, screaming chatter." "The

custom," says a writer on the subject, "of calling a bird 'she,' is, however, everywhere persisted in, at any rate amongst the uneducated." And in many of the popular rhymes this peculiarity may be noticed.

In some parts of the country it is the popular notion that the 21st of April is the day on which the cuckoo makes its first appearance ; and at Tenbury, in Worcestershire, it is a belief that it is never heard till Tenbury fair-day (April 20th), or after Pershore fair-day (June 26th). In Wales it is considered unlucky to hear the cuckoo before the 6th of April, but "you will have prosperity," is the common saying, "for the whole of the year if you first hear it on the 28th." According to some, the 14th of April is the time when the cuckoo's note is first heard, and many are the anxious ears that eagerly listen for it, as much significance is attached to this event. Thus, in the north of England, it is regarded as an unfortunate omen for anyone to have no money in his pocket when he hears the cuckoo for the first time in a season, and much care is taken to avoid such an occurrence. In Norfolk it is a widespread superstition that whatever you are doing when you first hear the cuckoo, that you will do most frequently all the year.* It was, formerly, a very common belief that if a young woman ran into the fields early in the morning to hear the cuckoo, and, as soon as she heard it, took off her left shoe and looked into it, she would

* See Howitt's ' Pictorial Calendar of the Seasons.'

there find a man's hair of exactly the same colour as
that of her future husband. In the 'Connoisseur,'
an allusion is made to this custom. "I got up last
May morning and went into the fields to hear the
cuckoo, and when I pulled off my left shoe I found a
hair in it exactly the same colour with his." Gay, too,
in his 'Shepherd's Week' (4th Pastoral), speaks of
it :—

> " When first the year I heard the cuckoo sing,
> And call with welcome note the budding spring,
> I straightway set a-running with such haste,
> Deb'rah that ran the smock scarce ran so fast ;
> Till, spent for lack of breath, quite weary grown,
> Upon a rising bank I sat adown,
> And doff'd my shoe, and by my troth I swear,
> Therein I spied this yellow frizzled hair,
> As like to Lubberkin's in curl and hue
> As if upon his comely pate it grew."

Cornishmen regard it as a good omen to hear the
first cuckoo from the right and from before them ; when
heard, however, from the left it is a sign of ill-luck.

In England, as well as in Germany, it is a belief
among the peasantry that the cuckoo, if asked, will
tell you by the repetition of his cry how many years
you have to live. Hence the rhyme :—

> " Cuckoo, cherry-tree,
> Good bird, tell me
> How many years have I to live."

Kelly, in his 'Indo-European Tradition and Folk-
lore,' ascribes the allusion to the cherry-tree, in this
and similar rhymes, to the superstition that before

the cuckoo ceases his song he must eat three good
meals of cherries. In Shropshire it was customary
for the labouring classes, as soon as they heard the
first cuckoo, to leave off work, and to devote the rest
of the day to merry-making, which went by the name
of the "cuckoo ale."

The cuckoo rhymes vary in different counties, and
nearly all agree as to the time of its arrival, although
they differ somewhat as to the date of its departure.
The following well-known rhyme is sung in many
places :—

> " In April
>   The cuckoo shows his bill ;
>   In May
>   He is singing all day ;
>   In June
>   He changes his tune ;
>   In July
>   He prepares to fly ;
>   In August
>   Fly he must."

In Sussex, says a correspondent of the 'Athenæum,'
there is a further addition :—

> " If he stay until September,
>   'Tis as much as the oldest man
>   Can remember."

In the allusion above to the change which takes
place in the cuckoo's cry, it should be noted, remarks
a writer in Mary Howitt's 'Pictorial Calendar of the
Seasons,' that its syllabled note is prolonged to *cuc-
cuckoo*, and not unfrequently ends in a mere repetition

of the first syllable, *cuc, cuc, cuc.* It is then about to comply with the request so pathetically urged by Chaucer :—

> "Now, good cuckowe, goe somewhere away."

In Derbyshire one rhyme very prevalent is as follows :—

> "The cuckoo is a merry bird,
>   She sings as she flies ;
> She brings us good tidings,
>   And tells us no lies.
> She sucks little birds' eggs,
>   To make her voice clear,
> That she may sing cuckoo
>   Three months in the year."

Among the Danes a curious custom is found in connection with the cuckoo. As soon as its voice is heard in the woods, every village girl kisses her hand, and asks the question, "Cuckoo, Cuckoo! When shall I be married?" The Swedes have a similar superstition, and many a peasant girl exclaims :—

> "Cuckoo grey, tell to me,
>   Up in the tree, true and free,
> How many years I must live and go unmarried."

In some districts the following proverb is much used :—

> "Cuckoo oats and woodcock hay
> Make a farmer run away."

This phrase, says a correspondent of 'Notes and Queries' (3rd series, vol. v. p. 450), means that if the

spring is so backward that the oats cannot be sown
till the cuckoo is heard, or the autumn so wet that the
latter-math crop of hay cannot be gathered in till the
woodcocks come over, the farmer is sure to suffer
great loss. In Norfolk, too, one may frequently hear
the poorer classes quoting the subjoined rhyme with
reference to their agricultural pursuits :—

> " When the weirling shrieks at night,
>   Sow the seed with the morning light ;
>   But 'ware when the cuckoo swells its throat,
>   Harvest flies from the mooncall's * note."

" When the cuckoo purls its feathers, the housewife
should become chary of her eggs," is a popular saying
in many parts of the country. In Wales the cuckoo
often goes by the name of "the Welsh Ambassador."
In Middleton's 'A Trick to Catch the Old One'
(act iv. sc. 5), Dampet says :—

" Why, thou rogue of universality, do I not know
thee ? This sound is like the cuckoo, the Welsh
Ambassador."

It has been suggested that the cuckoo is called by
this name in allusion to the annual arrival of Welsh-
men in search of summer and other employment. As
those wanderers might have entered England about
the time of the cuckoo's appearance, the idea that
the bird was the precursor of the Welsh might thus
become prevalent.

* Probably the nightingale. See 'Notes and Queries,' 1st series,
vol. ii. p. 419.

Cuckoos are believed to become sparrow-hawks in winter. The **Rev. H. B.** Tristram, **at a meeting of** the **British** Association held **at** Newcastle-on-Tyne, stated that **when** he once remonstrated with a **man** for killing a cuckoo, "the defence **was that** it was well-known that sparrow-hawks turned into cuckoos **in** summer." **In** Germany, after St. John's Day, it is **said to turn into** a hawk. **In** Scotland it is considered **lucky to be walking when** one first hears the cuckoo, and the peasants are accustomed to say :—

> "Gang and hear the gowk yell,
> Sit and see the swallow flee,
> See the foal before its mother's 'ee—
> 'Twill be a thriving year **wi' thee.**"

We **must** not omit to mention the following admirable **piece of advice contained in the** old Welsh proverb :—"**When thou hearest the cuckoo cry,** take timely **heed to** thy **ways ; for it may be that he warns thee to a** straighter **line of duty.**"

According to a pretty notion, the robin and the wren are said to cover with leaves or moss any dead bodies they may chance to find unburied, a belief which no doubt to a great degree found its origin in the old ballad of the Children in the Wood, wherein occurs the following stanza :—

> "And when they were dead,
> The robins so red
> Brought strawberry-leaves,
> And over them spread."

The idea is alluded to in Reed's Old Plays :—

> " Call for the robin redbreast and the wren,
> Since o'er shady groves they hover,
> And with leaves and flow'rs do cover
> The friendless bodies of unburied men."

And again thus pathetically by Drayton :—

> " Cov'ring with moss the dead's unclosed eye,
> The little redbreast teacheth charitie."

It is nearly everywhere considered unlucky to kill a robin, and in Cornwall boys are wont to exclaim :—

> " Who hunts the robin or the wren,
> Will never prosper, sea or land."

In Yorkshire, if a robin is killed, it is supposed that one of the cows belonging to the person, or family of the person, who killed it will give " bloody milk." A correspondent of ' Notes and Queries ' relates the following curious circumstances, which certainly furnish a most remarkable and striking coincidence, especially as he vouches for their accuracy and truth :—" A young woman, who had been living in service at a farmhouse, one day told her relatives how the cow, belonging to her late master, had given bloody milk after one of the family had killed a robin. A male cousin of hers, disbelieving the tale, went out and shot a robin purposely. Next morning her uncle's best cow, a healthy one of thirteen years, that had borne nine calves without mishap, gave half a canful of this ' bloody ' milk, and did so for three days in succession, morning and evening. **The** liquid was of a pink colour, which, after **standing in the** can, became clearer, and **when poured out, the** 'blood' or the deep red something like it, was seen **to** have settled to the **bottom. The** young man who **shot** the robin milked the cow himself on the second morning, still incredulous. **The farrier** was sent for, and the matter **furnished** talk to the village." Formerly, at Walton-le-Dale, **if a** farmer killed a swallow, it was believed **that his** cows would yield **blood** instead of milk. **This** superstition* is **also prevalent in the** greater part **of** Switzerland. And on this **account the** robin alone **of** all birds enjoys immunity **from the** gun of the Alpine herdsman.† In France, likewise, the robin generally meets **with** mercy at **the** hands of the sportsman, and in some **parts it** is almost looked upon **with** veneration.

Pott, in his 'Ode **to the** Robin' (1780, p. 27), alludes **to the** ill-luck that attends any **who** hurt it :—

> " For ever from his threshold fly,
> Who, void of honour, once shall try,
> With base, inhospitable breast,
> **To bar** the freedom of his guest.
> **Oh, rather seek** the peasant's shed,
> **For he will give** thee wasted bread,
> **And fear some** new calamity,
> Should any there spread snares for thee."

A correspondent **of** Chambers's ' Book **of** Days ' (vol. i. p. 678) **has the following curious** note:—" ' How

---

* ' Notes **and** Queries,' 4th series, vol. i. p. 329.
† See Tschudi, ' Animal Life in the Alps,' vol. ii. chap. iv.

badly you write,' I once said to a boy in our parish
school; 'your hand shakes so much that you can't
hold the pen steady. Have you been running hard or
anything of that sort?' 'No,' replied the lad, 'it
always shakes. I once had a robin die in my hand;
and they say that if a robin dies in your hand, it will
always shake.'" In Scotland, and also in some parts
of England, the song of the robin is thought to bode ill
to the sick person who hears it, and much uneasiness
is consequently caused when its notes or "weeping"
are heard near a house where anyone happens to be
sick. In the north of Devon, when a robin perches on
the top of a cottage, and utters its plaintive "weet," it
is believed that the baby in the cottage will die.

The robin is not altogether without a weather-lore;
for in the south-east of Ireland should it enter a house,
it is said to prognosticate hard weather, snow, frost, &c.
In Devonshire it often goes by the name of "Farewell
Summer."

There is a pretty Welsh legend connected with
the robin, which, says a correspondent of ' Notes and
Queries,' makes not only the Babes in the Wood, but
mankind at large, indebted to these deserving favourites. How could any child help regarding with
grateful veneration the little bird with bosom red,
when assured "that far, far, far away, is a land of
woe, darkness, spirits of evil, and fire. Day by day
does this little bird bear in his bill a drop of water to
quench the flame. So near the burning stream does

F

he fly, that his dear little feathers arc *scorched ;* and hence he is named Brou-rhuddyn (Breast-burnt). To serve little children, the robin dares approach the infernal pit. No good child will hurt the devoted benefactor of man. The robin returns from the land of fire, and therefore he feels the cold of winter far more than his brother birds. He shivers in the brumal blast ; hungry, he chirps before your door."

Whilst speaking of the robin, we must not omit to mention also that touching little legend, which attributes his red breast to his having tried to pluck a spike from the crown of thorns with which our blessed Lord's head was encircled, thus poetically described by Mr. John Hoskyns-Abrahall :—

> "Bearing his cross, while Christ passed forth forlorn,
> His godlike forehead by the mock crown torn,
> A little bird took from that crown one thorn.
> To soothe the dear Redeemer's throbbing head,
> That bird did what she could ; His blood, 'tis said,
> Down dropping, dyed her tender bosom red.
> Since then no wanton boy disturbs her nest ;
> Weasel nor wild cat will her young molest ;
> All sacred deem the bird of ruddy breast."

It is a common belief that the wren is the wife of the robin, and in many places it is considered highly unlucky to kill or injure it :—

> "The robin and the wren
> Are God Almighty's cock and hen.
> Him that harries their nest,
> Never shall his soul have rest.
> The martin and the swallow
> Are God Almighty's bow and arrow."

The following lines were obtained from Essex :*—

> " The robin and the redbreast,
>   The robin and the wren ;
> If ye take out o' their nest,
>   Ye'll never thrive agen !

> " The robin and the redbreast,
>   The martin and the swallow ;
> If ye touch one o' their eggs,
>   Bad luck will sure to follow."

"To hunt the wren," says Yarrell ('British Birds,' vol. ii. p. 178), "is a favourite pastime of the peasantry of Kerry on Christmas Day. This they do, each using two sticks, one to beat the bushes, the other to fling at the bird. It was the boast of an old man, who lately died at the age of one hundred, that he had hunted the wren for the last eighty years on Christmas Day." Hunting the wren was formerly a pastime very prevalent in the Isle of Man on Christmas Eve, and on St. Stephen's Day. This singular practice, Waldron informs us, was founded on a tradition that, in days gone by, a fairy of uncommon beauty exerted such undue influence over the male population, that she now and then induced many of them, by her sweet voice, to follow her footsteps, until by degrees she led them into the sea, where they perished. This cruel exercise of power had continued for so long a time, that at last fears were entertained lest the island should be exhausted of its. defenders, when luckily a knight-errant sprang up, who discovered a means of

* See Halliwell's ' Popular Rhymes.'

countervailing the charms used by this siren, and even
laid a plot for her destruction, which she only escaped
by taking the form of a wren. Though, however, she
evaded instant annihilation, a spell was cast upon her
by which she was condemned, on each succeeding New
Year's Day, to reanimate the same form, with the
definite sentence that she must ultimately perish by
human hand. In consequence of this legend, the
barbarous practice of hunting the wren was year by
year vigorously kept up. In Dr. William Drummond's
' Rights of Animals ' the cruelty practised towards the
wren in the south of Ireland is dwelt upon, and a
tradition narrated, attributing its origin to political
motives. This custom, however, has for the last thirty
years been put down by authority.* The following
is a specimen of the song that was sung on the
occasion :—

> " The wren, the wren, the king of all birds,
>   St. Stephen's Day was caught in the furze :
>   Although he is little, his family's great ;
>   I pray you, good landlady, give us a treat.
>
> " My box would speak if had but a tongue,
>   And two or three shillings would do it no wrong.
>   Sing holly, sing ivy— sing ivy, sing holly ;
>   A drop, just to drink it, would drown melancholy."

After killing the wren, the children exhibited the
slaughtered birds on an ivy bush decked with ribbons,
and carried them about ;—an allusion to which is
made in the above lines.

* See ' Saturday Review,' 1876, vol. xli. p. 314.

Like the robin and the wren, it is considered highly unlucky to kill a swallow, "perhaps," says Brand,[*] "from the idea of its being a breach of hospitality, each of these birds being in the habit of taking refuge in houses." The more probable reason, however, is that this superstition has come down to us from the ancients, by whom the swallow, says Ælian, was held sacred to their penates or household gods, and therefore preserved. The same they also honoured as the harbinger of the spring, and Athenæus relates that the Rhodians had a solemn song to welcome it in. The swallow is still partly regarded by us as an unlucky bird, and in many cases its presence is regarded as the forerunner of death. A correspondent of ' Notes and Queries,' when one day visiting the sick child of a poor woman—a girl about twelve—had the following remark made to her by the mother :—" A swallow lit upon her shoulder, ma'am, a short time since, as she was walking home from church, and that is a sure sign of death." On the other hand, it is deemed lucky for martins or swallows to build their nests on the roof of a house, but just the reverse for them to forsake a place which they have once tenanted. By the Germans, the swallow is much venerated, and its presence on a house is said not only to preserve it from storms and fire, but also from evil. With the Irish, the swallow is certainly not a favourite, for by the vulgar it is called the " devil's

[*] ' Popular Antiquities,' vol. iii. p. 193.

bird," from a strange belief that on everyone's head
there is a particular hair, which, if the swallow can
pluck off, dooms the wretched individual to eternal
perdition.   In Scotland, however, Mr. Henderson tells
us, the pretty little yellow-hammer goes by the name
of the " devil's bird," and hence a superstitious dislike
to it extends as far south as Northumberland.
Swallows, too, are not without their share of weather-
lore.   If they fly low, and often touch the water with
their wings, they are said to foretell rain.   Thus Gay,
in his first ' Pastoral,' says :—

> " When swallows fleet soar high and sport in air,
>   He told us that the welkin would be clear."

Parker, in his poem of ' The Nightingale,' published
in the year 1632, speaking of swallows, says :—

> " And if in any's hand she chance to dye,
>   'Tis counted ominous, I know not why."

There are scattered, here and there, many rhymes
respecting the swallow, in which it is coupled with
the robin, the martin, &c.   Thus, according to one,—

> " The martin and the swallow
>   Are God Almighty's birds to hollow."

Here the word hollow most probably, says Halliwell,
is a corruption of the verb *hallow*, to keep holy.
Again, in Essex, it is said :—

> " A martin and a swallow
>   Are God Almighty's shirt and collar."

The beautiful little bird, the yellow-hammer, to which allusion has already been made, is, says Chambers ('Popular Rhymes,' 1870, p. 191), the subject of an unaccountable superstitious notion on the part of the peasantry, in England as well as in Scotland, who believe that it drinks a drop, some say three drops, of the devil's blood each May morning, or as others affirm, Monday morning. Its nest therefore receives less mercy than that of almost any other bird. The boys address it in the following rhyme of reproach :—

> "Half a paddock, half a toad,
> Half a yellow yorling ;
> Drink a drap o' the de'il's bluid,
> Every May morning."

"The classical fable of the unhappy Philomela," says a correspondent of Chambers's 'Book of Days' (vol. i. 515), "may have given an ideal tinge of melancholy to the Daulian minstrel's midnight strain ; as well as an origin to the once, and even now not altogether forgotten, popular error, that the bird sings with its breast impaled upon a thorn." In an exquisite sonnet by Sir Philip Sidney, set to music by Bateson, in 1604, we read :—

> "The nightingale, as soon as April bringeth
>   Unto her rested sense a perfect waking,
> While late bare earth, proud of her clothing, springeth,
>   Sings out her woes, a thorn her song-book making,
> And mournfully bewailing,
>   Her throat in tunes expresseth,
>   While grief her heart oppresseth,
> For Tereus o'er her chaste will prevailing."

Shakspeare notices this myth :—

> " Everything did banish moan,
> Save the nightingale alone ;
> She, poor bird, as all forlorn,
> Leaned her breast up till a thorn,
> And there sung the doleful ditty,
> That to hear it was great pity."

There are no nightingales at Havering-at-Bower, runs the legend, because Edward the Confessor, being interrupted by them in his meditations, prayed that their song might never be heard again. The Rev. R. R. Faulkner, however, who was incumbent of Havering for over a quarter of a century, in his little work, entitled, 'The Grave of Emma Vale at Havering Bower,' says, "their sweet notes are still heard, chanting their Maker's praise amidst the shady groves of this pretty village." There is, too, a prevalent idea, we are informed, that the nightingale has never been heard in Yorkshire. Hargrove, in his 'History of Knaresborough' (1832), contradicts this notion, for he tells us :—" In the opposite wood, called Birkans Wood (opposite to the Abbey House), during the summer evenings, the nightingale

> " ' Sings darkling ; and in shadiest covert hid,
> Tunes her nocturnal note.' "

Andrew Boord, in his 'Book of Knowledge,' says that in St. Leonards Forest the nightingales are dumb :—" In the Forest of Saint Leonards in South-sex there doth never singe nightingale, althoughe the

Foreste rounde about in tyme of the yeare is re-
plenyshed with nightingales; they wyl singe round
about the Foreste and never within the precincte of
the Foreste; as divers keepers of the Foreste, and
other credible persons dwellyng there did show
me."

In some places there is a popular prognostication
from the fact of the cuckoo or nightingale being first
heard. Thus the poet Milton, in his 'Sonnet to the
Nightingale,' says :—

> "Thy liquid notes that close the eve of day,
> First heard before the swallow cuckoo's bill,
> Portend success in love."

This piece of folk-lore is also alluded to by Chaucer
in his poem entitled "The Cuckoo and the Nightingale." In the modernized version by Wordsworth, it
is said :—

> "But tossing lately on a sleepless bed,
> I of a token thought which lovers need :
> How among them it was a common tale,
> That it was good to hear the nightingale,
> Ere the vile cuckoo's note be uttered."

More than two hundred years ago, a learned Jesuit,
says a correspondent of Chambers's 'Book of Days'
(vol. i. p. 516), named Marco Bettini, attempted to
reduce the nightingale's song to letters and words ;
and towards the close of the last century, one
Bechstein, a German, improved on his attempt. In a
'Proper New Boke of the Armony of Byrdes'

(quoted by Dibdin, 'Top. Antiq.,' vol. iv. 381), of
unknown date, though probably before the year 1580,
the nightingale is represented as singing its Te
Deum :—

> " Tibi cherubin
> Et seraphin,
> Full goodly she dyd chaunt,
> With notes merely ;
> Incessabile
> Voce præclamant."

In the 'Worcester Herald' (May 17th, 1862), we
are told that "there is a tradition of hops having
been planted many years ago near Doncaster, and of
the ,nightingale making its first appearance about the
same time. The popular idea was, that between the
bird and the plant some mysterious connecting link
existed, but both the hop and the nightingale disappeared long ago." This bit of folk-lore, says
Cuthbert Bede ('Notes and Queries,' 3rd series,
vol. i. p. 447), is not a fact ; for in Huntingdonshire,
there is a large field by the side of the Great
Northern Road, which still retains the name of the
"Hop Grounds," and "helps to remind us of a time
when this county was described by Bede and William
of Malmesbury as 'the garden of England,' and was
rich in vines and hops, yet there is not a hop-yard
within a very extensive radius of this locality, nor has
been for centuries ; nevertheless the nightingales
abound in every direction, singing night and day

> " ' By the dusty roadside drear.' "

In Scotland, and the north of England, the country people have a curious notion, that if you are desirous of knowing what the lark says, you must lie down on your back in the field and listen, and you will then hear him say * :—

> "Up in the lift go we,
> Tehee, tehee, tehee, tehee !
> There's not a shoemaker on the earth
> Can make a shoe to me, to me !
> Why so, why so, why so ?
> Because my heel is as long as my toe."

It was anciently believed, that during the *Halcyon days*, or that time when the halcyon, or kingfisher, is engaged in hatching her eggs, the sea remained so smooth that the sailor might venture upon it without incurring any risk of storm or tempest ; a notion thus referred to by Dryden :—

> " Amidst our arms as quiet you shall be
> As halcyons brooding on a winter's sea."

and in Wild's ' Iter Boreale' we read :—

> " The peaceful kingfishers are met together
> About the decks, and prophesy calm weather."

Shakspeare in ' King Lear' (act ii. scene 1), alluding to another curious superstition connected with this bird, makes the Earl of Kent say :—

> " turn their halcyon beaks
> With every gale and vary of their masters."

---

* Chambers's ' Popular Rhymes of Scotland,' 1870, p. 192.

—the common belief being that a dead kingfisher, suspended from a cord, would always turn its beak in that direction from whence the wind blew, which is also alluded to by Marlow, in his 'Jew of Malta,' 1633 :—

> " But how now stands the wind ?
> Into what corner peers my halcyon's bill ?"

Sir Thomas Browne in his quaint fashion ('Vulgar Errors,' Bohn's Edit., vol. i. p. 270) has gone into the subject somewhat minutely, and says, it is "a conceit supported chiefly by present practice, yet not made out by reason or experience." Occasionally one may still see this bird stuffed and hung up in cottages ; a remnant, no doubt, of this old superstition. "I have once or twice," says Mrs. Charlotte Smith, "seen a stuffed bird of this species hung up to the beam of a cottage ceiling, and imagined that the beauty of the feathers had recommended it to this sad pre-eminence, till, on inquiring, I was assured that it served the purpose of a weather-vane ; and though sheltered from the immediate influence of the wind, never failed to show every change by turning its beak to the quarter whence the wind blew." *

In the north of England it is a notion very prevalent that when rooks desert a rookery which they have tenanted for a number of years, it foretells the coming downfall of the family on whose property it is.

* From a paper "On Shakspeare's Knowledge of Natural History," by J. H. Fennell, 'Gent. Mag.'

Unfortunately, however, for those who put credence in such a superstition, it only too often happens that these birds change from one place to another, without any of the dreadful consequences happening predicted by the foolishly credulous. It is commonly said too, that when a rookery is near a house, in the case of death, this bird will not leave the neighbourhood until the funeral has taken place.

The following rhyme is common in the North:—

> " On the first of March,
>   The crows begin to search ;
>   By the first o' April,
>   They are sitting still ;
>   By the first o' May,
>   They're a' flown away ;
>   Croupin' greedy back again,
>   Wi' October's wind and rain."

It is curious to find, says a writer in the 'Standard' (Jan. 26th, 1877), Cosmo di Medici, afterwards Grand-Duke of Tuscany, who visited England in the reign of Charles II., and subsequently wrote, or caused to be written, an account of his travels, giving especial notice to the rooks, which he tells us the nobles of England prided themselves on attaching to the neighbourhood of their castles, because they were regarded as " fowls of good omen." " No one, therefore," he adds, " is permitted to kill them, under severe penalties." Possibly, the great desire, says the same writer, of the late eccentric Vicar of Morwenstow to create a rookery in some tall trees near his parsonage, a matter which he made the subject of special prayer, was connected with this superstition.

In Looe, East Cornwall, it is a popular belief that rooks forsake an estate, if, on the death of the proprietor, no heir can be found to succeed him. The raven is another of the chosen birds of superstition, from its supposed longevity, and its frequent mention and agency in Holy Writ. Its supposed faculty of "smelling death," formerly rendered its presence, or even its voice, ominous to all, as

> " The hateful messenger of heavy things,
>   Of death and dolour telling."

Its unusually harsh croak is still, when illness of any kind is in the house, regarded as an inauspicious sound. Thus, Shakspeare in his "Othello," says :—

> " O, it comes o'er my memory
>   As doth the raven o'er the infected house,
>   Boding to all."

Spencer, too, speaks somewhat in the same strain :—

> "The ill-fac'd owle, death's dreadful messenger ;
>   The hoarse night raven, trompe of doleful dreere."

In Cornwall, the croaking of a raven over the house bodes evil to some member of the family. The following incident, quoted by Hunt in his 'Popular Romances,' illustrates this superstition.

"One day our family were much annoyed by the continued croaking of a raven over our house. Some of ·us believed it to be a token, others derided the idea ; but one good lady, our next-door neighbour, said, 'Just mark the day, and see if something does not come of it.' The day and hour were carefully noted. Months passed away, and unbelievers were loud in their boastings and inquiries after the token.

" The fifth month arrived, and with it a black-edged letter from Australia, announcing the death of one of the members of the family in that country. On comparing the dates of the death and the raven's croak, they were found to have occurred on the same day."

According to ancient authors ravens were formerly white, but were changed to black for babbling. Mr. John Barrow, in his 'Visit to Ireland,' says, "This bird was dedicated to Odin, who, as the traditional history of Ireland informs us, had two ravens, which were let loose every morning to collect intelligence of what was going on in the world, and which, on returning in the evening, perched upon Odin's shoulders, to whisper in his ear whatever information they might have collected ; and even now, as we learn from Alafsen and Povelsen, the Icelanders entertain superstitious notions regarding the raven. They believe this bird to be not only acquainted with what is going on at a distance, but also what is to happen in the future." Cicero, it is said, was forewarned by the noise and fluttering of ravens about him, that his end was near.

An old Cornish legend* avers that King Arthur is

* 'Traditions, Superstitions, and Folk-Lore,' 1872, p. 168.

still alive in the form of a raven, and certain superstitious persons, says Mr. Hardwick, refuse to shoot
these birds, from a fear that they might inadvertently
destroy the mythic warrior. Mr. Hawker in his
entertaining little book, 'Echoes from Cornwall,'
mentions this belief as existing in connection with the
chough—a bird which hovers around the western
coast,* and quotes these lines :—

> " And mark yon bird of sable wing,
>   Talons and beak all red with blood ;
>   The spirit of the long-lost king
>   Passed in that shape from Camlan's flood.

> " And still when loudliest howls the storm,
>   And darkliest lowers his native sky,
>   The king's fierce soul is in that form—
>   The warrior spirit threatens nigh."

The crow, too, has generally been regarded as a bird
of ill-omen ; a superstition which dates as far back as
the time of Virgil, who tells us how

> " Sæpe sinistra cava prædixit ab ilice cornix."

In Essex the peasants have a rhyme respecting the
crow almost similar to that connected with the
magpie. If crows fly *towards* you, then—

> " One's unlucky,
>   Two's lucky ;
>   Three is health,
>   Four is wealth ;
>   Five is sickness,
>   And six is death."

---

* 'Traditions, Superstitions, and Folk-Lore,' 1872, p. 168.

Throughout Lancashire **and** Yorkshire, the children **regard** with no friendly feelings this unfortunate bird, as appears from the subjoined rhyme :—

> " Crow, crow, get out of my sight,
>   **Or else I'll** eat thy **liver** and lights."

If **a crow cry, says** Bourne, it portends **some evil,** and when **it makes a** hoarse, hollow, **noise,** it presages foul weather.   **Crows** seem **to** have been **looked** upon as ominous **in most countries.   Thus** Butler, **in** his ' Hudibras,' says :—

> " Is it not om'nous in **all countries**
>   When crows **and ravens croak upon trees ?"**

The magpie is generally looked upon **as a** mysterious **bird,** and according to the popular rhyme—

> " **One is sorrow,** two mirth,
>   Three a wedding, four a birth,
>   Five heaven, six hell,
>   Seven the de'il's ain sell."

This varies **somewhat in** different localities, but in substance is the same.   Thus, to quote from Grose :— " It is unlucky to see first one magpie, and then more : but to see two, denotes marriage or merriment ; three, a successful journey ; four, **an** unexpected piece of good **news ; five, you** will shortly be in a great company."   **In** Lancashire we find this variation :—

> " One for anger,
>   Two for mirth,
>   Three for a wedding,
>   Four for a birth,

G

Five for rich,
Six for poor,
Seven for a witch ;
I can tell you no more."

Another version has the last four lines thus :—

" Five for a fiddle,
Six for a dance,
Seven for England,
Eight for France."

In Devonshire, in order to avert the ill-luck, from seeing a single magpie, the peasant spits over his right shoulder three times, repeating the following words :—

" Clean birds by sevens,
Unclean by twos ;
The dove, in the heavens,
Is the one I choose."

And, in Yorkshire, to break the same charm, various practices are in use : One is to raise the hat as a salutation, and then to sign the cross on the breast, and another to make the same sign by crossing the thumbs. In Lancashire, says Brand,* " among the vulgar, it is accounted very unlucky to see two magpies (called there pynots, in Northumberland pyanots) together." In Scotland, the same superstition holds respecting this bird, and an old writer quaintly remarks, that "many an old woman would more willingly see the devil, who bodes no more ill-luck than he brings, than a magpie perching on a

* ' Popular Antiquities.'

neighbouring tree." In Morayshire, and no doubt in other parts of Scotland, it is believed that magpies flying near the windows of a house portend a speedy death to some inmate.* We must also not omit to quote what Shakspeare has said about the magpie. Thus in Henry VI. (act v. scene 6) we are told how—

> " The raven rook'd her on the chimney's top,
> And chattering pies in dismal discord sung."

And in Macbeth :—

> " Augurs, and understood relations, have
> By magot-pies, and choughs, and rooks, brought forth
> The secret'st man of blood."

Magpies, says a writer in the 'Standard' (Jan. 26th, 1877), are mysterious everywhere, but our English magpie stories pale before those of the true Northland. A lady, we are told, living near Carlstad, in Sweden, grievously offended a Finn woman who came into the court of her house, asking for food. The woman was told "to take that magpie hanging up on the wall, and eat it." She took the bird and disappeared, with an evil glance at the lady who had been so ill-advised as to insult a Finn, whose magical powers, it is well known, far exceed those of the gipsies. Nothing happened for a time ; but by-and-by the lady began to observe that wherever she went one of the magpies always made its appearance in her path. Presently the number increased ; and the lady, who had first been amused, became troubled, and tried to drive them

* See chapter on " Death Superstitions."

away by various devices. All was to no purpose. She could not move without a large company of magpies ; and they became at length so daring as to hop on her shoulder, pull her dress, and peck at her feet as she walked. When she could bear it no longer, she shut herself up in her house ; but the magpies were always waiting at the door, and hopped in whenever it was opened. Then she took to her bed in a room with closed shutters ; yet even this was not an effectual protection, for the magpies kept tapping at the shutters day and night. The death of the lady is not recorded. Possibly she is still "dreeing her weird ;" but it is fully expected that, die when she may, all the magpies in Wermland will be present at her funeral.

Alexander Ross, in his Appendix to the 'Arcana Microcosmi,' informs us that in the time of King Charles VIII. of France, "the battle that was fought between the French and Britains, in which the latter were overthrown, was foreshewed by a skirmish between the magpies and jackdaws."

The half nest of the magpie, says Halliwell, in his 'Popular Rhymes,' is accounted for by a rural ornithological legend : "Once upon a time when the world was very young, the magpie, by some accident or another, although she was quite as cunning as she is at present, was the only bird that was unable to build a nest. In this perplexity, she applied to the other members of the feathered race, who kindly undertook to instruct her. **So, on** a day appointed, they assembled **for** that purpose, **and the** materials having been collected, the blackbird said, 'Place that stick there,' suiting the action to the word, as she commenced the work. 'Ah!' **said** the magpie, 'I knew that afore.' The other birds followed with their suggestions, but to every piece of advice the magpie kept saying, '**Ah! I** knew that afore.' **At** length, when the bridal habitation was half-finished, the patience of the company was fairly exhausted by the pertinacious conceit of the pye, so they all left **her** with **the** united exclamation, 'Well, mistress mag, **as you seem** to know all about it, you may e'en finish the nest yourself.' **Their** resolution was obdurate and final, **and** to this day the magpie exhibits the effects of partial instruction by **her** miserably incomplete abode."

Smith,* **in** his 'History of Cork,' says the magpie was not known in Ireland seventy years before **the** time at which he wrote, about 1746. Tradition says, also, that they were driven over to Ireland from England during a storm. Sir William Hooker, in his 'Tour in Iceland,' in 1809, remarks that a legend in that island **says,** the **magpie was** imported there by the English out of spite. In Norway, that the magpie **may** share the festivities of the season, the inhabitants place **a sheaf of corn at the** end of their houses. **Mr.** Henderson, in his 'Folk-Lore of the Northern Counties **of** England,' gives the following

* See Yarrell's 'British Birds,' 1856, vol. ii. p. 120.

curious anecdote upon the magpie. He says, "Well do I remember, when a boy ten or twelve years old, driving an old lady in a pony-carriage to visit a friend in a secluded part of the county of Durham. Half our journey was made, when, without a word of warning, the reins were suddenly snatched out of my hand, and the pony brought to a stand. Full of astonishment, I looked to my companion for some explanation of this assault on my independence ; I saw her gazing with intense interest on a magpie then crossing the road. After a pause of some seconds, she exclaimed, after a sigh, 'Oh! the nasty bird! Turn back! turn back!' and back we turned." This certainly is a startling illustration of the power of superstition.

An old tradition explains the origin of the ill-luck that is supposed to arise from meeting a magpie, in the following way :—It was the only bird that refused to enter the ark with Noah and his folk, preferring to perch itself on the roof of the ark, and to jabber over the drowning and perishing world. Ever since, it has been regarded as unlucky to meet this defiant and rebellious bird.

Reginald Scott, in his 'Discovery of Witchcraft,' says, "that to prognosticate that guests approach to your house, upon the chattering of pies or haggisters (haggister in Kent signifies a magpie) is altogether vanity and superstition."

In Scotland and the north of England, the plaintive

note of the chaffinch, says **Chambers,*** is interpreted
as a sign of rain. When, therefore, the **boys** hear it,
they first imitate it, and then rhymingly refer **to the**
expected consequences :—

"Weet, weet !—Dreep, dreep !"

From earliest times, the owl has been regarded as a
most unlucky bird, and its dismal voice has been looked
upon not only as the omen of misfortune, but even of
death. A correspondent of 'Book of Days' (vol. ii.
p. 732) informs us that two of these birds, "of enormous size, premonish the noble family of Arundel of
Wardour of approaching mortality. Whenever these
two solemn spectres are seen perched on a battlement
of the family mansion, it is only too well known that
one of its members will soon be summoned out of
this world." In Reed's 'Old Plays' (vi. p. 357), it is
said that—

"When screech-owls croak upon the chimney tops,
It's certain that you of a corse shall hear."

The ancients held this bird in the utmost abhorrence,
and even Rome itself underwent a lustration, because
one of them strayed into the capital. Thus Butler, in
his 'Hudibras,' tells us,—

"The Roman senate, when within
The city walls an owl was seen,
Did cause their clergy with lustrations
(Our synod calls humiliations)
The round-fac'd prodigy t'avert
From doing town and country hurt."

---

* 'Popular Rhymes,' 1870, p. 190.

The owl, according to various old legends, was originally of noble parentage. Waterton, in his 'Essays on Natural History' (1838, p. 8), quotes the following ballad, which thus describes this unfortunate bird's altered condition :—

> "Once I was a monarch's daughter,
>   And sat on a lady's knee,
> But am now a nightly rover,
>   Banished to the ivy tree.
> Crying, Hoo, hoo, hoo, hoo, hoo, hoo,
>   Hoo, hoo, hoo, my feet are cold ;
> Pity me, for here you see me
>   Persecuted, poor, and old."

Shakspeare alludes to another legend. In 'Hamlet' (act iv. scene 5) he makes Ophelia exclaim : "They say the owl was a baker's daughter. Lord, we know what we are, but know not what we may be."

Douce gives the legend as follows :—"Our Saviour went into a baker's shop where they were baking, and asked for some bread to eat : the mistress of the shop immediately put a piece of dough into the oven to bake for him ; but was reprimanded by her daughter, who, insisting that the piece of dough was too large, reduced it to a very small size ; the dough, however, immediately began to swell, and presently became a most enormous size, whereupon the baker's daughter cried out, 'Heugh, heugh, heugh !' which owl-like noise probably induced our Saviour to transform her into that bird for her wickedness."

Dasent, in his 'Popular Tales from the Norse,' gives

another account of this tradition, in which, however, in place of the owl the woodpecker is substituted:—
" In those days when our Lord and St. Peter wandered upon earth, they came to an old wife's house, who sat baking. Her name was Gertrude, and she had a red mutch on her head. They had walked a long way, and were both hungry, and our Lord begged hard for a bannock to stay their hunger. Yes, they should have it. So she took a little tiny piece of dough and rolled it out, but as she rolled it, it grew until it covered the whole griddle.

"Nay, that was too big; they couldn't have that. So she took a tinier bit still; but when that was rolled out it covered the whole griddle just the same, and that bannock was too big, she said; they couldn't have that either.

"The third time she took a still tinier bit, so tiny that you could scarce see it; but it was the same story over again—the bannock was too big.

"'Well,' said Gertrude, 'I can't give you anything; you must just go without, for all these bannocks are too big.'

"Then our Lord waxed wroth, and said, 'Since you loved me so little as to grudge me a morsel of food, you shall have this punishment—you shall become a bird and seek your food between bark and bole, and never get a drop to drink save when it rains.'

"He had scarce said the last word before she was turned into a great black woodpecker, or Gertrude's bird, and flew from her kneading-trough right up the chimney. And till this very day you may see her flying about, with her red mutch on her head, and her body all black, because of the soot in the chimney; and so she hacks and taps away at the trees for her food, and whistles when rain is coming, for she is ever athirst, and then she looks for a drop to cool her tongue." The woodpecker's cry is said to denote wet. The woodpecker, from its vociferous cry when rain is impending, has been popularly called "the rain-bird"; and in many country districts it is held in no small estimation from its prognosticating wet; and Wallis, in his 'History of Northumberland,' tells us that it is called in that county by the common people, "Rain-fowl." Both these terms are analogous to the Pluviæ aves of the Romans, who for the same reason gave them this designation. The woodpecker is also called the yaffle, or yaffil, in Surrey and Sussex. "This name," says Yarrell ('British Birds,' vol. ii. p. 148), "has reference to the repeated notes of the bird, which have been compared to the sound of a laugh." White, of Selborne, says, "The woodpecker laughs;" and in the popular poem of "The Peacock at Home," the following couplet occurs :—

> "The skylark in ecstasy sang from a cloud,
> And chanticleer crow'd, and the yaffil laughed loud."

The possession of peacock's feathers is said to bring ill-luck and misfortune to the owner. This may be accounted for * from what Palgrave says in his 'Central and Eastern Arabia' (vol. i. p. 286), where, according to Mahometan tradition, the peacock opened the wicket of Paradise to admit the devil. Mr. Llewellyn Jewitt † tells us that in Derbyshire and the surrounding counties this superstition is prevalent, and that he has seen people "perfectly horrified when a child or other person has unwittingly brought a peacock's feather into the house," as it is believed to bring loss and various disasters, including even illness and death to the inmates. Peacocks, when they make a loud and shrill noise, are said to predict rain ; and in Lupton's 'Notable Things,' we read that "the oftener they cry, the more rain is signified."

It was long ago believed among the common people that at the time of cock-crowing the midnight spirits forsook this world, and went to their proper places. This opinion is very ancient, and is mentioned by the Christian poet Prudentius, who flourished at the beginning of the fourth century. In one of his hymns he says :—

> " They say the wandering powers that love
>   The silent darkness of the night,
>   At cock-crowing give o'er to rove,
>   And all in fear do take their flight."

This idea is illustrated by Shakspeare in ' Hamlet,'

* ' Notes and Queries,' 3rd series, vol. viii. p. 332.
† ' Notes and Queries,' 3rd series, vol. ix. p. 187.

where the ghost was "about to speak, when the cock
crew," and "faded at the crowing of the cock."

The disappearance of spirits at cock-crow is a
frequent fancy of the poets. Spenser says of one of
his spirits :—

> " The morning cock crew loud,
> And at the sound it shrunk in haste away,
> And vanished from our sight."

Butler, in his ' Hudibras,' tells how—

> " The cock crows, and the morning grows on,
> When 'tis decreed I must be gone."

Blair, too, in his ' Grave ' says—

> " The tale
> Of horrid apparition, tall and ghastly,
> That walks at dead of night, or takes his stand
> O'er some new-open'd grave ; and, strange to tell,
> Evanishes at crowing of the cock."

In Devonshire and Cornwall, when the cock crows
more than usually, it is said to be " a sign that a
stranger is coming." The same idea exists, also, in
other parts, as, for instance, on the borders of Shropshire and Montgomeryshire. In some places, the
cock-crowing denotes a change of weather, while in
others, fine weather. An old proverb tells us :—

> " If the cock crows on going to bed,
> He's sure to rise with a watery head."

In the midland counties it is said that—

> " If the cock moults **before the hen,**
> We shall have the weather thick and thin ;
> If the hen moults **before the cock,**
> We shall have weather as hard as a block."

In Derbyshire,* the peasants believe that "if the hens gather on a rising ground, and trim their feathers, it is a sure sign of rain." And "if the cock stays on the roost longer in the morning than usual, and crows there, it is a sign of wet."

Formerly, it was customary in Derbyshire for girls to peep through the key-holes of house-doors, before opening them on St. Valentine's Day ; when, if fortune was good to them, and they saw a cock and hen in company, it was regarded as a certain omen that the person interested would be married before the year was out. Croker, in his ' Researches in the South of Ireland,' affirms that in the year 1305, a woman was charged with having sacrificed nine red cocks to her familiar spirit. The Buddhists of Ceylon, and the low-castes in the south of England, still sacrifice red cocks to their evil spirits. Mr. Hunt † relates the following anecdote, showing with what supernatural attributes the cock is credited in Cornwall :—

" A farmer in Towednack, having been robbed of some property of no great value, was resolved, never-

* From a paper by Mr. T. Ratcliffe " On the Folk-Lore of Domestic Fowls," in ' Long Ago,' 1873, vol. i. p. 81.

† ' Popular Romances of West of England.'

theless, to employ a test which he had heard the 'old people' resorted to for the purpose of catching a thief. He invited all his neighbours into his cottage, and when they were assembled, he placed a cock under the 'brandice' (an iron vessel formerly much employed by the peasantry in baking, when this process was carried out on the hearth, the fuel being furze and ferns). Everyone was directed to touch the brandice with his or her third finger, and say, 'In the name of the Father, Son, and Holy Ghost, speak.' Everyone did as they were directed, and no sound came from beneath the brandice. The last person was a woman, who occasionally laboured for the farmer in his fields. She hung back, hoping to pass unobserved amidst the crowd. But her very anxiety made her a suspected person. She was forced forward, and most unwillingly she touched the brandice, when, before she could utter the words prescribed, the cock crew. The woman fell faint on the floor, and when she recovered, she confessed herself to be the thief, restored the stolen property, and became, it is said, 'a changed character from that day.'" In Cornwall, it is often said that a whistling maid and a crowing hen in one house, is an infallible sign of the down-fall of some in it ; hens are even killed for crow-ing by night. In the 'British Apollo' we find the query,—

> " When my hens do crow,
> Tell me if it be ominous or no."

In Kent, and other counties, there is a common
and pretty superstition connected with chickens,
which is thus described by Mary Allen, in her ' Poems
for Youth ' (1810):—

> " The little chickens, as they dip
>   Their beaks into the river,
>   Hold up their heads at every dip,
>   And thank the Giver."

Cuthbert Bede, relates in ' Notes and Queries '
(5th series, vol. vi. p. 24) the following piece of folk-
lore connected with the hatching of ducks' eggs :—
" A farmer's wife, in Rutland, was promised a
' setting ' of ducks' eggs by the wife of another
farmer, who sent the eggs at nine o'clock in the evening. ' I cannot imagine how she could have been so
foolish,' said the first named, when she mentioned the
matter to me on the following day. I inquired as to
the foolishness, and was told that ducks' eggs brought
into a house after sunset, would do no good, and
never be hatched."

There is a Lancashire superstition which identifies
the plover with the transmuted soul of a Jew. When
seven of them are seen together, they are called the
" seven whistlers," and their sound, it is said, foretells
misfortune to those who hear it. A correspondent of
' Notes and Queries ' thus alludes to this odd piece
of superstition :—" One evening a few years ago,
when crossing one of our Lancashire moors, in company with an intelligent old man, we were suddenly

startled by the whistling overhead of a covey of plovers. My companion remarked that when a boy the old people considered such a circumstance a bad omen, 'as the person who heard *the wandering Jews,*' as he called the plovers, was sure to be 'overtaken with some ill-luck.' On questioning my friend on the name given to the birds, he said, ' There is a tradition that they contain the souls of those Jews who assisted at the crucifixion, and in consequence were doomed to float in the air for ever.' When we arrived at the foot of the moor, a coach, by which I had hoped to complete my journey, had already left its station, thereby causing me to finish the distance on foot. The old man reminded me of the omen."

The appearance of the dotterel, that " highly esteemed migratory visitant " * is regarded by shepherds as a sign of coming winter, and hence the adage :—

"When dotterel do first appear, it shows that frost is very near ;
But when the dotterel do go, then you may look for heavy snow."

In Hampshire, according to a common, but of course most erroneous idea, swans are said generally to be hatched during a thunderstorm. This, however, is a very old piece of superstition, for Lord Northampton, in his 'Defensative against the Poyson of Supposed Prophecies ' (1583) says :—" It chaunceth sometimes to thunder about that time and season of the yeare when swannes hatch their young ;

* See Brand's ' Popular Antiquities,' vol. iii. p. 218.

and yet no doubt it is a **paradox** of simple men to thinke that a swanne cannot hatch without **a cracke of** thunder." Pliny * alludes to a superstition by which swans are said to sing sweetly before their death, but falsely, he tells us, as proved through his own observation. Sir Thomas Browne, in his 'Vulgar Errors' (**Bohn's Edit.,** 1852, vol. i. p. 357), has some quaint **remarks on** this subject, giving us the following explanation of its origin :—" From great antiquity, and before the melody of Syrens, the musical note of swans hath been commended, and they sing most sweetly before their death ; for thus we read in Plato, that from the opinion of *metempsychosis*, or transmigration **of** the souls of men into the bodies of beasts most suitable unto their human condition, after his death Orpheus the musician became a swan ; thus was it the bird **of** Apollo, the god of music, by the Greeks ; and an hieroglyphick of music among the Egyptians, from whom the Greeks derived the conception ;—hath been the affirmation of many Latins, and **hath not** wanted assertors almost from every nation."

In Scotland swans are looked upon as good prog- nosticators of the weather. Coleridge, speaking of this superstition, wittily remarks :—

> " Swans **sing** before they **die** ; 'twere no bad thing,
> Should certain persons die before they sing."

The common people in the North Riding **of** York-

* 'Hist.' x. 23.

shire believe that once upon a time the cushat, or ring-dove, laid its eggs upon the ground, and that the peewit, or lapwing, made its nest on high ; but that one day they made an agreement to exchange their localities for building. Hence the peewit, in consequence, now expresses its disappointment at the new arrangement in the subjoined words :—

> " Peewit, peewit !
> I coup'd my nest and I rue it."

The cushat,* however, rejoices that she is safe out of the reach of mischievous boys :—

> " Coo, coo, come now,
> Little lad,
> With thy gad,
> Come not thou."

In the South of Scotland the lapwing is still looked upon as an unlucky bird. Mr. Chatto, in his ' Rambles in Northumberland and the Scottish Border,' refers to "the persecution to which the Covenanters were exposed in the reign of Charles II. and his bigoted successor ; " and, quoting Dr. Leyden,† alludes to the tradition that "they were frequently discovered to their pursuers by the flight and screaming of the lapwing." Hence the fact of this bird being regarded as unlucky in Scotland.

The very ancient Lincolnshire family, the Tyrwhitts, bear three peewits for their arms ; and an old tradition

---

* See Brockett's ' Glossary of North Country Words.'
† Yarrell's ' British Birds,' 1856, vol. ii. p. 518.

informs us, "that it was in consequence of the founder of their family having fallen in a skirmish, wounded, and being saved by his followers, who were directed to the spot where he lay by the cries of these birds, and their hovering near him." *

Montagu gives a curious legend respecting the wood-pigeon prevalent in Suffolk. "The magpie, it is said, once undertook to teach the pigeon how to build a more substantial and commodious dwelling; but, instead of being a docile pupil, the pigeon kept on her old cry of 'Take two, Taffy! take two!' The magpie insisted that this was a very unworkmanlike manner of proceeding, one stick at a time being as much as could be managed to advantage; but the pigeon reiterated her 'Two, take two,' till Mag, in a violent passion, gave up the task, exclaiming, 'I say that one at a time's enough; and, if you think otherwise, you may set about the work yourself, for I will have no more to do with it!' Since that time the wood-pigeon has built her slight platform of sticks, which certainly suffers much in comparison with the strong, substantial structure of the magpie." The cooing of the wood-pigeon, it is said, means—

" Take two-o coo, Taffy !
Take two-o coo, Taffy !"

It is not an uncommon superstition, that no one can die *happy* on a bed of pigeon's feathers. As an illus-

* Yarrell's ' British Birds,' 1856, vol. ii. p. 519.

H 2

tration of this, a correspondent of ' Notes and Queries' informs us that one day he met a servant with a basket full of pigeon's feathers, that she was about to consign to the dusthole. On being questioned as to the reason of this act, she replied that the feathers of the pigeon, and of all birds of game, were generally thrown away, as no person could die happy when lying on a bed that contained any. From the same source, we read of an instance where a man on the verge of death was actually removed by his relations from his bed to the floor, as they suspected that game feathers were in the bed, and that therefore it was impossible for him "to die easily." If a pigeon accidentally settles on a table, it is considered a sign of sickness, and if on a bed or chimney, of death.

It is reckoned a sure sign of death in a house if a white pigeon is observed to settle on a chimney.

Sea-gulls are considered ominous. In Sir John Sinclair's 'Statistical Account of Scotland,' the minister of Arbirlot, in the county of Forfar, informs us that "when they appear in the fields, a storm from the south-east generally follows; and when the storm begins to abate, they fly back to the shore." They are sometimes called "sea-mews," and it is said that early in the morning, when they make a gaggling more than ordinary, they prognosticate stormy weather.

In Scotland the following rhyme is prevalent :—

> " Sea-gull, sea-gull, sit on the sand ;
> It's never good weather when you're on the land."

CHAPTER IV.

ANIMALS.

The Dog — Cat — Horse — Mouse — Bat — Lamb — Pig — Hare — Goat — Rabbit — Ass — Hedgehog — Snail.

THE dog was held by the Egyptians as an object of adoration, from its being the representative of one of the celestial signs; and by the Indians as one of the sacred forms of their deities.

> " The Egyptians worshipped dogs, and for
> Their faith made internecine war."

It is still, even in our own country, oftentimes the cause of superstition. It is, for example, nearly everywhere a common notion that the howling of this faithful and intellectual companion of man is unlucky, and generally to be regarded as prognosticating misfortune of some kind or other. Scattered here and there, we find various charms for averting the consequences believed to follow this sign of ill-omen ; among which, by way of illustration, we may mention one practised in Staffordshire : When you hear a dog howl, take off your shoe from the left foot, and spit upon the sole, place it on the ground bottom upwards, and your foot upon the place you sat upon, which will not only

preserve you from harm, but stop the howling of the
dog. In the 'British Apollo' (1708) we have the
question asked, "Whether dogs howling may be a
fatal prognostic or no ? to which the following answer
is given :—We cannot determine, but 'tis probable
that out of a sense of sorrow for the sickness or
absence of his master or the like, that creature may
be so disturbed." This superstition is a very ancient
one, and is noticed by Pausanias, who relates how
before the destruction of the Messenians, the dogs
set up a fiercer howling than they were wont to do ;
and Virgil, alluding to the Roman misfortunes in the
Pharsalic war, says :—

> "Obscœnique canes, importunæque volucres,
>   Signa dabant."

In Lancashire * the life of a dog is sometimes said
to be bound up with that of his master or mistress.
When either dies the other cannot live. It has been
suggested whether this may not be a remnant of the
old belief in the transmigration of souls.

Dogs are said to have extraordinary quickness in
understanding character. It is believed that they
instinctively avoid ill-tempered persons; and if they
follow any stranger, it is generally a person of kind
and cheerful disposition. Among the Highlanders
great care is taken that dogs do not pass between
a couple that are going to be married, as much ill-

* Harland and Wilkinson, 'Lancashire Folk-Lore,' p. 142.

luck is supposed to result from such an occurrence. In
Ireland it is considered unfortunate to meet a barking
dog early in the morning, and, on the other hand, just
as fortunate for one to enter a house the first thing in
the day. Dogs are not without their weather-lore.
Thus, when they eat grass, it is a sign of rain ; if they
roll on the ground and scratch, or become drowsy and
stupid, a change in the weather may be expected.
As in the case of the cat, most of their turnings and
twistings are supposed to be prognostications of something.

Formerly, a custom existed in Hull of whipping all
the dogs that were found running about the streets on
the 10th of October, and so common was this practice
at one time, that every little urchin considered it his
duty to prepare a whip for any unlucky dog that
might be seen wandering in the streets on that day.
Tradition, says a correspondent of ' Notes and Queries '
(1st series, vol. viii. p. 409), assigns the following
origin to the custom :—Previous to the suppression of
monasteries in Hull, it was the custom for the monks
to provide liberally for the poor and the wayfarer who
came to the fair held annually on the 11th October,
and while bringing in this necessary preparation the
day before the fair, a dog strolled into the larder,
snatched up a piece of meat, and decamped with it.
The cooks gave the alarm, and when the dog got into
the street, he was pursued by the expectants of the
charity of the monks, who were waiting outside the

gates, and made to give up the stolen joint. Whenever, after this, **a** dog **showed his** face while this annual preparation was going on, he **was** instantly beaten off. Eventually this was taken up by the boys, and, until the introduction of the new police, was rigidly **put in** practice by them every 10th of October.

A similar custom was, in bygone days, kept up at York on St. Luke's Day: hence the day was called "Whip-dog-Day." Its origin is uncertain, but tradition assigns it to the following circumstance :—that, **in** some time of Popery, a priest celebrating mass at this festival, in some church in York, unfortunately dropped the host after consecration, which was suddenly snatched up and swallowed by a dog that lay under the communion table. **The** profanation of this sacred act occasioned the death of the dog, and a persecution began **which was** kept up on the anniversary **of** the day.

Cats, from their great powers of resistance, are commonly said to have nine lives ; hence, Ben Jonson, in 'Every Man in his Humour,' says :—"'Tis a pity you **had** not ten lives—a cat's and your own." In ancient times this domestic animal was honoured as an emblem of the moon, from the great changeableness, says Timbs, of the pupil of the eye, which in the daytime is a mere narrow line, dilatable in the dark to a luminous **globe. On this account,** it was so highly esteemed among the **Egyptians, as to** receive sacrifices, and even to have stately temples erected to its honour. Whenever a cat died, Brand* tells us, all the family shaved their eyebrows; and Diodorus Siculus relates that a Roman happening accidentally to kill a cat, the mob immediately gathered around the house where he was, and neither the entreaties of some principal men sent by the king, nor the fear of the Romans, with whom the Egyptians were then negotiating a peace, could save the man's life.

Dingley, in his 'Tour Round Wales' (1800, vol. ii. p. 210), narrates that in Wales, if any person killed the cat that was about the king's palace, "she was to be taken by the tail, and her head touching the floor, so much wheat was to be forfeited for the offence, as being thrown around her, would cover the top of her tail."

In the Middle Ages the cat was a very important personage in religious festivals. At Aix, in Provence,† on the festival of Corpus Christi, the finest tom cat of the country, wrapped like a child in swaddling clothes, was exhibited in a magnificent shrine to public admiration. Every knee was bent, every hand strewed flowers, or poured incense; and pussy was treated in all respects as the god of the day. On the festival, however, of St. John (June 24th), poor Tom's fate was reversed. A number of cats were put in a wicket basket, and thrown alive into the midst of a large

---

* 'Popular Antiquities,' 1849, vol. ii. p. 38.
† Mill's 'History of the Crusades.'

fire, kindled in the public square by the bishop and his clergy. Hymns and anthems were sung, and processions were made by the priests and people, in honour of the sacrifice.

In England the superstitious still hold the cat in high esteem, and oftentimes when observing the weather, attribute much importance to its various movements. Thus, according to some, when they sneeze it is a sign of rain; and Herrick, in his 'Hesperides,' tells us how

> " True calendars, as pusses eare,
> Wash't o're to tell what change is neare."

It is a common notion that when a cat scratches the legs of a table, it is a prognostic of change of weather. John Swan, in his 'Speculum Mundi' (Cambridge, 1643), writing of the cat, says :—" She useth therefore to wash her face with her feet, which she licketh and moisteneth with her tongue ; and it is observed by some that, if she put her feet beyond the crown of her head in this kind of washing, it is a signe of rain." Indeed, in the eyes of the superstitious, there is scarcely a movement of the cat which is not supposed to have some significance.

It is commonly said that cats are exceedingly fond of valerian (*V. officinalis*), and in Topsell's 'Four-footed Beasts' (1658, p. 81), we find the following curious remarks :—" The root of the herb valerian (called Phu), is very like to the eye of a cat, and where-

soever it groweth, if cats come thereunto, they instantly dig it up for the love thereof, as I myself
have seen in mine own garden, for it smelleth moreover
like a cat." There is also an English rhyme on the
plant marum to the following effect :—

> " If you set it,
> The cats will eat it ;
> If you sow it,
> The cats will know it."

Cats are by many supposed to suck the breath of
young children, and so cause their death. In the
'Annual Register' (January 25th, 1791) occurs the
following paragraph :—"A child of eighteen months
old was found dead near Plymouth ; and it appeared
on the coroner's inquest that the child died in consequence of a cat sucking its breath, thereby occa-
sioning a strangulation." There is, of course, no truth
whatever in this foolish superstition, and "this extremely unphilosophical notion of cats preferring
exhausted to pure air is," says a correspondent of
Chambers's 'Book of Days' (vol. ii. p. 39), " frequently
a great cause of annoyance to poor pussy, when, after
having established herself close to baby, in a snug,
warm cradle, she finds herself ignominiously hustled
out under suspicion of compassing the death of her
quiet new acquaintance, who is not yet big enough to
pull her tail." In Suffolk, cats' eyes are supposed to
dilate and contract with the flow and ebb of the tide.
In Lancashire the common people have an idea that

those who play much with cats never have good health.

In some parts black cats are said to bring good luck, and in Scarborough,* a few years ago, sailors' wives were in the habit of keeping one, thinking thereby to ensure the safety of their husbands at sea. This, consequently, gave black cats such a value that no one else could keep them, as they were nearly always stolen. There are various proverbs which attach equal importance to this lucky animal, as, for example :—

> " Whenever the cat o' the house is black,
> The lasses o' lovers will have no lack."

And again :—

> " Kiss the black cat,
> An' 'twill make ye fat ;
> Kiss the white ane,
> 'Twill make ye lean."

In Cornwall, says Hunt, those little gatherings which come on children's eyelids, locally called "whilks," are cured by passing the tail of a black cat nine times over the place. If a ram cat, the cure is more certain. In Ireland it is considered highly unlucky for persons to take a cat with them when removing. Consequently, cats, says a correspondent of 'Notes and Queries' (4th series, vol. iv. p. 505), often suffer terribly in Dublin, being mercilessly left to the sympathy of any who may chance to take compassion upon them.

* Henderson's 'Folk-Lore of the Northern Counties,' p. 171.

In some counties, for example Devonshire and Wiltshire, it is believed that a May cat—or, in other words, a cat born in the month of May—will never catch any rats or mice, but, contrary to the wont of cats, will bring into the house snakes and slow-worms, and other disagreeable reptiles. In Huntingdonshire it is a common saying that "a May kitten makes a dirty cat." If a cat should leap over a corpse, it is said to portend misfortune. Gough, in his 'Sepulchral Monuments,' says that in Orkney, during the time the corpse remains in the house, all the cats are locked up, and the looking-glasses covered over. In Devonshire a superstition prevails that a cat will not remain in a house with an unburied corpse, and stories are often told how on the death of one of the inmates of a house, the cat has suddenly made its disappearance, and not returned again until after the funeral. The sneezing of the cat, says Brand ('Popular Antiquities,' 1849, vol. iii. p. 187), appears to have been considered as a lucky omen to a bride who was to be married on the succeeding day.

In Scotland there is a children's rhyme upon the purring of the cat :—

> " Dirdum drum,
> Three threads and a thrum ;
> Thrum gray, thrum gray !"

There is a somewhat slang phrase, " to grin like a Cheshire cat," that is, to display the teeth and gums when laughing. A curious explanation has been given of this phrase,* that Cheshire **is** a county palatine, and the cats, when they **think** of it, are so tickled with the notion that they can't help laughing.

In South Lancashire the following tradition is current †: — A gentleman was one evening sitting cosily in his parlour, reading or meditating, when he was interrupted by the appearance of a cat, which came down the chimney, and called out, "Tell Dildrum Doldrum's dead!" He was naturally startled by the occurrence, and when shortly afterwards **his** wife entered, **he** related to her what had happened, and her own cat, which accompanied her, exclaimed, "Is Doldrum dead?" and immediately rushed up the chimney, and was heard of no more. Of course there were numberless **conjectures** upon **such a** remarkable occurrence, but the general opinion appears to be that Doldrum had been king of Catland, and that Dildrum was the next heir. A similar legend is current in Northumberland.

One of the frauds of witchcraft was, says Timbs, the witch pretending to transform herself into a certain **animal,** the favourite and most usual transformation being **a** *cat;* **hence** cats were tormented by the ignorant vulgar.

Steevens, the commentator on Shakspeare, states that in some counties in England **a** cat was formerly

---

* Hotten's 'Slang Dictionary,' 1864, p. 99.
† 'Notes and Queries,' 2nd series, vol. x. p. 463.

closed up with a quantity of soot in a cask suspended on a line. He who beat out the bottom of the cask as he ran under it, and was nimble enough to escape the contents, was regarded as the hero of this inhuman diversion, which was terminated by hunting to death the unfortunate cat.

In Lancashire it is regarded as unlucky to allow a cat to die in a house. Hence,* when they are ill, they are usually drowned. At Christchurch, Spitalfields, there is a benefaction for the widows of weavers under certain restrictions, called "cat and dog money." And there is a tradition in the parish that money was given in the first instance to cats and dogs. †

The horse, in this country, has always been an object of the highest interest, and our ancestors were, says Bell ('History of British Quadrupeds'), from the earliest periods, celebrated for the excellence of their breeds of this useful animal. When Cæsar landed on the shores of Kent, he was received by the cavalry and war-chariots belonging to the defending army. It is not surprising, therefore, that the horse has its quota of folk-lore. Many regard it as lucky to find a horseshoe, a notion very common in country places, where one may often see nailed over the doorway an old cast-off horseshoe. In some places they are supposed to keep off witches, and misfortune; thus, in Gay's fable of

* Harland and Wilkinson, 'Lancashire Folk-Lore,' p. 141.
† See Edwards's 'Old English Customs,' p. 54.

" The Old Woman **and her Cats,**" the supposed witch
complains :—

> " Straws laid across my path retard ;
>   The horseshoe's nail'd, each threshold's **guard.**"

When **Dr. James,*** then a poor apothecary, had
invented **the** fever-powder, he was introduced to
Newbery, **of** St. Paul's Churchyard, **to** vend the
medicine for him. One Sunday morning, **as** James
was on his way to Newbery's country-house at Vaux-
hall, in passing over Westminster Bridge, seeing **a**
horseshoe lying **in the road,** and considering it to be
a sign of good luck, he put the shoe **into** his pocket.
As Newbery was a shrewd **man, he** became James's
agent for the **sale of** the fever-powder ; whilst the
doctor ascribed all his success **to the** horseshoe, which
he subsequently **adopted as the crest** upon his carriage.
Douce considers that **the practice** of nailing horseshoes to thresholds resembles that of driving nails into
the walls of cottages among the Romans, which they
believed to be an antidote against the plague.

Aubrey, in his 'Miscellanies,' informs **us that "it
is a thing very common** to nail horseshoes on the
thresholds **of doors ; which is to hinder** the power of
witches that **enter** the house. **Most** of the houses of
the West-end of London **have the** horseshoe on the
threshold. It should **be a horseshoe that** one finds."
Further **on he adds,** "under the **porch** of Staninfield

* See **Timbs's** 'Things not Generally **Known,'** 1856, p. 146.

Church, in Suffolk, I saw a tile with a horseshoe upon
it, placed there for this purpose, though one would
imagine that holy water alone would have been sufficient. I am told there are many other instances."
Nelson, who was of a somewhat superstitious turn of
mind, had very **great faith in** the luck of a horseshoe,
and one was **nailed to the mast of the ship** 'Victory.'

There **is a** certain amount of good **or** bad luck, **says**
a correspondent **of** 'Notes and Queries' (**5th series,**
vol. **vii. p. 64),** attached **to** horses having one or **more**
white feet or legs. It is very lucky to own a horse
whose fore-legs are both equally "white stockinged;"
but if one fore and one hind leg on the same side are
white, it is unlucky. It is unlucky when **one** leg only
of the four is "white stockinged," but if opposite legs,
as off fore, and near hind, are white, very lucky. A
versified set of instructions on buying white-footed
horses runs thus :—

> " One white foot—buy a horse ;
> Two white feet—try a horse ;
> Three white feet—look well about him ;
> Four white feet—do without him."

In the neighbourhood of Stoke-in-Teignhead,
Devonshire, the following rhymes are current :—

> " If you have a horse with four white legs,
> Keep him not a day ;
> If you have a horse with three white legs,
> Send him **far** away ;
> If you have a horse with two white legs,
> Sell him to a friend ;
> And if you have a horse with **one white leg,**
> **Keep** him to his end."

I

In Yorkshire, it is looked upon as unlucky to meet a white horse on leaving home, and in order to avert the ill-omen one must spit on the ground.

The plant moonwort was in former days supposed to possess the quality of drawing the shoes from the feet of horses.   Thus we read * :—

> " And horse that, feeding on the grassy hills,
> Tread upon moon-woort with their hollow heels,
> Though lately shod, at night goe barefoot home,
> Their maister musing where their shooes become.
> O moon-woort ! tell us where thou hidst the smith,
> Hammer, and pincers, thou unshod'st them with ?
> Alas ! what lock or iron engine is't
> That can thy subtile secret strength resist,
> Sith the best farrier cannot set a shoe
> So sure, but thou (so shortly) canst undo ? "

In Lancashire † a *hogstone* with a hole through, tied to the key of the stable doors, is said to protect the horses ; and if hung up at the bed's head, the farmer and his family.   From the same source we learn that " in some of the rural districts of Lancashire, belief in witchcraft is still strong.   Many believe that others have the power to bewitch cows, sheep, horses, and oxen, and even persons to whom the witch has an antipathy.   On one occasion a respectable farmer asserted that his horse was bewitched into a stable through a loophole twelve inches by three !   The fact, he said, was beyond doubt, for he had locked the

---

* Du Bartas.
† Harland and Wilkinson, 'Lancashire Folk-Lore,' p. 154.

stable door himself when the horse was in the field, and had kept the key in his pocket."

To meet with a shrew-mouse * in going a journey is said, by the Northamptonshire peasantry, to be unlucky. The harvest-mouse, it is also believed, cannot cross a path which has been trod by man.

It is difficult to account for the prejudices which have always existed against that harmless and interesting little animal, the bat,† which has not only furnished an object of superstitious dread to the ignorant, but has proved to the poet and painter a fertile source of images of gloom and terror. The strange combination of character of beast and bird, which the bat was believed to possess, gave to Virgil the idea of the Harpies, and Aristotle speaks of them as having feet like birds, but wanting them as quadrupeds. In some parts of England the common term for the bat is flittermouse, corrupted into flintymouse. In Scotland, when the boys see this animal flitting about in the evening, they shout,—

> "Bloody, bloody bat,
> Come into my hat;"

strongly believing in the potency of their charm.

In Shropshire, one of the methods of discovering who one's partner for life is to be, consists in procuring the blade-bone of a lamb, and after pricking it at

---

* See p. 223.   † Thomas Bell, F.R.S.

midnight with **a penknife, in repeating the** following
charm :—

> " 'Tis not this bone I mean to pick,
> But my love's heart I wish to prick ;
> If he comes not, and speaks, to-night,
> I'll prick, and prick 'till it be light."

In Lancashire, it is thought, in spring, lucky to see
the first lamb's head, but equally unlucky to see its
tail.   Another piece of superstition consists in noticing when you see for the first time this little animal,
whether its head or tail is turned towards you.   If the
former, you will have plenty **of meat to** eat during
the year; if the latter, you may·**look for** nothing but
milk and vegetables.*

Pigs are not without their little portion of folk-lore,
for we are informed that **the Filey** fishermen will not
go to sea on any day when they have either seen or
met a pig the first thing in the morning ; and in
Ireland, to see pigs running about the farmyard with
straws in their mouth, foretells an approaching storm.

Grose tells us that **" if** going on a journey on
business a sow cross the road, you will probably meet
with a disappointment, if not a bodily accident, before
you return home.   **To** avert this, **you** must endeavour
to prevent her crossing you ; and if that cannot be
done, you must ride round **on fresh** ground : if the
sow is with her litter **of pigs, it is** lucky and denotes a
successful journey."   **The same** superstition prevails

* **Henderson's** ' Traditions of the Northern Counties.'

in Germany, where the peasant considers it unlucky to meet a herd of swine.

The hare was used in divination by the ancient Britons, and was never killed for the table.* Borlase, in his 'Antiquities of Cornwall,' relates a remarkable way of divining recorded of Boadicea, Queen of the Britons:—"When she had harangued her soldiers to spirit them against the Romans, she opened her bosom and let go a hare, which she had there concealed, that the augurs might thence proceed to divine. The frighted animal made such twistings and windings in her course, as, according to the then rules of judging, prognosticated happy success. The joyful multitude made loud huzzas ; Boadicea seized the opportunity, approved their ardour, led them straight to their enemies, and gained the victory."

In Northamptonshire, if a hare runs along the street or mainway of a village, it portends fire to some house in the immediate vicinity. Sir Thomas Browne says, " If a hare cross the highway, there are few above three-score years that are not perplexed thereat, which, notwithstanding, is but an augurial terror, according to that received expression, 'Inauspicatum dat iter oblatus lepus.'" The hare was formerly esteemed a melancholy animal, and its flesh was supposed to produce melancholy in those who ate it. An old medical writer informs us how " hare-flesh engendreth melancholy bloude." This idea, says Timbs, was not

* See Brand's 'Popular Antiquities,' 1849, vol. iii. p. 203.

quite forgotten in Swift's time; in his 'Polite Conversation,' Lady Answerall, being asked to eat hare, replies: "No, Madam; they say, 'tis melancholy meat." Another old notion respecting hares—and one, too, supported by respectable ancient authorities —was that they yearly changed their sex. Fletcher, in his 'Gentle Shepherd,' says:—"Hares that yearly sexes change." The hare, too, was supposed to be so timid that it never—not even in sleep—closed its eyes. Chapman has drawn from this superstition a fine epithet on the death of Prince Henry :—

> " Relentless Rigor, and Confusion faint,
>   Frantic Distemper, and hare-eyed Unrest."

There is a popular notion relative to goats: they are supposed, says Brand,* never to be seen for twenty-four hours together; and that once in that space, they pay a visit to the devil, in order to have their beards combed. This is common both in England and Scotland. Martin, in his 'Description of the Western Islands,' says it was an ancient custom among them to hang a he-goat to the boat's mast, in order to ensure by this means a favourable wind.

The rabbit, like the hare, is looked upon as ominous, for to use the words of Mr. Tylor ('Primitive Culture,' vol. i. p. 109), "the Cornish miner turns away in horror when he meets an old woman or a rabbit on his way to the pit's mouth."

A common superstition attaching to the ass is that

* 'Popular Antiquities,' vol. ii. p. 517.

the marks on its shoulders were given as memorials of our Saviour riding upon it. In the North Riding of Yorkshire, however, there is a tradition * that these marks "were in consequence of Balaam's striking it, and as a reproof to him and memento of his conduct."

One cause of the superstitions attached to the hedge-hog is owing to the peculiar noise it makes, which is alluded to by Shakspeare in 'Macbeth,' where the witches round the caldron are represented as say-ing :—

> "Twice the brindled cat hath mewed,
> Twice and once the hedge-pig whin'd," &c.

The sound of its voice is similar to that of a person snoring, or breathing very hard ; and as heard, says a correspondent of 'Notes and Queries,' in the still silence of the night, might be mistaken by the fearful and superstitious for the moaning of a disturbed spirit. Our ancestors regarded the hedgehog as a prognosti-cator of the weather. An old writer tells us—

> "As hedge-hogs doe fore-see ensuing stormes,
> So wise men are for fortune still prepared."

In 'Poor Robin's Almanack,' too, for the year 1733, we find these curious lines :—

> "Observe which way the hedge-hog builds her nest,
> To front the north, or south, or east, or west ;
> For if 'tis true that common people say,
> The wind will blow the quite contrary way :

---

* Brand's 'Popular Antiquities,' vol. iii. p. 363.

> If by some secret **art** the hedge-hogs know,
> So long before, which **way** the winds will blow,
> She has an art which **many a** person lacks,
> That thinks himself **fit to make almanacks.**"

A common amusement among children consists in charming snails, in order to induce them to put out their horns—the following couplet in the southern counties being repeated on the occasion :—

> " Snail, snail, come out of your hole,
>   **Or else** I'll beat you as black as a coal."

In the northern counties, we find another version which runs thus :—

> " Snail, snail, **put out your horns,**
>   I'll give **you bread and barley-corns.**"

In certain **districts of Scotland, it is** regarded as a token of fine **weather, if the snail obeys** the command to put out its horn :—

> " Snailie, snailie, shoot out your horn,
>   And tell us if it will be a bonnie day the morn."

Snail charms, it may **be** noted, are not peculiar **to English** children, but are found on the Continent. **Thus, for** instance, in Silesia, the children **are in the** habit of singing :—

> " Snail, snail, slug slow,
>   **To me thy** four horns show ;
>   If thou dost not show me thy four,
>   I will throw thee out of the door,
>   For the crow in the gutter,
>   To eat for bread and butter." *

---

* See Halliwell's ' Popular Rhymes,' p. **177.**

Snails were much used in days gone by in love divinations; a practice alluded to by Gay in his ' Shepherd's Week ' :—

> " Last May-day fair I searched to find a snail,
>   That might my secret lover's name reveal.
>   Upon a gooseberry bush a snail I found,
>   For always snails near sweetest fruit abound.
>   I seiz'd the vermin, home I quickly sped,
>   And on the hearth the milk-white embers spread.
>   Slow crawl'd the snail, and if I right can spell,
>   In the soft ashes marked a curious L ;
>   Oh ! may this wondrous omen lucky prove,
>   For L is found in Lubberkin and Love."

Snails, too, it would seem, were deemed good for a cough in times past. Mrs. Delany* writes in January, 1758 :—" Does Mary cough in the night ? Two or three snails boiled in her barley-water or tea-water, or whatever she drinks, might be of great service to her ; taken in time, they have done wonderful cures. She must know nothing of it. They give no manner of taste. It would be best nobody should know it but yourself, and I should imagine six or eight boiled in a quart of water, and strained off and put into a bottle, would be a good way, adding a spoonful or two of that to every liquid she takes. They must be fresh done every two or three days, otherwise they grow too thick."

There is a notion prevalent all over Scotland, says Chambers ('Popular Rhymes,' 1870, p. 202), " that an unusually large species of snail—probably the *Helix pomatia*—was kept by the monks in former days

* Extracted from ' Book of Days,' vol. i. p. 198.

about their convents and monasteries, and that it is still rife about the ruins of religious houses. The following story, from its universality, seems to have some truth at bottom. In a time of long enduring famine in a past age, when all people looked attenuated and pale from low diet, it was observed with surprise of two poor old women that they continued to be fat and fair. They were suspected of witchcraft, as the only conceivable means of their keeping up the system at such a time, were seized, and subjected to examination. With much reluctance, and only to escape a threatened death of torment, they confessed that, in the previous autumn, when the state of the harvest gave token of coming dearth, they had busied themselves in collecting snails, which they salted as provisions; and by dieting on these creatures, which furnished a wholesome, if not an agreeable food, they had lived in comparative comfort all the winter. The discovery in their house of the barrel, still containing a large amount of this molluscous provision, confirmed the tale; and they were set at liberty, not without some approbation of their foresight, and the pious wisdom they had shown in not rejecting any healthful fare which Providence had placed at their command."

CHAPTER V.

INSECTS—REPTILES.

The Bee — Ant — Spider — Butterfly — Moth — Dragon-fly — Fly — Daddy-longlegs — Gnat — Cricket — Wasp — Flea — Ladybird — Snake — Glow-worm — Toad.

OUR forefathers, says Couch,* appear to have been amongst those who considered bees as possessing a portion "divinæ mentis"; for there is a degree of deference yet paid to them which would scarcely be offered to beings endowed with only ordinary animal instinct. Indeed, the varied kinds of superstitions connected with these remarkable little insects presuppose the idea that they possess a certain amount of understanding or instinct whereby they are able to take cognizance of things which otherwise they could not do. Thus, to remove bees on any day but Good Friday would, it is said in Cornwall, most certainly ensure their death. In Bedfordshire, it is by no means uncommon for the peasantry to sing a psalm in front of hives in which bees are not doing well, as afterwards they are sure to thrive. In Yorkshire there is a custom, which has been revived, more or less, by the country people, ever since the alteration of the style,

* 'History of Polperro,' p. 168.

of watching, on the midnight of the new and old
Christmas Eve, by the beehives, in order to determine
on the right Christmas from the loud humming noise
which they suppose the bees will make when the birth
of our Saviour took place.

The sale of bees is considered by some a very unlucky
proceeding ; and they are not unfrequently transferred from one owner to another, with the tacit understanding that a bushel of corn—the constant value of
a swarm—is to be given in return. In Sussex, we
are informed, no one would think of buying a stock
of bees, or of paying for them in anything else but
gold or hay—half-a-sovereign is the usual price.
Virgil's precept is followed everywhere :—

" Tinnitusque cie, et matris quate cymbala circum ;"

the instruments used for ringing them down being
generally the frying-pan and one of the house door-
keys. In allusion to this practice, we find the following remarks in 'Tusser Redivivus,' 1744, p. 62 :—" The
tinkling after them with a warming-pan, frying-pan,
kettle, is of good use to let the neighbours know you
have a swarm in the air, which you claim wherever it
lights ; but I believe of very little purpose to the re-
claiming of the bees, who are thought to delight in no
noise but their own."

Borlase, in his 'Antiquities of Cornwall,' tells us
that " the Cornish to this day invoke the Spirit
Browny, when their bees swarm ; and think that their
crying Browny, Browny, will prevent their returning

into their former hive, **and** make them pitch and form
a new colony.

As to the time of their swarming, there are many
rhymes, of which **we give a specimen** :—

> "A swarm of bees in May
> **Is worth a** load of hay ;
> A swarm of bees in June
> Is worth a silver spoon ;
> A swarm of bees in **July**
> Is not worth a butterfly."

Tusser, **in his ' Five Hundred Points of** Husbandry,'
under the month of **May, says** :—

> "Take heed to thy bees, that are ready to swarme,
> The losse thereof **now is a crown's worth of** harme."

It is a common saying in Hampshire that **bees
are** idle or unfortunate whenever there are wars. **In**
Northamptonshire, a notion prevails that they will not
thrive in a quarrelsome family. Stolen bees, too,
will not flourish, but will by degrees **pine away and**
die. In Suffolk it is looked upon as unlucky **for a**
stray swarm of bees to settle on a person's premises,
unclaimed by their owner. "Going to my father's
house," says a correspondent of Chambers's ' Book **of**
Days' (vol. **ii.** p. 752), one afternoon, I found the
household in a state of excitement, as a stray swarm
of bees had settled on the pump. A hive had been
procured, and the coachman and I hived them
securely. After this had been done, I was saying that
they **might think themselves fortunate** in getting a

hive of bees so cheap ; but I found that this was not agreed to by all, for one man employed about the premises looked very grave, and shook his head. On my asking him what was the matter, he told me in a solemn undertone that he did not mean to say that there was anything in it, but people *did* say that if a swarm of bees came to a house, and were not claimed by their owner, there would be death in the family within the year ; and it was *evident* that he believed in the omen. As it turned out, there was a death in my house, though not in my father's, about seven months afterwards, and I have no doubt but that this was taken as a fulfilment of the portent." In Cumberland, there is a popular notion that when bees die, their owner will soon die also. A vulgar prejudice prevails too in many places in England, that, when bees remove or go away from their hives, the owner of them will die soon after.* In Rutlandshire,† if a bee fly in at the window, it is a sure sign of a visitor.

A superstition very prevalent, not only in this country but also abroad, consists in announcing to bees the death of their master, as unless this is done, it is believed they will either all die or desert the hive, and in some parts the hives are even put in mourning. Many curious anecdotes are told of the misfortune befalling bees where this practice has not been strictly adhered to. "A neighbour of mine," says a correspondent of the 'Book of Days' (vol. i. p. 753),

---

* See Brand's ' Popular Antiquities,' 1849, vol. ii. p. 300.
† Also in Buckinghamshire.

"bought a hive of bees at an auction of the goods of a farmer, who had recently died. The bees seemed very sickly, and not likely to thrive, when my neighbour's servant bethought him that they had never been put in mourning for their late master ; on this he got a piece of crape and tied it to a stick, which he fastened to the hive. After this the bees recovered, and when I saw them they were in a very flourishing state ; a result which was unhesitatingly attributed to their having been put into mourning." In the neighbourhood of North Bovey, Devonshire,* a similar belief still exists.

"All of 'em dead, sir, all the thirteen! What a pity it is!"

"What's a pity, Mrs. ——? Who's dead?"

"The bees, to be sure, sir. Mrs. Blank, when she buried her husband, forgot to give the bees a bit of mourning, and now, sir, all the bees be dead, though the hives be pretty nigh full of honey. What a pity 'tis folks will be so forgetful!"

Mrs. —— continued to explain, that whenever the owner or part owner of a hive died, it was requisite to place little bits of black stuff on the hive, otherwise the bees would follow the example of their owner.

Mrs. ——'s husband, who listened while this scrap of folk-lore was being communicated by his wife, now added, "My wife, sir, be always talking a lot of nonsense, sir ; but this about the bees is true, for I've seed it myself."

* 'Report of the Devonshire Association,' 1876, vol. viii. p. 51.

In Tymm's 'Topography' we find an allusion to
this custom : " The inhabitants of Cherry Burton
believe in the necessity of clothing the bees in mourning at the death of the head of a family, to secure the
prosperity of the hive. An instance occurred in July,
1827, in a cottager's family, when a black scarf was
suspended to each hive, and an offering of a pounded
funeral biscuit, soaked in wine, was placed at the
entrance with great solemnity. In Hampshire, when
the head of a family who keeps bees dies, it is usual
for a person, after his death, at once to repair to the
hives, and gently tapping them, to say :—

> " Bees, bees, awake !
>   Your master is dead,
>   And another you must take."

Unless this is done, it is said they will very soon all
die or fly away. In other places, this intelligence is
communicated to the little community by one of the
inmates first knocking with the key of the house-
door three times against the hive, and repeating the
doleful news. In Germany, this curious custom is
still further carried out, says Mr. Tylor ('Primitive
Culture'), for not only is the sad message "given to
every beehive in the garden and every beast in the
stall, but every sack of corn must be touched, and
everything in the house shaken, that they may know
the master is gone." In Westphalia, it is customary
to announce formally to the nearest oak any death

that has occurred in a family. In some places bees are invited to funerals, and a formal invitation is sent to them. At Bradfield, a primitive little village on the edge of the Moors, in the parish of Ecclesfield, this custom is kept up, and has been from time immemorial.

We may also mention another instance of this popular belief of bees being affected by the death of a member of a family, narrated by a correspondent of 'Notes and Queries :'—" In Cheshire I overtook an old farmer's wife who had from fifteen to twenty hives of bees when I was last at her house, a couple of years ago. 'Well, Mrs. ——,' I said, 'how have the bees done this year ?' 'Ah!' she replied, 'they are all gone. When our Harriet lost her second child, a many of them died. You see, they were under the window where it lay ; and then when Will died last spring, the rest all died too ; at least some of them went away and left their honey, but the rest died. I bought a hive of bees again, but they have not swarmed, and they have not done much good. Some folks pretend to say that death has nothing to do with bees ; but you may depend upon it, it has. I always say that bees are very curious things.' 'Yes,' I said, 'they are very curious things.'"

In the 'Argus' newspaper of September 13th, 1790, we read :—" A superstitious custom prevails at every funeral in Devon of *turning* **round** the beehives that belonged to the deceased, if he had any, and that at

K

the moment the corpse is carried out of the house. At a funeral some time since at Collumpton of a rich old farmer, a laughable circumstance of this sort occurred ; for, just as the corpse was placed in the hearse, and the horsemen to a large number were drawn up in order for the procession of the funeral, a person called out, ' Turn the bees ! ' when a servant, who had no knowledge of such a custom, instead of turning the hives round, lifted them up, and then laid them down on their sides. The bees thus hastily invaded, instantly attacked and fastened on the horses and their riders. It was in vain they galloped off, the bees as precipitately followed, and left their stings as marks of their indignation. A general confusion took place, attended with loss of hats, wigs, &c., and the corpse during the conflict was left unattended ; nor was it till after a considerable time that the funeral attendants could be rallied in order to proceed to the interment of their deceased friend." This odd superstition is prevalent in many counties. Thus, in Cheshire, an old blacksmith, says a correspondent of ' Notes and Queries ' (2nd series, vol. viii. p. 243), lamented to me the ill-success which had attended his bee-keeping ever since the death of his wife, attributing it to his having neglected to turn the hives round when that event occurred.

In Lincolnshire, not only at funerals but at weddings, they give a piece of the funeral biscuit and wedding cake to the bees, informing them at the

same time of the name of the party dead or married.
It is said that if the bees do not know of the former
they sicken and die; and if ignorant of the latter,
they become very irate and sting everyone within
their reach. Bees are also believed to foretell the
weather. Thus, when many enter a hive, and none
leave it, rain is at hand. Hence the rhyme :—

> "If bees stay at home,
> Rain will soon come ;
> If they fly away,
> Fine will be the day."

Virgil, in the Fourth 'Georgic' (191–194) mentions
this idea :—

> " Nec vero a stabulis pluvia impendente recedunt
> Longius, aut credunt cœlo adventantibus Euris ;
> Sed circum tutæ sub mœnibus urbis aquantur."

Willsford, in his 'Nature's Secrets' (p. 134), says :—
" Bees, in fair weather, not wandering far from their
hives, presage the approach of some stormy weather."

In Lancashire,[*] dreaming of bees is counted fortunate, because they are industrious :—

> " Happy the man who dreaming sees
> The little humble busy bees
> Fly humming round their hive."

If the bees sting you, it is a sign of bad luck,
crosses and difficulties.

In Cornwall it is wrong to destroy a colony of
ants, which are called by the peasantry "Muryans,"

---

[*] Harland and Wilkinson, 'Lancashire Folk-Lore,' p. 148.

as it is believed that they are small people—one of the fairy tribe—in a state of decay from off the earth.

It is considered as unlucky to hurt or kill a spider, as it is lucky to let one live. Thus, in Kent, the following couplet is found :—

> " If you wish to live and thrive,
> Let a spider run alive."

In Northamptonshire the small spiders called " Money-spinners " prognosticate good luck ; and, in order to propitiate them, they must be thrown over the left shoulder. In some places, it is said that if a spider be found on a person's clothes, it is an omen that he will shortly have money, upon which superstition old Fuller thus moralises :—" When a spider is found upon our clothes, we use to say, some money is coming towards us. The moral is this :—such who imitate the industry of that contemptible creature, by God's blessing, weave themselves into wealth, and procure a plentiful estate." Willsford, in his ' Nature's Secrets,' speaking of the peculiarities attaching to certain plants, tells us that " in autumn (some say) in the gall or oak apple, one of these three things will be found, if cut in pieces—a fly, denoting want ; a worm, plenty ; but if a spider, mortality." In the supplement to the ' Athenian Oracle,' the fly in the oak apple is explained as denoting war ; the spider, pestilence ; the small worm, plenty.

Even the little butterfly, that flits brightly about in

the summer sky, and alighting on some fragrant
flower adds a further beauty to its graceful form,
is not without a folk-lore. In Devonshire, anyone
neglecting to kill the first he may see in the season,
will have, it is generally supposed, ill-luck for the
remainder of the year. As an illustration of this
superstition, Hunt, in his 'Popular Romances of the
West of England,' quotes the following, given by a
young lady:—"The other Sunday, as we were walking
to church, we met a man running at full speed, with
his hat in one hand and his stick in the other. As
he passed us, he exclaimed, 'I shan't hat 'en now, I
b'lieve.' He did not give us time to inquire what he
was so eagerly pursuing ; but we presently overtook
an old man, whom we knew to be his father, and who,
being very infirm, and upwards of seventy, generally
hobbled about by the aid of two sticks. Addressing
me, he observed, 'My *zin*, a took away wan a my
sticks, miss; wan't be abble to kil'n now though,
I b'lieve.' 'Kill what?' said I ; 'Why, 'tis a butterfly, miss, the *furst* heeth a zeed for the year; and
they zay that a body will have cruel bad luck if a
ditn 'en kill a furst a zeeth.'"

In Gloucestershire there is a superstition that if
the first butterfly you see in the opening year is *white*,
you will eat white bread during the remainder of the
year, which is another way of saying that you will
have good luck; if, however, the first is brown, it is
said that you will eat brown bread—that is, be un-

lucky. In Nottinghamshire it is regarded as great an omen to see three butterflies together as three magpies.

In Somersetshire there exists a cruel custom among the children, who, when they have caught a certain kind of large white moth, which is locally termed a *Miller*, chant over it this rhyme :—

> " Millery ! Millery ! Dousty-poll !
> How many sacks hast thou stole ?"

The poor creature is then put to death for the imagined misdeeds of his human namesake.

In Yorkshire the country people used to call, and even now occasionally do so, night-flying white moths, " souls."

In some parts of the Isle of Wight, says Halliwell, in his interesting and amusing little volume, 'Popular Rhymes,' "dragon-flies are found of a peculiarly large size, and their colours are extremely beautiful. There is an old legend respecting them which is still current. It is supposed by the country people that their sting or bite is venomous, as bad as that of a snake or adder, and perhaps from this belief their provincial name of snake-stanger, or snake-stang, is derived. It is said that these insects can distinguish the good children from the bad when they go fishing ; if the latter go too near the water, they are almost sure to be bitten ; but when the good boys go, the dragon-flies point out the places where the fish are by settling on the banks, or flags, in the proper direction."

It is a common idea that if a fly falls into the glass from which anyone has been drinking, it is a certain omen of prosperity to the drinker.

During harvest time, reapers often take very great care not to injure a large kind of daddy-longlegs—popularly known by them as the harvestman—under the superstitious notion that it is unlucky to kill one.

In the Eastern Counties of England, says Halliwell ('English Popular Rhymes'), and perhaps in other parts of the country, children chant the following lines when they are pursuing the gnat :—

> "Gnat, gnat, fly into my hat,
> And I'll give you a slice of bacon."

In Lancashire,* crickets about a house are said to be lucky, and to do no harm to those who treat them well. It is believed, however, that they eat holes in the worsted stockings of such members of the family as kill them.

In Northamptonshire it is said that the first wasp seen in the season should always be killed. By so doing, one secures to himself good luck and freedom from enemies throughout the year.†

Fleas, it has been observed, and other parasitic insects, never infest a person who is near death ; and so frequently has this, says Mr. Timbs, been remarked, that it has become one of the popular signs of approaching dissolution. This is, he adds, " in

* Harland and Wilkinson's 'Lancashire Folk-Lore,' p. 156.
† Sternberg's 'Northamptonshire Glossary,' 1851, p. 160.

all probability, caused **by the alteration in the state of**
the fluids immediately under the skin, either in quality
or quantity. **It must be** upon the same principle that
women and children **are** always more infested with
the bed-bug, and other parasitic insects, than old men,
whose sub-cutaneous fluids are scanty, and their skin,
in consequence, more rigid and **dry.**" Willsford, **in** his
'Nature's Secrets' **(1658,** p. 130), tells **us** that the
"little sable beast (called a *flea*), if much thirsting
after blood, it argues rain."

In some parts **of Sussex** the ladybird is called the
lady-bug ; and in others, fly-golding, **or** God **Al-**
mighty's Cow. This little **insect** is not without its
folk-lore, for the **children set it** on their finger,
saying :—

> " Bishop, **Bishop** Barnabee,
> Tell me when **my** wedding **shall be ;**
> If it be to-morrow day,
> Ope your wings **and fly** away."

In Lancashire, too, the children say :—

> " Lady-bird, lady-bird, fly away home ;
> Your house is on fire and your children will burn."

And in Yorkshire there is another version :—

> " Cusha-coo-lady, fly away home ;
> Thy house is a-fire and all thy bairns gone."

In Scotland there is a popular **rhyme** to this effect :—

> "Lady, Lady Landers,
> Lady, Lady Landers,
> Take up your coats about your head,
> **And** fly away to Flanders."

Scattered here and there throughout the country, we find a good deal of folk-lore connected with that most disagreeable of all reptiles—the snake. In Cornwall it is believed that the dead body of a serpent,* bruised on the wound it has occasioned, is an infallible remedy for its bite. Thus has originated the following rhyme :—

> " The beauteous adder hath a sting,
> Yet bears a balsam too."

In Devonshire we find the following remedy resorted to :—A chicken is killed, and the wound thrust into the stomach, and there allowed to remain till the bird becomes cold. If the flesh of the bird, when cold, assumes a dark colour, it is believed that the cure is effected, and that the virus has been extracted from the sufferer ; if, however, on the other hand, the flesh retains its natural colour, then the poison has been absorbed into the system of the bitten person. A correspondent of ' Notes and Queries ' (4th series, vol. iv. p. 507), tells us that he has observed nearly the same mode of cure for the bite of a snake practised amongst the Hottentots in the Kat River settlement, on the eastern frontier of Cape Colony. A few feathers are plucked from the breast of a fowl, and a small incision made in the skin, to which the wound is applied ; after some time the process is repeated ;

* See ' Popular Romances of the West of England,' 1871, p. 415 ; also Brand's ' Popular Antiquities,' 1849, vol. iii. p. 270.

the fowl, it is said, meantime gradually dying as the poison extracted from the wound operates upon it.

Mr. Hawkes ('Footprints of Former Men in Far Cornwall') gives the following remedy, as related to him by an inhabitant of the parish of Morwenstow, and is certainly highly comical:—"Cut a piece of hazlewood, and fasten a long bit and short one together in form of a cross; then lay it softly upon the wound, and say thrice, blowing out the words aloud, like one of the Commandments:—

> " Underneath this hazelin mote,
>   There's a braggoty worm with a speckled throat;
>   Nine double is he :
>   Now from nine double to eight double,
>   And from eight double to seven double,
>   And from seven double to six double,
>   And from six double to five double,
>   And from five double to four double,
>   And from four double to three double,
>   And from three double to two double,
>   And from two double to one double,
>   And from one double to no double,
>   No double hath he !"

This charm, of course, like all others, has never been known to fail, except from people's obstinacy and want of faith.

In Sussex there is a superstition that the slow-worm has certain words engraven on his belly :—

> " If I could hear as well as see,
>   No man of life should master me."

Another version of the same rhyme is :—

> "If I could hear as well as I can see,
> No man nor beast should pass by me."

There has always been an aversion to toads. The older poets clothed him, says Sir William Jardine, in his notes on White's 'Natural History of Selborne' (1853, p. 42), "in a garb ugly and venomous;" and one of our master bards has, likened the Evil Spirit to him, as a semblance of all that is devilish and disgusting :—

> "Him they found,
> Squat like *a toad*, close at the ear of Eve,
> Assaying with all his devilish art to reach
> The organs of her fancy."

Thus we are taught, and the feeling is handed down from family to family, to loathe a harmless animal. The bite is innocent of any after consequences, and we never saw a toad attempt to bite. The exudation of the skin is only used in self-defence. This, however, is a disputed point, and naturalists are divided in their opinion.*

Herrick, in his 'Hesperides,' mentions the following "charm, or allay, for love" :—

> "If so be a toad be laid
> In a sheep-skin newly flaid,
> And that ty'd to man, 'twill sever
> Him and his affections ever."

---

* See Cuvier's 'Animal Kingdom.'

According to a very old belief, there is a violent antipathy between a toad and a spider, and that they "poisonously destroy each other," says Sir Thomas Browne ('Vulgar Errors,' book iii.), "is very famous, and solemn stories have been written of their combats, wherein the victory is generally ascribed to the spider." Erasmus tells a ridiculous story of a monk found asleep on his back, with a toad squatted upon his mouth. The brethren, carefully conveying the monk, placed him immediately under the web of a spider, who instantly descended upon and at length slew the toad, and delivered the monk from an ugly death.

CHAPTER VI.

CHARMS.

Madness — Hydrophobia—Epilepsy—Shingles—Sciatica—Hiccough—Stopping Blood—Sprain—Thrush—Consumption — Goitre—Wen — Cancer— Sore-eyes—Whooping-cough — Toothache — Earache —Headache —Ague —**Cramp**— Warts— Small-pox — Measles — Burn — Ringworm — Scarlet-fever — Boils — Sting of Nettle — Prick of Thorn.

EVERY country has its own peculiar belief in what perhaps may best be called charm-magic—the supposed cure of certain diseases by the instrumentality of charms. This is a species of superstition, which, curious to say, is not by any means confined to the ignorant and uneducated, but often shared in by those who lay claim to possessing not only knowledge, but its invaluable accompaniment, common sense. Charm-formulas are frequently actual prayers, and not always of a very reverential tone. Sometimes they are mere verbal forms, without the slightest meaning, yet they are repeated with equal care and solemnity, as some inherent magic is believed to be embodied in them. As will be seen in the following pages, there are charms supposed to be curative of "all the ills that flesh is heir to."

Borlase notices, in his ' Natural History of Cornwall,'

(p. 302), a very singular method of curing madness,
mentioned, too, by Carew, as practised in the parish
of Altarnum, which consisted in placing "the dis-
ordered in mind on the brink of a square pool filled
with water from St. Nun's Well. The patient,
having no intimation of what was intended, was,
by a sudden blow on the breast, tumbled into the
pool, where he was tossed up and down by some
persons of superior strength till, being quite debili-
tated, his fury forsook him; he was then carried
to church, and certain masses were sung over him.
The Cornish call this immersion *boossenning*, from
beuzi or bidhyzi, in the Cornu-British and Armoric,
signifying to dip or drown." Casting mad people
into the sea, says Mr. Pettigrew, in his 'Superstitions
connected with Medicine and Surgery' (1844, p. 63),
or immersing them in the water until nigh drowned,
have been recommended by high medical authorities
as a means of cure. Boerhaave has an aphorism
(1123) to this effect:—"Præcipitatio in mare, sub-
mersio in eo continuata quamdiu ferre potest princeps
remedium est."

Sir Walter Scott alludes to this practice in his
'Marmion':—

> "Thence to St. Fillan's blessed well,
> Whose spring can frenzied dreams dispel,
> And the crazed brain restore :"

and in a note he adds, "There are in Perthshire
several wells and springs dedicated to St. Fillan,
which are still places of pilgrimage and offerings,

even among the Protestants. They are held powerful in cases of madness, and in cases of very late occurrence, lunatics have been left all night bound to the holy stone, in confidence that the saint would cure and unloose them before morning."

The following extract from the 'Pall Mall Gazette' for Oct. 12th, 1866, illustrates a singular remedy for hydrophobia, still practised in Buckinghamshire :— "At an inquest held on the 5th of October at Bradwell, on the body of a child of five years of age, which had died of hydrophobia, evidence was given of a practice almost incredible in civilized England. Sarah Mackness stated that at the request of the mother of the deceased, she had fished the body of the dog, by which the child had been bitten, out of the river, and had extracted its liver, a slice of which she had frizzled before the fire, and had then given it to the child to be eaten with some bread. The dog had been drowned nine days before. The child ate the liver greedily, drank some tea afterwards, and died in spite of this strange specific." Such superstition as this can hardly be understood in the nineteenth century.

The 'Maidstone Gazette' of September 12th, 1848, gives a curious piece of superstition on this point :— "So strong a hold has the genius of superstition among the peasantry of South Wales, that a woman recently bitten by a mad donkey was sent to the churchyard of St. Edrins to eat the grass, which, it is believed, has the peculiar property of being an antidote to hydrophobia."

From an old manuscript receipt-book of cookery, medicine, and lucky days and signs, quoted by a correspondent of ' Notes and Queries,' we extract the following :—" Against the bite of a mad dog—write upon an apple, or on fine white bread, ' O king of glory, come in peace.' Pax. Max., D. inax.

> " Swallow this three mornings fasting ;
> Also, Hax, Max, Adinax, Opera, Chudor."

The hair of a dog, says Timbs, in his useful little book, ' Things not Generally Known ' (1856, p. 76), " when burnt, was formerly prescribed as an antidote against the effects of intoxication ; hence a man too much excited by drink at night is recommended to take a hair of the same dog the next morning, as a means of gradually counteracting his state of debility ; but the dram is now substituted for the hair." This reminds us of the following passage from ' La Gitanilla,' one of Cervantes' *novelas* :—" A young man on approaching a gipsy camp by night, was attacked and bitten by dogs. An old gipsy woman undertook to cure his wounds, and her procedure was : She took some hairs of the dogs, and fried them in oil, and having first washed with wine the bites he had in his left leg, put the hairs and oil upon them, with a little chewed green rosemary over them ; she then bound the wounds up with clean cloths, and made the sign of the cross over them." This was one of the many instances of the ancient homœopathic doctrine, says Mr. Tylor ('Primitive Culture,' vol. i. p. 761), that what hurts will also cure: it is mentioned in the Scandinavian Edda, "Dog's hair heals dog's bite."

The elder tree has been especially employed in epilepsy. In Blochwick's 'Anatomie of the Elder' (1655, p. 52), we read of an amulet made of the elder growing on a sallow :—"If in the month of October, a little before the full moon, you pluck a twig of the elder, and cut the cane that is betwixt two of its knees, or knots, in nine pieces, and these pieces, being bound in a piece of linen, be in a thread so hung about the neck that they touch the spoon of the heart, or the sword-formed cartilage ; and, that they may stay more firmly in that place, they are to be bound thereon with a linen or silken roller wrapt about the body, till the thread break of itself. The thread being broken and the roller removed, the amulet is not at all to be touched with bare hands, but it ought to be taken hold on by some instrument, and buried in a place that nobody may touch it."

The following paragraph is from the 'Times' of March 7th, 1854, and is interesting as showing the almost incredible height to which superstition is capable of reaching :—"A young woman, living in the neighbourhood of Halsworthy, North Devon, having for some time past been subject to periodical fits of illness, endeavoured to effect a cure by attendance at the afternoon service at the parish church, accom-

L

panied by thirty young men, her near neighbours.
Service over, she sat in the porch of the church, and
each of the young men as they passed out in succession, dropped a penny into her lap; but the last,
instead of a penny, gave her half-a-crown, taking from
her the twenty-nine pennies. With this half-crown in
her hand she walked three times round the com-
munion-table, and afterwards had it made into a
ring, by the wearing of which she believed she would
recover her health.

This piece of folk-lore, slightly varied, exists elsewhere. Thus, in Herefordshire, a ring, called "a sacrament shilling," made out of a shilling taken from the
offertory, is occasionally used as a remedy for fits;
and the 'Staffordshire Advertiser' tells us that on
Christmas Day, 1874, a labourer's wife in Wiltshire
came to a clergyman of the parish and asked for a
sacrament shilling in exchange for one which she
tendered. On inquiry, it appeared that her son was
subject to fits, and that the only certain remedy was
to hang a sacrament shilling round the patient's neck.
This must be obtained by first collecting a penny a
piece from twelve maidens, then exchanging the pence
for an ordinary shilling, and then again exchanging
the shilling for a sacrament one. When this rule has
been carefully followed out, it has never been known
to fail. The following extract from the 'Stamford
Mercury' (Oct. 8th, 1858), chronicles another piece of
superstition of by no means a pleasing kind:—"A

collier's wife recently applied to the sexton of Ruabon Church for ever so small a **portion of a human** skull **for** the purpose **of** grating **it** similar to ginger, to be afterwards added **to some** mixture which she **intended** giving to her daughter **as a** remedy against **fits, to** which she was subject." **This** practice **exists more or** less all over **the country.**

There is **an** irritating **herpetic** disease which, like a girdle, **gradually encircles the** body, whence its English name **of the** *shingles* (**Latin,** *cingulum*). "**By an** imagination **not difficult to** understand," says Mr. Tylor,* "the **disease is** attributed **to a sort of** coiling snake ; **and I remember a** case in **Cornwall where a** girl's family waited **in great fear to see if the creature** would stretch all **round her,** the **belief being that if** the snake's head and tail met, **the patient would die."** Turner, in his 'Diseases of the Skin' (p. 82), notices a common charm among old **women for** the shingles : the blood **of a black** cat, taken **from the** cat's tail, and smeared **on the** part affected. **In the** only case, however, **in which** he saw this superstition **practised, it** caused considerable mischief.

Near **Exmoor,** Devonshire, and **also in parts of** Cornwall, **a curious** and uncommon charm called the "bone-shave," exists for the cure **of** sciatica. The patient lies **on his** back **on** the bank of a brook or stream, placing by his **side,** betwixt him and the **water, a** straight stick or **staff,** and, while in this

* 'Primitive Culture,' vol. i. p. 278.

position, the following **lines are** repeated by way of incantation :—

> "Bone-shave right,
> Bone-shave straight,
> As the water runs by the stave,
> **Good** for the bone-shave."

There **are many** charms for sciatica[*] common **to** Devon **and** Cornwall—the knuckle bone **of a** leg **of mutton, a raw** potato, **a** piece of loadstone; either of these **carried** in the **trouser's** pocket or round **the neck is** supposed **to be** a cure. A Cornish cure consists in wetting the forefinger of the right hand with spittle, and **crossing** the front of the left shoe **or** boot three times, **repeating the** Lord's Prayer backwards.

To cure that **troublesome little** complaint hiccough when it **comes perhaps, as it often** does, at the most inconvenient **time, the** following **rhyme** must be repeated secretly :—

> "Hickup, hickup, go away,
> **Come** again another day :
> Hickup, hickup, when I bake,
> **I'll give** to you a butter-cake."

It is needless **to** say that it seldom refuses to obey this polite command.

In Devonshire, the following charm is used for

---

[*] Cumming's 'Churches and Antiquities **of** Cury and Gunwalloe,' 1875, **p. 238.**

stopping blood :—" Our Blessed Saviour was born in Bethlehem and baptized in the river Jordan :—

> The waters were wild and rude ;
> The Child Jesus was meek, mild, and good.

He put his foot into the waters, and the waters stopped, and so shall thy blood."

The charm for a sprain, often made use of, is as thus :—" As Our Blessed Lord and Saviour Jesus Christ was riding into Jerusalem, His horse tripped and sprained His leg. Our Blessed Lord and Saviour blessed it, and said :—

> ' Bone to bone, and vein to vein,
> O vein, turn to thy rest again ! '
> M. N., so shall thine, in the name," &c.

In Scotland, when a person has received a sprain, it is customary to consult an individual practised in casting what is called the "wrested thread." This consists of a thread spun from black wool, on which are cast nine knots, and is tied round the sprained limb. During the time the operator is putting this on, he repeats in a muttering voice, inaudible even to the by-standers, these words :—

> " The Lord rade (rode),
> And the foal slade (slipped) ;
> He lighted,
> And she righted.
> Bone to bone,
> And sinew to sinew,
> Heal in the Holy Ghost's name ! "

To cure the thrush, take the child to a running stream, draw a straw through its mouth, and repeat the verse, "Out of the mouth of babes and sucklings," &c.

Formerly, many physical charms were in use for consumption. In the province of Moray, Scotland, Mr. Shaw tells us that in consumptive and hectic diseases, the inhabitants pair the nails of the fingers and toes of the patient, put them in a rag cut from his clothes, then wave their hand with the rag thrice round his head, crying *Deas Soil;* after which the rag is buried in some unknown place. This is a practice similar to that recorded by Pliny, as practised by the Magicians and Druids of his time.[*] In Somersetshire, to cure this terrible disease, the person so afflicted is either carried or led through a flock of sheep as they are let out of the fold in the morning. Very soon after this has been done, it is believed that the complaint will gradually begin to disappear until the patient entirely regains his former health and vigour.

In Surrey, a sovereign cure for the goitre was to form the sign of the cross on the neck with the hand of a corpse. In Launceston and its neighbourhood, the poor people believe that this complaint is cured by the patient going before sunrise on the first of May to the grave of the last young man who has been buried in the churchyard, and applying the

[*] See Pettigrew's 'Medical Superstitions,' 1844, p. 72.

dew collected—by passing the hand three times from the head to the foot of the grave—to the part affected. This piece of superstition exists in the neighbourhood of Plymouth as appears from the 'Times' of May 9th, 1855 :—" At an early hour on the morning of the 1st of May, a woman, respectably attired, and accompanied by an elderly gentleman, applied for admittance to the cemetery at Plymouth. On being allowed to enter, they proceeded to the grave of the last man interred ; and the woman, who had a large wen in her throat, rubbed her neck three times each way on each side of the grave, departing before sunrise. By this process it was expected the malady would be cured." In Sussex, the peasants use the following remedy for the cure of a " large neck." A common snake,* held by its head and tail, is slowly drawn nine times across the front of the neck of the person affected, the reptile being allowed, after every third time to crawl about for a time. Afterwards it is put alive into a bottle, corked up, and buried in the ground. The idea is that as the snake decays the swelling disappears.

It was a notion some years ago that toads had the power of sucking the poison of cancer from the system ; but it was doubtless perfectly erroneous, and like most other folk-lore of a similar nature mere superstition. In White's 'Selborne' (Letters 18 and 21) it will be seen that he did not, for a moment, credit

---

* 'Notes and Queries,' 1st series, vol. iii. p. 404.

the report then (1768) common as to persons suffering from this cruel complaint being cured by toads.

In the West of England, "if an invalid goes out for the first time and makes a circuit, this circuit," says Hunt ('Popular Romances of the West of England'), "must be with the sun; if against the sun there will be a relapse."

The following extract from the 'Exeter and Plymouth Gazette' (March 15th, 1877) illustrates a strange superstition practised at Braunton, Devonshire, as an eye-cure :—"A woman residing in the above-named locality recently made a house-to-house visit, begging penny pieces ; her idea being, when the amount collected reached four shillings and sixpence, she would purchase a pair of ear-rings, the wearing of which was supposed to cure her bad eyesight. She was only to seek the pence from males, and was not to say 'please' nor 'thank you,' or the spell would be broken. On asking one inhabitant, she was very sensibly told that it would be better for her to lay out the money she was collecting in food for her family, but she replied that she had faith in the charm." In the neighbourhood of Banbury, in Oxfordshire, the rain which may happen to fall on Holy Thursday is carefully preserved, and bottled, as a specific remedy for sore eyes. Charms, says Mr. Pettigrew,* were often employed for the cure of worms, accompanied with a form of prayer. Brand† quotes a manuscript which contains an exorcism

* 'Medical Superstitions,' 1844.   † 'Popular Antiquities.'

against all kinds of worms which infest the body ; it is to be repeated three mornings as a certain remedy.

In Cornwall, a curious remedy * is made use of for whooping-cough, namely, a slice of bread and butter to be eaten by the patient, or a piece of a cake given by a married couple whose Christian names are John and Joan. According to the 'Birmingham Gazette' (1867) a child from Clent in Worcestershire, suffering from the whooping-cough, was some years ago taken to the finger-post at Broom ; the parents placed it on the cross of a donkey's back, rode it round the post nine times, and, not to impede the donkey's progress, cut away part of the hedge near the post. The child was reported from this time to have been perfectly cured. It is, indeed, difficult, as in the majority of similar charms, to discover the supposed connection between the disease and the remedy. In one of the principal towns of Yorkshire, it was once customary for parents to take their children afflicted with whooping-cough to a neighbouring convent, where the priest allowed them to drink a small quantity of holy water out of a silver chalice, which the little sufferers were strictly forbidden to touch. By Protestant, as well as by Roman Catholic parents, this was considered an excellent remedy. In Gloucestershire, a good cure for whooping-cough is a roasted mouse eaten by the patient. In some parts of Devonshire, it is believed that if a child be carried fasting on

* 'Bygone Days in Devon and Cornwall.' Mrs. Whitcombe, 1874, p. 147.

a **Sunday** morning into three parishes, he will soon get much better.   In Lancashire,* it is commonly said to a parent whose child is suffering **from** this complaint, " Yo' mun tak him onto **th'** whoite-moss every **day** if yo' want'nt cure him o' that chin-cough ; " and here **and** there in Yorkshire, "Owl **broth**" is considered as **a** certain specific.   In Staffordshire, there are several remedies **for** this disease.   Hanging an empty bottle up **the** chimney is considered an infallible **cure.**†

In Norfolk, and its neighbourhood, when a child **is** seized with whooping-cough, a common house spider **is** caught, tied up **in a** piece of muslin, and pinned **over** the mantel-piece.   **So long as** the spider lives, **the** cough will continue ; **but when it** dies, the cough **in** a very short time will disappear.   On the border ground of Suffolk **and** Norfolk a **hole** is dug in a meadow, and into this **the** little sufferer is placed in a bent position, head downwards.   The flag cut in making **the hole is** then placed over him, and the child remains **in** the hole until he coughs.   **It is** thought **that** if the charm be done in the evening, with only the father **or** mother to witness it, the child will soon recover.‡   **It** is a common superstition prevalent in many parts **of** England, to **inquire** of anyone riding **on a** pyebald horse § of **a remedy** for the whooping-

* English Dialect Society, ' Lancashire Glossary,' 1875, p. 74.
† See page 47.
‡ Glyde's ' Norfolk **Garland**,' 1872, **p. 31.**
§ See ' **Folk-Lore on** the Horse,' p. 113.

cough, and whatever may be named is regarded as an infallible specific.* A correspondent of 'Notes and Queries' tells us that when staying in a village in Oxfordshire, he was informed by an old woman that she and her brothers were cured of whooping-cough in the following way. They were required to go the first thing in the morning to a hovel at a little distance from their house, where a fox was kept, carrying with them a large can of milk. This they set down before the fox, and when he had taken as much as he cared to drink, the children were to share what was left among them.

It was formerly a very prevalent idea—and one, too, not confined to our own country—that toothache was caused by a little worm, having the form of an eel, which gradually gnawed a hole in the tooth. This notion is still to be met with in Germany, and is mentioned by Thorpe in his 'Northern Mythology' (vol. iii. p. 167), who quotes a North German incantation, beginning:—

> "Pear tree, I complain to thee ;
> Three worms sting me."

It exists, too, even in China and New Zealand,† and in the latter the following charm is used :—

> "An eel, a spinyback ;
> True indeed, indeed : true in sooth, in sooth.
> You must eat the head
> Of said spinyback."

---

* Pettigrew, 'Medical Superstitions,' 1844, p. 73.
† See Shortland's 'Traditions and Superstitions of the New Zealanders.'

Shakspeare in 'Much Ado about Nothing' (Act. ii. scene 2), speaks of this curious belief :—

> "*D. Pedro.* What ! sigh for the toothache ?
> *Leon.* Where is but a humour or a worm."

This superstition was common some years ago in Derbyshire, where there was an odd way of extracting, as it was thought, the worm. A small quantity of a mixture, consisting of dried and powdered herbs, was placed in a tea-cup or other small vessel, and a live cake from the fire was dropped in. The patient then held his or her open mouth over the cup, and inhaled the smoke as long as it could be borne. The cup was then taken away, and a fresh cup or glass, containing water, was put before the patient. Into this cup the person breathed hard for a few moments, and then, it was supposed, the grub or worm could be seen in the water. In Orkney, too, toothache goes by the name of "the worm ;" and, as a remedy, the following charm, called "wormy lines," is written on a piece of paper, and carried by the person affected in some part of his dress :—

> " Peter sat on a marble stone weeping ;
>   Christ came past, and said, ' What aileth thee, Peter ? '
>   ' O my Lord, my God, my tooth doth ache.'
>   ' Arise, O Peter ! go thy way ; thy tooth shall ache no more.' "

In Staffordshire, a dead person's tooth carried in the pocket is held to be a cure for the toothache ; and in Wiltshire, it is believed by the labouring classes that if you take the fore-legs of a "want" (i.e. a mole) and one of its hind-legs, and put them into a bag, and wear the whole about your neck, you will never be troubled with the toothache. In Cornwall, this complaint, according to the superstitious, not only can be easily and speedily cured by biting from the ground the first fern that appears in spring, but it is also believed that this act will prevent the person from suffering from this complaint during the remainder of the year. A nail driven into an oak tree is reported to be a cure for this pain.

In Sussex, they say if you always clothe your right leg first, i.e. if you generally put the right stocking on before the left; right leg into the trousers before the left, &c., you will never suffer from toothache. In Norfolk, the toothache is called the "love pain," and consequently the sufferer does not receive much sympathy.

In Gloucestershire, to cure the earache the following means are resorted to: a snail is procured, and, being pricked, the exuded froth is allowed to drop into the ear.

Some years ago there resided at Cambridge an old man, called the "Duke of York," who earned his living by sitting on the steps of King's College Chapel, and showing to the numerous strangers who visited that beautiful structure, live specimens of the common English snake (*Coluber natrix*). This man added to his earnings by selling the sloughs, or cast-off skins of

these reptiles, as being excellent remedies for every
kind of pain in the head, when bound round the fore-
head and temples. Grose tells us that a halter
wherewith anyone has been hanged, if tied about the
head, will cure the headache. Moss, growing upon a
human skull, if dried and powdered, and taken as snuff,
is no less efficacious.

Charms for the cure of ague are very prevalent in
most parts of the country, differing, of course, according to the locality; some are very simple, whereas
others are just the reverse, not only requiring much
faith on the part of those who invoke them, but much
trouble. This charm is extracted from an old diary
of 1751, but was in use as recently as 1871 :—" When
Jesus came near Pilate, He trembled like a leaf, and
the judge asked Him if He had the ague. He
answered, He neither had the ague nor was He
afraid ; and whosoever bears these words in mind
shall never fear ague or anything else." This style
of phraseology, which is very common in charm invocations, is certainly of a most irreverent character, and
does not commend itself to the favour of those who
value the sanctity of the sacred name of Christ.

A very respectable ecclesiastic once told me, says a
correspondent of ' Notes and Queries,' the following
fact which had occurred within his own experience.
Having learnt from a young person that she had been
subject to the ague, but had never had any return of
it since she had worn a spell for its cure, he explained

to her the sinful nature of such superstitions, and advised her to put away the spell. For a long time she declined, alleging that if she removed it from her neck, or opened it, she would have a return of the ague. At length, however, she yielded to the priest's exhortation, took off the spell, and handed it to him. It was a small paper, sealed up. He opened it, and read its contents to her as follows :—

"Ague, farewell!
Till we meet in hell."

"There," said he, "how do you like the bargain?" The poor young woman was horrified, and declared her decided preference for the return of her malady. In Gloucestershire, a common antidote for ague is a live garden snail, sewed up in a bag, and worn round the neck for nine days. The bag is then opened, and the snail thrown into the fire, when it is said to shake like the ague, and after this the patient is never troubled with the tedious complaint. In Somersetshire, to cure ague, the poor catch a large spider and shut it up in a box. As it pines away, so in proportion is the disease supposed to wear itself out. It is curious to find how much reliance is not unfrequently placed upon this foolish notion. It shows, however, as in all other similar cases, how strong a hold superstition has kept on the minds of our country people ; and this, too, in spite of the great advancement everywhere of education.

A few years ago, we are informed that there lived near Deeping St. James, Lincolnshire, an old woman who stood in great repute with her neighbours for her cure of ague, which consisted of a small glass of gin with a pinch of candle snuff in it, for which she levied contributions on the snuffers of her neighbourhood. Another charm for this troublesome complaint was to be said up the chimney, by the eldest female of a family, on St. Agnes' Eve. It ran thus :—

> " Tremble and go !
> First day shiver and burn :
> Tremble and quake !
> Second day shiver and learn :
> Tremble and die !
> Third day never return."

Mr. Pettigrew, in his 'Medical Superstitions' (1844, p. 71), relates the following amusing narrative, of considerable interest, relating to Sir John Holt, Lord Chief Justice of the Court of King's Bench, 1709, who, it is said, "was extremely wild in his youth, and being once engaged with some of his rakish friends in a trip into the country, in which they had spent all their money, it was agreed they should try their fortune separately. Holt arrived at an inn at the end of a straggling village, ordered his horse to be taken care of, bespoke a supper and a bed. He then strolled into the kitchen, where he saw a little girl of thirteen, shivering with the ague. Upon making inquiry respecting her, the landlady told him that she was

her only child, and had been ill nearly a year, notwithstanding all the assistance she could procure for
her from physic. He gravely shook his head at the
doctors, bade her be under no further concern, for that
her daughter should never have another fit. He then
wrote a few unintelligible words in a court hand on a
scrap of parchment, which had been the direction
affixed to a hamper, and, rolling it up, directed that it
should be bound upon the girl's wrist, and there
allowed to remain till she was well. The ague returned
no more ; and Holt, having remained in the house a
week, called for his bill. 'God bless you, sir,' said the
old woman, 'you're nothing in my debt, I'm sure. I
wish, on the contrary, that I was able to pay you for the
cure which you have made of my daughter. Oh ! if I
had had the happiness to see you ten months ago, it
would have saved me forty pounds.' With pretended
reluctance he accepted his accommodation as a re-
compense, and rode away. Many years elapsed ; Holt
advanced in his profession of the law, and went a
circuit, as one of the judges of the Court of King's
Bench, into the same county, where, among other
criminals brought before him, was an old woman
under a charge of witchcraft. To support this accu-
sation, several witnesses swore that the prisoner had a
spell with which she could either cure such cattle as
were sick, or destroy those that were well, and that in
the use of this spell she had been lately detected, and
that it was now ready to be produced in court. Upon

M

this statement the judge desired that it might be
handed up to him. It was a dirty ball, wrapped
round with several rags, and bound with packthread.
These coverings he carefully removed, and beneath
them found a piece of parchment, which he immediately recognized as his own youthful fabrication.
For a few moments he remained silent : at length,
recollecting himself, he addressed the jury to the following effect :—' Gentlemen, I must now relate a
particular of my life, which very ill suits my present
character, and the station in which I sit ; but to
conceal it would be to aggravate the folly for which
I ought to atone, to endanger innocence, and to
countenance superstition. This bundle, which you
suppose to have the power of life and death, is a
senseless scrawl which I wrote with my own hand and
gave to this woman, whom for no other reason you
accuse as a witch.' He then related the particulars
of the transaction, with such an effect upon the minds
of the people, that his old landlady was the last person tried for witchcraft in that county." Again, the
possibility of transplanting or transferring the disease,
was, says Mr. Pettigrew, once commonly entertained.
By breaking a salted cake of bran and giving it to a
dog, the malady has been supposed to be transferred
from the patient to the animal.

In Hampshire, the patient makes three crosses
with white chalk on the back of the kitchen chimney
—a large one in the middle, and a smaller one on

each side; as the smoke from the fire obliterates them, so will the ague disappear. This ought to be done just as the fit is coming on.*

In Harland and Wilkinson's 'Lancashire Folk-Lore' (p. 88), we are informed that "casting out the ague" was but another name for "casting out the devil," "for it was his possession of the sufferer that caused the body to shiver and shake. One man, of somewhat better education than his neighbours, acquired a reputation for thus removing the ague by exorcism, and was much resorted to for many years for relief." These charms, if they teach anything, certainly show the power of faith, and it has been truly remarked that oftentimes faith does more for a patient than the remedy itself.

In days gone by it was customary with the kings of England to hallow certain rings on Good Friday, the wearing of which was believed to prevent illness. The custom took its rise from a ring, long preserved with great veneration in Westminster Abbey, which was reported to have been given to King Edward (probably the Confessor) by some persons coming from Jerusalem. The rings consecrated by the sovereign were called "cramp rings," and there was a special service for their consecration. Andrew Boorde, in his 'Breviary of Health,' speaking of the cramp, says:—"The kynge's majestie hath a great helpe in this matter in halowyng crampe ringes, and so geven without money

* 'Athenæum,' August 11th, 1849.

M 2

or petition."   Scattered here and there throughout
the country, we find still lingering on many remnants
of old charms for averting this complaint, all, of
course, equally supposed to be efficacious.   Thus a
cork under the pillow is said in Devonshire to be a
certain cure for cramp,* and Pepys in his 'Diary'
(vol. ii. p. 415) gives this charm :—

> " Cramp, be thou faintless,
>   As our Lady was sinless
>   When she bare Jesus."

In the neighbourhood of Penzance, the following is
considered an infallible cure :—" On going to rest, put
your slippers under the bed, and turn the soles upwards."   In the north of England, it was formerly the
custom for boys who were in the habit of swimming
to wear an eel's skin about their naked leg, as this
was supposed to be a sure preventive against cramp.
The bone of a hare's foot was considered a good
remedy.   In Withal's Dictionary (1608) we find :—

> "The bone of a haire's foot closed in a ring,
>   Will drive away the cramp whenas it doth wing."

Charms for the cure of warts are very numerous, and
are still much in use.   Lord St. Alban, in his 'Natural
History,' alluding to their cure by rubbing them with
something that is afterwards allowed to waste away
and decay, says :—"I had from my childhood a wart
upon one of my fingers ; afterwards, when I was about
sixteen years old, being then at Paris, there grew upon

---

* ' Notes and Queries,' 1st series, vol. vi. p. 601.

both my hands a number of warts, at the least an hundred in a month's space. The English ambassador's lady, who was a woman far from superstitious, told me one day, she would help me away with my warts: whereupon she got a piece of lard with the skin on, and rubbed the wart all over with the fat side; and amongst the rest, the wart which I had from my childhood; then she nailed the piece of lard, with the fat towards the sun, upon a post of her chamber window, which was to the south. The success was, that within five weeks' space all the warts went quite away; and that wart which I had so long endured, for company. But at the rest I did little marvel, because they came in a short time, and might go away in a short time again, but the going away of that which had stayed so long doth yet stick with me. They say the like is done by the rubbing of warts with a green elder stick, and then burying the stick to rot in muck." A common charm, practised by the peasantry throughout the country, consists in procuring a bean-shell, and rubbing the wart with it, and then secretly taking it under an ash-tree, and repeating these words :—

> " As this bean shell rots away,
> So my wart shall soon decay."

Some people obtain an elder stick, cut a nick or notch for each wart, touch the wart with the notch, and then secretly bury the stick.

In Cornwall, there are various ways of curing warts. A piece of flesh is taken secretly, and rubbed over them ; and it is believed **that as the** flesh decays, so in like manner the warts will vanish. In some places, an apple **is** deemed potent against warts, an idea prevalent also in Germany. Another method is as thus :—Some mysterious vagrant desires them to be carefully counted, and marking the number on the inside of his **hat,** leaves the neighbourhood, when the warts also disappear. A Devonshire cure * consists in taking a piece of twine, tying it in as many knots as one has warts, touching each wart with a knot, and then throwing the twine behind one's back into some place where it may soon decay—a pond **or** hole in the earth—but one **must** keep the matter secret. When the twine is decayed, the warts will disappear without any pain or trouble.

In Gloucestershire, one of the cures for a wart is to pierce **a snail** as many times as you have warts in number, then to stick the snail on a blackthorn in the hedgerow ; **as** the creature dies, so will the warts **wane and** disappear. In Staffordshire, it is said, that **if a person suffering with** warts rub them over with **a dead man's hand, they** will **soon disappear.** There **are** many other remedies prescribed, **such as** stealing **a piece of beef, rubbing them with it,** and then burn- **ing the beef, or rubbing them,** night and morning, **with** fasting spittle, **or with the tail** of a tortoise-

* **Brand's** ' Popular Antiquities,' 1849, vol. iii. p. 277.

shell tom cat in May. In Kent, it is believed that if a
person watches for the opportunity when a funeral is
passing, and then, wetting the forefinger with saliva,
rubs the wart three times in the same direction, saying
each time, "My wart goes with you," taking care that
this is done without its being observed, a cure will
soon be effected.

The following charm is practised in all parts of
Ireland, and is believed by even the more intelligent
classes, to be an effectual cure * :—Take a small stone,
less than a boy's marble, for each wart, and tie them
in a clean linen bag, and throw it out on the highway.
Then find out a stone in some field or ditch with a
hollow in which rain or dew may have lodged, and
wash the warts seven times therein, and after the
operation whoever picks up the bag of stones will
have a transfer of the warts. Another remedy consists in procuring a wedding-ring, and in pricking or
touching the wart with a gooseberry thorn passed
through it. We might mention many more of these
supposed remedies ; but those we have quoted are
sufficient to show that even nowadays no little reliance is placed upon what, after all, is childish superstition.

Cuthbert Bede records in 'Notes and Queries' a
preservative against infection, which he met with in
a Huntingdonshire village, where there were several
cases of small-pox. "An old cottager," he says,

* 'Notes and Queries,' 3rd series, vol. viii. p. 146.

"told me that the best way to prevent the disease from spreading was, to open the window of the sick-room at sunset, in order to admit the gnats ; who would load themselves with the infection, and then fly forth and die. 'Smoking and whitewash, and tar-water, are fools to them gnats,' said my informant, who placed the most implicit reliance on his scrap of folk-lore." Some carry on their person a small bag containing camphor, under the notion that it wards off any kind of infection.

"My nurse," says a correspondent of the same useful little periodical, "declared that I and my brother were cured of the measles by having hair cut from the nape of each of our necks, and then separately placed between two slices of bread and butter. She says she anxiously watched for a strange dog to pass (no other being efficacious). She gave him the bread and butter, and as he ate it without loathing she was sure we should be cured. He then went away, and of course never came again, for *he* died of the measles—miserably, no doubt, poor fellow, having travelled off with the disease of three affected children." Brand * tells us that in the neighbourhood of Gloucester whooping-cough is cured in the same way. In some places it is said that a roasted mouse is an excellent cure for measles, and many wonderful remedies are of course on record.

In Sussex, and also in Devonshire, within the last

* 'Popular Antiquities,' 1849, vol. iii. p. 289.

forty years, the following charm was used for the
cure of a burn or scald :—

> "Two angels from the north,
>   One brought fire, the other brought frost ;
>   Out, fire !
>   In, frost !
>   In the name of the Father, Son, and Holy Ghost."

This, with but slight variation, is found in Norfolk :—

> "An angel came from the north,
>   And he brought cold and frost ;
> An angel came from the south,
>   And he brought heat and fire ;
> The angel came from the north,
>   Put out the fire.
> In the name of the Father, and of the Son, and of the Holy Ghost."

In illustration of the above, we quote the paragraph below from the 'Pall Mall Gazette' of the 23rd
of November, 1868 :—"The child of a Devonshire
labourer died from scalds caused by its turning over
a saucepan. At the inquest the following strange
account was given by Ann Manley, a witness :—'I
am the wife of James Manley, labourer. I met Sarah
Sheppard about nine o'clock on Thursday coming on
the road with the child in her arms, wrapt in the tail
of her frock. She said her child was scalded : then
I charmed it, as I charmed before, when a stone
hopped out of the fire last Honiton Fair and scalded
its eye. I charmed it in the road. I charmed it by
saying to myself, " There was (*sic*) two angels come
from the north, one of them brought fire and the other

frost ; out, fire, in, frost," &c. I repeat this three times ; this is good for a scald. I can't say it is good for anything else. Old John Sparway told me this charm many years ago. A man may tell a woman the charm, or a woman may tell a man ; but if a woman tells a woman, or a man a man, I consider it won't do any good at all."

In Shetland, to cure a burn, these words are used :—

> " Here come I to cure a burnt sore ;
> If the dead knew what the living endure,
> The burnt sore would burn no more."

The person then blows three times upon the burnt place. Whenever anyone, too, is affected with that unpleasant complaint, ringworm, he is directed to take a little ashes between his forefinger and thumb, three successive mornings, before breakfast, and, holding the ashes to the diseased part, to say :—

> " Ringworm ! ringworm red !
> Never mayst thou spread or speed,
> But aye grow less and less,
> And die away among the ases (ashes)."

The Irish, formerly (and even now occasionally), when anyone was attacked with scarlet fever, cut off some of the sick person's hair, and put it down the throat of an ass. By this means the disease was supposed to be charmed away from the patient, and to attack the poor ass instead.

In Devonshire, "Every old woman has her remedy for boils," says Mr. Chanter ('Report and Transactions of the Devonshire Association,' 1867, vol. ii. p. 39), "some of them of a very ludicrous nature. I was favoured with a new and rather ghastly recipe, which I copy in full:—

"'To cure a friend of boils :—Go into a churchyard on a dark night, and to the grave of a person who has been interred the day previous ; walk six times round the grave, and crawl across it three times. If the sufferer from boils is a man, this ceremony must be performed by a woman, and the contrary. The charm will not work unless the night is quite dark.' There is an appended note. 'This remedy was tried by a young woman in Georgeham Churchyard,' but with what result is not told ; the inference was that it succeeded."

Another charm consists in poulticing the boil for three days and nights, and then placing the poultices with their cloths in the coffin of anyone lying dead, and about to be buried.

In Devonshire, a curious charm, consisting in creeping under an arched bramble, is used to cure blackhead, or pinsoles, as they are sometimes called. A contributor to the 'Transactions of the Devonshire Association' (1877, vol. ix. p. 96) tells us that the person affected by this troublesome malady is to creep hands and knees under or through a bramble three times with the sun : that is from east to west. The bramble must be of peculiar growth ; that is, it must form an arch, rooting at both ends, and if it reaches into two proprietors' lands, so much the better. Thus, if a bramble grows on the hedge of one owner, and a branch, of which the end takes root, extends into the field of another, the best form for working the charm is provided. In some parts, dock-tea is taken as being an infallible remedy for boils. This beverage is produced from the root, well boiled, so as to yield an essence of a not very agreeable flavour.

To cure the sting of a nettle, the person stung must rub the leaves of a dock over the part affected, repeating at the same time :—

> " Nettle in, dock out,
> Dock rub nettle out."

This charm is as old as Chaucer's time, for in ' Troilus and Cresside,' is the following passage :—

> " Thou biddest me that I should love another
> All freshly newe, and let Cressidé go.
> It li'th not in my power, levé brother ;
> And thoughe I might, yet would I not do so.
> But can'st thou playen racket to and fro,
> *Nettle in, dock out,* now this, now that, Pandare ?
> Now foulé fall her for thy woe that care."

This appears to be, too, a proverbial expression implying inconstancy.

In some parts of **Cornwall,** the following recipe is given for **the prick of a thorn** :—

> "Happy man, that Christ was born !
> He was crowned with a thorn ;
> He was pierced through the skin,
> For to let the poison in :
> But His five wounds, so they say,
> Closed before He passed away.
> In with healing, out with thorn :
> Happy man that Christ was born."

It is not unlike one known in Yorkshire :—

> "Unto the Virgin Mary our Saviour was born,
> And on His head He wore a crown of thorn :
> If you believe this true, and mind it well,
> This hurt will never fester nor swell."

Sufficient instances have been quoted to show how varied are the charms in use throughout the country ; and it is surprising, in these days of medical science, that they should still be so prevalent. It proves the force of long-standing superstition, and how difficult it is to remove certain ideas, however whimsical and fallacious, when once they have taken deep root in the mind.

CHAPTER VII.

BIRTH—BAPTISM.

THERE still linger on, throughout England, many curious superstitions connected with human birth, all of which invest this momentous event with an atmosphere of the supernatural. Thus, in Lancashire there is· a strong dread* of "the witches or fairies coming secretly and exchanging their own ill-favoured imps for the newly born infant; and various charms are used to prevent the child from being thus stolen away." Shakspeare alludes to this notion when he makes King Henry IV., speaking of Hotspur in comparison with his own profligate son, say :—

> "O that it could be prov'd,
> That some night-tripping fairy had exchang'd,
> In cradle-clothes, our children where they lay,
> And call'd mine Percy, his Plantagenet !
> Then would I have his Harry, and he mine."

This idea prevails, too, in Scotland, and Pennant informs us that in his day infants were carefully watched till the christening was over, lest they should

* Harland and Wilkinson, 'Lancashire Folk-Lore.'

be stolen or changed by the fairies. Spenser, also, mentions this superstition :—

> " From thence a fairy thee unweeting reft,
>   There as thou slep'st in tender swadling band,
>   And her base elfin brood there for thee left ;
>   Such men do changelings call, so chang'd by fairy theft."

Gay, in his fable of the Mother, Nurse, and Fairy, laughs at the superstitious idea of changelings. He represents a fairy speaking thus :—

> " Whence sprung the vain, conceited lye,
>   That we the world with fools supplye ?
>   What ! give our sprightly race away
>   For the dull, helpless sons of clay !
>   Besides, by partial fondness shown,
>   Like you, we doat upon our own.
>   Wherever yet was found a mother,
>   Who'd give her booby for another ?
>   And should we change with human breed,
>   Well might we pass for fools indeed."

In some places it is believed that children born at midnight have the power of seeing ghosts, whereas in Devonshire it is said that those born by daylight never see such things. Great importance, too, is paid by many to the day of the week on which a child is born* ; as each day is supposed to bestow upon it certain characteristics ; and hence the superstitious believe that they can prognosticate the character of a child from the day of its birth. Certain seasons are thought to be more propitious for births than others. In Cornwall, children born in May are called " May

---

* See chapter on Days of the Week.

chets," and kittens cast in May are invariably
destroyed, for

> "May chets
> Bad luck begets."

Good Friday and Easter Day, are both considered,
says Brand ('Popular Antiquities,' 1849, vol. ii.
p. 87), lucky days for changing the caps of young
children. If a child tooths first in the upper jaw,
it is considered ominous of its dying in infancy.
Children, too, prematurely wise, are said not to be
long-lived, a notion which we find mentioned by
Shakspeare, in his Richard III.

In Leicestershire, the first time a new-born child
pays a visit, it is presented with an egg, a pound of
salt, and a bundle of matches. In some parts of
Lancashire,* as well as in Yorkshire, Northumberland,
and other counties, when an infant for the first time
goes out of the house, in the arms of the mother or the
nurse, the family or families visited present it with an
egg, some salt, a little loaf of bread, and now and then
with a small piece of money. These gifts are supposed
to ensure that the child shall never stand in need of
the common necessaries of life. It was formerly customary, and the practice has not yet wholly died out,
of providing a large cheese and a cake, and cutting
them at the birth of a child. Pieces of these were
distributed among all the houses in the vicinity. If
the child was a boy, the pieces of cheese were sent to

* Harland and Wilkinson's 'Lancashire Folk-Lore.'

the males ; if a girl, to the females, each member of a family receiving a portion ; visitors also came in for their share. These were called the "Groaning Cake and Cheese." Misson, in his 'Travels in England,' says, " The custom here is not to make great feasts at the birth of their children ; they drink a glass of wine, and eat a bit of a *certain cake ;* which is seldom made, but upon these occasions."

In Oxford it was the practice to cut the "Groaning Cheese" in the middle, and by degrees to form it into a large kind of ring, through which the child was passed on the day of its christening. In the North Riding of Yorkshire, at the birth of the first child, the first slice of the "Sickening Cake," is cut into small pieces by the medical man, and distributed amongst the unmarried of the female sex, under the name of "dreaming bread." Each takes a piece, places it in the foot of the left stocking, and throws it over the right shoulder. The anxious expectant must then retire to bed backwards, without uttering a word, and if she fall asleep before twelve o'clock, her future partner will appear to her in her dream.

In some parts of North Lancashire,* it is customary to have a tea-drinking on the birth of a child. All the neighbours and friends are invited, and both tea and rum are plentifully distributed. After tea, each visitor pays a shilling towards the expense of the "birth feast," and the remainder of the evening is spent in

* Harland and Wilkinson, 'Lancashire Folk-Lore,' p. 26.

social gossip and amusements. In many country
parishes a child is invariably called by the name of
the saint on whose day it may happen to have been
born ; and any omission of this custom is believed
to bring it ill-luck It not unfrequently is the
case, therefore, that children are found with very
strange names, which can only be explained by a
reference to this practice. Herrick, in his 'Hesperides,'
has the following charms for the preservation of young
children :—

> "Bring the holy crust of bread,
> Lay it underneath the head ;
> 'Tis a certain charm to keep
> Hags away while children sleep.
> Let the superstitious wife
> Near the childs heart lay a knife ;
> Point be up, and haft be down
> (While the gossips in the towne).
> This, 'mongst other mystick charms,
> Keeps the sleeping child from harmes."

"The well-known toy," says Brand, "and a piece of
coral at the end, which is generally suspended from the
necks of infants to assist them in cutting their teeth, is
supposed to have originated in an ancient superstition,
which regarded coral as an amulét against fascination.
It was thought, too, to preserve and fasten the teeth
in men." Plat, in his 'Jewel Home of Nature and
Art,' says, "Coral is good to be hanged about children's
necks, as well to rub their gums as to preserve them
from the falling sickness: it hath also some special
sympathy with nature, for the best coral being worn

about the neck will turn pale and wan if the party
that wears it be sick, and comes to its former colour
again as they recover health." Thus Stevens, in the
'Three Ladies of London' (1584), says :—

> "You may say jet will take up a straw,
>   Amber will make one fat,
>   Coral will look pale when you be sick, and
>   Chrystal will staunch blood."

Curious to say, the same belief exists among the
West Indian negroes, who affirm that the colour of
coral is always affected by the state of the wearer's
health—it becoming paler in ill-health. In Sicily it is
very much worn as an amulet by persons of all ranks.
In an old Latin work, dated 1536, it is said, "Wytches
tell that this stone (coral) withstandeth lightenynge.
It putteth of lightenynge, whirlewynde, tempeste, and
stormes fro shyppes and houses that it is in."

It is a Norfolk superstition that when there are
boys and girls to be baptized, the boy must come
first, or else the girl will have a beard. In other
places, too, this odd notion prevails. There is a
notion prevalent in many parts of England that
a child who does not scream when sprinkled with
water at baptism, will not live long. Martin, in his
' History of St. Kilda,' tells us that it was customary
for the inhabitants always to baptize their children on
a Saturday, from a superstitious notion that if this
ceremony were observed on another day they would
die.

It was formerly the custom for the sponsors at baptisms to present the children with spoons—commonly termed apostle spoons, because the figures of the twelve apostles were carved on the tops of the handles. Rich sponsors gave twelve, those in poorer circumstances gave as many as they could afford. It is in allusion to this custom that when Cranmer professes to be unworthy of being sponsor to the young princess, Shakspeare makes the king reply :—

> " Come, come, my lord, you'd spare your spoons."

Many of these spoons are preserved in various museums. Bishop Corbet, in a poem on the Birth of Prince Charles, says :—

> " When private men get sons, they get a spoon,
> Without eclipse, or any star at noon ;
> When kings get sons, they get withal supplies
> And subsidies."

" In Scotland," says Brand ('Popular Antiquities,' vol. ii. 1849, p. 73), "children dying unbaptized were supposed to wander in woods and solitudes, lamenting their hard fate, and were said to be often seen." In the north of England it is thought very unlucky to go over their graves, or, as it is vulgarly called, "unchristened ground." In the 'Gentle Shepherd,' Bauldry, describing Manse as a witch, says of her :—

> " At midnight hours o'er the kirk-yard she raves,
> And howks unchristen'd weans out of their graves."

There is a curious superstition that an unbaptized child cannot die. The 'Morning Herald' of the 18th June, 1860, alludes to a case of attempted infanticide near Liverpool. It appeared that the unhappy mother, having entered a gentleman's grounds, placed her child on the ground and covered it with sods. Fortunately the child was discovered, and its life saved. The mother was apprehended, and charged with having attempted to destroy her child. She confessed her guilt, and added that she had previously succeeded in getting the child baptized, as she believed it could not otherwise have died.

CHAPTER VIII.

MARRIAGE.

MANY superstitions are connected with that momentous crisis in human life—marriage. Those who are anxious to enter upon the nuptial state would do well to acquaint themselves with some of these, as in the eyes of the credulous they are looked upon with no small amount of anxiety. It is impossible, indeed, to say how many an unmarried lady regards her fate or lot in life as the result of a special providence which revealed itself to her in the form of some supernatural occurrence. Thus, to see a future spouse in a dream, says Grose ('Provincial Glossary,' 1811, p. 117), "the parties inquiring must lie in a different county from that in which they commonly reside ; and, on going to bed, must knit the left garter about the right-legged stocking, letting the other garter and stocking alone ; and, as they rehearse the following verses, at every comma knit a knot :—

'This knot I knit,
To know the thing I know not yet ;
That I may see
The man (woman) that shall my husband (wife) be ;
How he goes, and what he wears,
And what he does all days and years.'

Accordingly, in a dream, the desired one will appear, with the insignia of his trade or profession." If a lady completes a patchwork quilt without assistance, she will never be married, and the reason assigned for this piece of folk-lore is, says a correspondent of 'Notes and Queries' (2nd Series, vol. xii. p. 490), that patch-work is generally made a social occupation, and a person must move very little in society, or be of un-social temper, to do such a thing alone. The lady, too, who reads the Marriage Service entirely through will never be married. It often happens that those who are too anxious to get married die old maids.

St. Agnes's Eve was, in days gone by, much observed by young maidens who wished to know when and whom they should marry. It was required that on this day they should not eat, which was called "St. Agnes's Fast." * Keats, in one of his poems, alludes most pathetically to this superstition :—

> " St. Agnes's Eve ! Ah ! bitter chill it was !
>   The owl, for all his feathers, was a-cold ;
>   The hare limp'd trembling through the frozen grass,
>   And silent was the flock in woolly fold.
>
>   *   *   *   *
>
>   They told me how, upon St. Agnes's Eve,
>   Young virgins might have visions of delight ;
>   And soft adorings from their loves receive,
>   Upon the honey'd middle of the night,
>   If ceremonies due they did aright ;
>   As supperless to bed they must retire,
>   And couch supine their beauties, lily white ;

---

* Thiselton Dyer's ' British Popular Customs,' p. 46.

Nor look behind, nor sideways, but require
Of Heaven, with upward **eyes, for all** that they desire.
   *   *   *   *

              Her vespers done,
Of all its wreathed pearls **her hair she frees ;**
Unclasp'd her warmed jewels **one by one ;**
  Loosens her fragrant bodice ; **by degrees**
  Her **rich** attire creeps rustling to her **knees :**
Half-hidden, like a mermaid in **sea-weed,**
  Pensive awhile she dreams awake, and sees,
In fancy, fair St. Agnes in her bed,
But dares **not** look behind, or all the charm **is fled."**

Formerly, too, in Scotland, a number of young men and women met together on St. Agnes's Eve at midnight, went, one by one, to a certain field, and threw in some grain, after which they repeated the following rhyme :—

    " Agnes sweet, **and Agnes fair,**
    Hither, hither, **now repair ;**
    Bonny Agnes, let me see
    The lad who is to marry **me."**

The shadow of the destined bride or bridegroom was supposed to be seen in a looking-glass **on** this very night. Similar superstitions seem to have **been practised on** St. Mark's Eve. In 'Poor Robin's Almanack' for 1770, we read how—

    "On St. Mark's Eve, at twelve o'clock,
    The fair maid will watch her smock,
    To find her husband in the dark,
    By praying unto good St. Mark."

It was a popular superstition that if any unmarried **woman fasted on** Midsummer Eve, and at midnight

laid a clean cloth, with bread, cheese, and ale, and then
sat down as if about to eat—the street door being left
open—the person whom she was afterwards to marry
would come into the room and drink to her by
bowing ; and, after filling the glass, would leave it on
the table, and, making another bow, retire.* It is
difficult to understand how even the most credulous
could have been foolish enough to believe in such
childish fancies : the fact, however, remains, and is
a striking proof of the power of superstition over the
mind. In Scotland, many love-charms are still invoked
on Hallow Eve ; an enumeration of which may be
found in Burns's 'Notes upon Halloween.'

In Dorsetshire, girls use their shoes as a means
of divining who their future husbands are to be. At
night, on going to bed, a girl places her shoes at
right angles to one another, in the form of a T,
saying :—

> " Hoping this night my true love to see,
> I place my shoes in the form of a T."

"Two young unmarried girls," says Halliwell,†
"must sit together in a room by themselves, from
twelve o'clock at night till one o'clock the next morning, without speaking a word. During this time each
of them must take as many hairs from her head as
she is years old, and, having put them into a linen
cloth with some of the herb, true-love, as soon as the

---

* See Grose's ' Provincial Glossary,' 1811, p. 47.
† ' Popular Rhymes.'

clock strikes one, she **must burn every hair separately,**
saying :—

> ' I offer **this my sacrifice,**
> To him **most** precious **in** my eyes ;
> I charge thee now come forth **to me,**
> That I this minute may thee **see ;'**

upon which her husband will appear, **and walk** round
the room, and then vanish.   The same event happens
to both the girls, **but** neither sees the other's **lover."**

Fire burning on one side of a grate is the sign of a
wedding.   What connection, however, this can have
with marriage it is impossible to say, as it generally
happens where there is a greater current of air on one
side of the room than **on the** other.   In Shropshire,
those curious to ascertain **who their** future partners
are to be, fetch at **twelve o'clock at** night from the
nearest churchyard **a** half brick, which they place
under their pillows, as, by this means, **they are** sure
to **dream about** courtship **and marriage.**

In Yorkshire it is a common saying :—" Be sure
when you go to get married that you don't go in **at**
one door and out at another, or you will always **be**
unlucky."

In the West of England, to **choose a wife, "** ascertain," says **Hunt ('Popular** Romances **of the** West
of England '), " **the day of the young** woman's birth,
and refer to **the** first chapter **of** Proverbs.   Each verse
from the 1st to the 31st is supposed to indicate,
either directly **or indirectly, the character, and** to
guide the searcher—the verse corresponding with her
age indicating the woman's character."

We might enumerate many more of these love-charms ; but those quoted are sufficient to show their nature ; and it is not a little surprising to find how, even now-a-days, many young people are credulous and superstitious enough to put confidence in them ; and, in doing so, only too often mistake their own imagination and fancy for what they believe to be a supernatural revelation.

Many superstitious notions are still retained as to the times of the year when it is regarded as lucky or otherwise to marry. The month of May has at all times been considered as unlucky for marriages; a notion which dates back eighteen centuries ago, up to the time of Ovid,* who alludes to the Roman objection to marriage in this month :—

> " Nec viduæ tædis eadem, nec virginis apta
>   Tempora.   Quæ nupsit, non diuturna fuit.
>   Hac quoque de causa, si te proverbia tangunt,
>   Mense malas Maio nubere volgus ait."

Pennant, in his 'Tour in Scotland' (1790, vol. i. p. 111), tells us that a Highlander never begins anything of consequence on the day of the week on which the third of May falls, which is styled *La Sheachanna na bleanagh,* or the dismal day.   And from other sources, it appears, that marriage is carefully avoided throughout this month.

Jeaffreson, in his 'Brides and Bridals' (1873, vol. i. p. 292), says that he is disposed to refer the evil reputation of marriages solemnized in May to the

---

* ' Fasti,' book v. 487.

Church's absolute rule, forbidding weddings between Rogation and Whitsunday. **When** the Church prohibited marriage during the greater part of May, timid and pious folk were wont **to say—**

> " Marry in May, and you'll rue the day."

In **Sir** John Sinclair's Statistical Account of Scotland, **the** minister **of** Logierait, in Perthshire, mentioning **the** superstitious practices **in the** parish, **says :—"None** choose to marry in January **or** May ; **or to have** their banns proclaimed in the end **of** one **quarter of the year, and to** marry in the beginning of **the** next." The following **proverb from** Ray, marks another superstition :—

> " Who marries between the sickle and the scythe,
> Will never thrive."

Which is not unlike one **common in** East Anglia :—

> "Marry in Lent,
> And you'll live to repent."

It **is very** generally believed that **it is unlucky** to marry **on the** feast of St. Joseph, and **this day** is therefore specially avoided. " It is supposed," says a writer in Chambers's ' Book **of** Days ' (vol i. p. 719), **"that** as this **day** fell in **Mid Lent, it** was the reason **why** all the Councils **and** Synods of the Church forbade marriage **during that season of** fasting ; indeed, all penitential days and vigils throughout the year were considered unsuitable for this joyous ceremony."

In a curious old almanac for the year 1559, "by Lewes Vaughan,* made for the Merydian of Gloucestre," we find "the tymes of weddinges when it begynneth and endeth. Jan. 14, weding begin. Jan. 21, weddinge goth out. April 3, wedding be. April 29, wedding goth out. May 22, wedding begyn."

"Childermas, or Holy Innocents' Day, has been at all times a black day in the calendar," says Brand, "of impatient lovers." On account of this superstition, few marriages ever take place ; being generally postponed until the ensuing day.†

A piece of modern doggerel, says Jeaffreson ('Brides and Bridals,' vol. i. p. 295), "declares that Monday, Tuesday, and Wednesday are all good, in different ways, for marriage ; that Saturday, having no power over destiny for blessing or cursing, is open to no grave objection ; and that Thursday is scarcely less unpropitious than Friday for wedlock." The lines are as follow :—

> " Monday for wealth,
> Tuesday for health,
> Wednesday the best day of all ;
> Thursday for crosses,
> Friday for losses,
> Saturday no luck at all."

* See Brand's ' Popular Antiquities,' vol. ii. p. 168.
† See Thiselton Dyer's ' British Popular Customs,' 1876, p. 498.

A piece of counsel, highly esteemed by prudent lovers of old time in Cheshire, was, " Better wed over the mixen than over the moor," i. e. choose a wife of a known stock near your own farmyard rather than wed a strange girl from the other side of the Staffordshire moorlands.

Short engagements are generally recommended, for—

> " Happy is the wooing
> That is not long in doing."

Although too hasty marriages are to be avoided, for, says the proverb, " Marry in haste and repent at leisure."

The principal customs formerly observed at weddings, are curiously collected in the following passage,* where the scornful lady declares her determination not to marry a boaster :—

> " Believe me, if my wedding smock were on,
> Were the gloves bought and giv'n, the licence come,
> Were the rosemary branches dipp'd, and all
> The Hippocras and cakes eat and drunk off,
> Were these two arms incompass'd with the bands
> Of bachelors, to lead me to the church,
> Were my feet at the door—were ' I John ' said,
> [Namely, ' I John take thee Mary,' in the Marriage Service]
> If John should boast a favour done by me,
> I would not wed that year."

In some of the midland and northern counties, it is customary on the evening of the Sunday when the banns of marriage are published for the first time, to

* Beaumont and Fletcher, ' Scornful Lady,' i. 1.

announce the fact with a merry peal from the church
bells. This peal is called the "Spur Peal," and the
Sunday, "Spur Sunday." * To put in the spurrings is
to give notice to the clergyman to publish the banns ;
and to be "spurred up" is to have had the banns
published for three Sundays. Mr. Hunter, in his
'Glossary of Hallamshire Words,' tells us that to *spurr*
is an old English word, equivalent to *ask*. In one of
the Martin Marprelate tracts, an interlocutor in a dia-
logue says, " I pray you, Mr. Vicker, let me *spurre* a
question to you, if I may be so bold." Another
custom connected with the publishing of banns exists
in Nottinghamshire, and is described in the following
extract from the 'Notts Guardian' of April 28th,
1853 :—"Wellow. It has been a custom from time
immemorial in this parish, when the banns of marriage
are published, for a person, selected by the clerk, to
rise and say, 'God speed them well,' the clerk and
congregation responding, Amen ! Owing to the recent
death of the person who officiated in this ceremony,
last Sunday, after the banns of marriage were read,
a perfect silence prevailed, the person chosen, either
from want of courage or loss of memory, not performing his part until receiving an intimation from the
clerk, and then, in so faint a tone as scarcely to be
audible. His whispered good wishes, were, however,
followed by a hearty Amen, mingled with some
laughter in different parts of the church." In Perth-

* 'Notes and Queries,' 1st series, vol. vi. pp. 243, 329.

shire,* ill-luck is thought **to pursue** the married couple **who** have their banns **published at** the end of one, and are married **at the beginning of** another quarter of a year.

The wedding-ring—that all important little article in the marriage ceremony—has given **rise** to very many superstitious ideas, to recount only **a** quarter of which would require far more space than we can give here. As illustrations of these, however, subjoined are **a** few which may be regarded as fair specimens.

In the first place, then, the wedding-ring is said to be worn on the fourth finger, in accordance with an old but erroneous belief, that a small artery ran from this finger to the heart.† "This," says Wheatley ('Book of Common Prayer'), " is now contradicted by experience, but several eminent authors, **as well** Gentiles as Christians, **as** well **physicians as** divines, were formerly of this opinion, and therefore they thought this finger the properest to bear this pledge of love, that from thence it might **be** conveyed, as it were, to the heart."

According to an old proverb—

> " As your wedding-ring wears,
>   Your cares will wear away."

Another version says :—

> " You'll live **out your cares.**"

---

* Jeaffreson, ' Brides and Bridals,' vol. i. p. 294.
† See Sir Thomas Browne's Works, vol. i. p. 386.

It is regarded as unlucky by very many when the wedding-ring comes off the finger, whether from accident or forgetfulness on the part of the newly-married wife. It is certain, however, that no importance is to be attached to such a piece of superstition ; as, in such a case, there would be but very few happy marriages, considering how about three-fourths, perhaps, of the wedding-rings sooner or later come off the fingers of those who wear them.

Another idea, too, by no means uncommon, is that when a lady's wedding-ring has worn so thin as to come in pieces, she or her husband will die—in other words, that with the wearing away of the wedding-ring, so, too, married life gradually wears away. Perhaps, we have here an answer to the often asked question of modern days, Why do ladies encumber themselves with such heavy wedding-rings ? Another common notion is, that if a wife should be unfortunate enough to break her wedding-ring, she will shortly lose her husband. In illustration of this superstition, a correspondent of 'Notes and Queries' tells us that part of the year 1857 he spent in North Essex, where a dreadful murder deprived a most respectable family of the farming class of its industrious head. "Ah !" said the poor widow, when I visited her shortly afterwards, " I thought I should soon lose him, for I broke my ring the other day ; and my sister too lost her husband after breaking her ring. It is a sure sign."

Atkinson, in his 'Memoirs of the Queen of

O

Prussia,' says : " The betrothal of the young couple (Frederic and **Sophia Charlotte, first** King and Queen of Prussia) speedily **followed.** I believe it was during the festivities attendant upon **this** occasion that the ring **worn by** Frederic, in memory **of his** deceased wife, with **the** device of clasped hands, **and** the motto ' *à jamais,*' suddenly broke, which was looked upon as an ómen that this union, likewise, was to **be of** short duration."

A **slice of** the bride-cake,* thrice drawn through the wedding-ring, and laid under the head of aṅ unmarried man **or** woman, **is believed to** make them dream of their future **wife or husband.** The same practice is observed in the North **with a piece of** the groaning cheese. †

In Somersetshire **it is said that the** ring-finger stroked along **any sore or** wound will **soon** heal it. All **the** other fingers **are** poisonous, especially the fore-finger.

Rings ˙**were** formerly given away at weddings. **Anthony Wood** relates of Edward Kelly, a "famous philosopher" **in** Queen Elizabeth's time, that " Kelly, who was **openly** profuse beyond the modest limits of **a sober** philosopher, did give away in gold wire rings (or rings twisted **with three gold** wires) at the marriage of one of his maid-servants, to **the** value of £4000."

A correspondent of '**Notes** and Queries' tells us

---

* 'Notes and Queries,' 3rd series, vol. x. p. 469.
† Grose's 'Provincial Glossary,' 1811, p. 47.

that, in the district about **Burnley, it is** customary to
put the wedding-ring into the posset, as after serving
it out, the unmarried person whose **cup contains**
the ring will **be the first of** the **company to** get
married. **In** Ireland **it** is a common belief that finding
the ring in a piece of Michaelmas **pie will** ensure **the**
possessor an **early marriage.**

It **is a** common superstition, especially in Ireland,
that **a marriage lacks validity unless solemnized with**
a gold **ring. Mr. Wood, in his 'Wedding Day in all**
Ages and Countries," says that at a **town in the**
south-east **of** Ireland, a person **kept a few gold**
wedding-rings for hire, and when parties **who were**
too poor to purchase a ring of **the necessary precious**
metal were about **to be married, they obtained the**
loan **of** one, and paid **a** small **fee for the same,** the
ring being returned **to the owner** immediately after
the ceremony. **In some places it is** customary **for**
the same ring to be used for many marriages, **for** which
purpose **it remains in the custody of the priest.**

The **bride's veil** originated **in the Anglo-Saxon**
custom of **performing the** marriage **ceremony under a**
square piece of cloth, **called the care-cloth, held at**
each corner **by a tall man** over **the bridegroom and**
bride to conceal her maiden blushes. Something like
this care-cloth, says Brand ('Popular Antiquities,'
1849, **vol. ii. p.** 142), " is used by **the modern** Jews, **from**
whom **it** has probably **been** derived into the Christian
Church : ' There **is a** square vestment called Taleth,

with pendents **about** it, put over **the head of the** bridegroom and bride together.'"   .

The reason why the orange blossom is worn by
brides is not satisfactorily **known.** The general
opinion seems to be that it was originally adopted as
an emblem of fruitfulness. It has also been suggested
that **this** custom was introduced by French milliners,
and that the flower in question was selected for its
beauty, rather than for any symbolical reason.   A
correspondent of 'Notes and Queries' tells us that
the practice has been derived from the Saracens,
amongst whom the orange blossom was regarded as
a symbol of a prosperous marriage ; and this is partly
to be accounted for by the fact that, in the East, the
orange tree bears ripe fruit and blossom at the same
time.

Rosemary, too, was formerly worn very extensively
at weddings.   In **an old** ballad, entitled ' The Bride's
Good-morrow,' we read :—

> " Young men and maids do ready stand,
>   With sweet rosemary in their hand,
>   A perfect token of your virgin's life ;
>   To wait upon you they intend,
>   Unto the church to make an end,
>   **And God** make thee a joyfull wedded wife."

The rosemary **was** first dipped in scented water ;
and thus in Beaumont and Fletcher's ' Scornful Lady '
it is inquired " Were the rosemary branches dipped ? "
From Ben Jonson's old **play, the** ' Tale of a Tub,' we
learn that it was usual for the bridesmaids, on the

bridegroom's **first** appearance on the wedding-day, **to present him** with a bunch of rosemary, ornamented with ribbons. Turf, speaking of the intended bride-groom's first arrival, says :—" Look, an' the wenches ha' not found un out, and do present un with a van **of** rosemary, and bays enough **to** vill a bow-pott, or trim the head of my **best** vore-horse ; we shall all **ha'** bride-laces, or point, **I zee."** Bay, too, was also in **use,** as is apparent **from** allusions in old writers.* Herrick, in his ' Hesperides,' **says :—**

> "**This** done, we'll draw lots, who shall buy,
>   And guild the baies and rosemary."

In an old wedding sermon (for in former **times, it** must be remembered, these were **very common) by** Dr. Hacket, dated 1607, **the use of rosemary at** weddings is thus set forth :—

" Ros marinus, the rosemary, **is** for married **men ;** the which, **by name,** nature, and continued use, **man** challengeth as properly belonging **to** himself. **It** overtoppeth **all the** flowers **in the** garden, boasting man's rule. **It** helpeth **the** braine, strengtheneth **the** memorie, **and is very** medicinable for **the** head. Another property **of the** rosemary is, it affects the heart. Let the ros marinus, this flower of men, ensigne of your wisdom, love, and loyaltie, be carried not only in your hands, but in your heads and hearts." **F**ormerly flowers were strewn from the house of the betrothed along the road to the church—a practice

* See Brand's ' Popular Antiquities,' vol. ii. pp. 121–123.

frequently alluded to by old writers and poets. Rowe,
in his 'Happy Village' (1796), says :—

> "The wheaten ear was scatter'd near the porch,
> The green bloom blossom'd strew'd the way to church ;"

and Shakspeare alludes to the custom :—

> "Our bridal flowers serve for a buried corpse."

A pleasing custom exists at Knutsford, in Cheshire.
On the occasion of a wedding, as soon as the bride
has set out for the church, a relative spreads on the
pavement before her house a quantity of silver-sand,
called "greet," in the form of wreaths of flowers, and
writes, with the same material, wishes for her happiness. This is soon copied by others, and if the bride
and bridegroom be favourites, there may be seen
before most of the houses numerous flowers in sand.

It was formerly believed that a union could never
be happy if the bridal party, on their way to church,
were unfortunate enough to meet one of the following animals, viz. :—a hare, a dog, a cat, a lizard, or
serpent ; while on the other hand, if a spider, toad, or
wolf came across their path, they were sure to have
prosperity and happiness. Many precautions were
consequently taken to avert any of these supposed
ill-omens, especially as oftentimes implicit confidence
was placed in them ; and there are numerous records
which tell of fainting and terror-stricken brides from
their having been the victims of such foolish fears.
Pliny, in his 'Natural History' (10th book, chapter viii.),

mentions that in his day the circos, a kind of tame
hawk, was looked upon as an auspicious omen at
weddings—a proof of the antiquity of this kind of
superstition. Perhaps, however, now-a-days, no greater
dread is occasioned among the credulous than by the
appearance of the raven :—

> " Which, seldom boding good,
> Croak their black auguries from some dark wood."

This, when seen over the head either of the bridegroom or bride, is regarded as the harbinger of
coming misfortune or sorrow — its presence alone,
even for a minute or so, being sufficient in the eyes of
the fanciful to dampen the joy of such a bright
occasion. It is curious, too, to observe how, in the
event of certain marriages having turned out un-
happily, the occurrence of this superstition has been
much commented upon, and the deduction drawn that
the issues of such marriages are exactly what might
have been expected.

It is a good omen for the sun to shine upon the
bride, an allusion to which we find in Herrick's
' Hesperides ' :—

> " While that others do divine,
> Blest is the bride on whom the sun doth shine."

If it rains while the wedding party are on their
journey either to or from church, then a life of
unhappiness is to be expected. In a letter from
Chamberlain to Dudley Carleton, dated July 10th,

1603, he says :—" Mr. Winwood was married on Tuesday, with much thunder and lightning and rain. The ominous weather and dismal day put together might have made a superstitious man startled, but he turned all to the best, and so may it prove." *   It is considered unlucky in some places for a woman to marry a man whose surname commences with the same letter as her own.   Hence the saying :—

" To change the name, and not the letter,
    Is a change for the worse, and not for the better."

This superstition exists also in Philadelphia, no doubt carried there by some of our own countrymen. In the South of England it is regarded as unlucky for a bride about to go to the church to look in the glass after she is completely dressed.   Hence, very great care is taken to put on a glove or some article after the last lingering and reluctant look has been taken in the mirror.   The idea is that any young lady who is too fond of the looking-glass will be unlucky when married.   It is a Yorkshire belief, and by no means a pleasant one, that whoever goes to sleep first on the marriage night, will be sure to die first ; this, they say, is as true as Scripture.   Hence, as may be imagined, few dare to close their eyes at such a prophetical time, and so by keeping awake leave in uncertainty that dismal piece of information which otherwise would be foretold to them.

* Brand's ' Popular Antiquities,' vol. ii. p. 170.

The modern honeymoon trip had its birth in the last days of George II., and became, says Jeaffreson,* " a recognized bridal institution in the aristocratic world in the earlier years of George III.'s reign. Many years passed before modest gentlefolk in the middle rank of life presumed to imitate their betters in respect to this convenient custom. The change of usage was, however, so agreeable to lovers of both sexes that the new fashion became yearly more general, so that by the end of the last century it was unusual for a bride, having the slightest claims to gentility, to pass the evening of her wedding-day under her father's roof."

In Yorkshire, hot water is often poured over the door-steps of the hall door as the bride and bride-groom drive away ; and the belief is that before it dries up, another marriage is sure to be agreed upon. A writer in the 'Athenæum' (November 16th, 1867) says :—" At a wedding in Holderness, the other day, at which my granddaughter assisted, a ceremony was performed there I had not observed before. As soon as the bride and bridegroom had left the house, and had the usual number of old shoes thrown after them, the young folks rushed forward, each bearing a tea-kettle of boiling water, which they poured down the front door-steps, that other marriages might soon flow, or as one said, 'flow on.'" This piece of folk-lore goes by the appellation of "keeping the threshold

* ' Brides and Bridals.'

warm for another bride." A correspondent of 'Notes and Queries' (1st series, vol. vii. p. 545) tells us that being present on the occasion of a wedding at a town in the East Riding of Yorkshire, he witnessed the following piece of divination : On the bride alighting from her carriage at her father's door, a plate covered with morsels of bride-cake was flung from a window of the second storey upon the heads of the crowd congregated in the street below; the divination consisting in observing the fate which attends its downfall. If it reach the ground in safety, without being broken, the omen is a most unfavourable one. If, on the other hand, the plate be shattered in pieces (and the more the better), the auspices are looked upon as most happy. It is difficult to understand upon what principle this conclusion is arrived at, as indeed the shattering of the plate would rather seem to imply ill-luck. The same custom exists, too, in Allendale, Northumberland, where on the bride's entry of her father's house after the marriage, she is met at the door, a veil thrown over her head, and a quantity of cake pitched over her. In Scotland * we find a similar practice observed. The mother or nearest female relative of the bridegroom attends at his house to receive the newly-married pair. She is expected to meet them at the door with a currant bun in her hands, which she breaks over the head of the bride before entering the house. It is considered very

---

* 'Notes and Queries,' 1st series, vol. xi. p. 420.

unlucky should the currant bun be broken by mistake
over the head of any person but that of the bride.
Herrick alludes to this practice :—

> " While some repeat
> Your praise, and bless you, sprinkling you with wheat."

The custom of throwing an old shoe after the bride
is still believed to propitiate success, and is kept up
in most places with as much enthusiasm as ever. It
has been suggested, however, that it is not thrown for
luck only, but that it was originally "a symbol of re-
nunciation of dominion and authority over her by her
father or guardian ; and the receipt of the shoe by the
bridegroom, even if accidental, was an omen that the
authority was transferred to him." In the Bible "the receiving of a shoe was an evidence and symbol of assert-
ing or accepting dominion or ownership ; the giving
back the shoe the symbol of rejecting or resigning it."
Thus in Deuteronomy (chap. xxv.) the ceremony of
a widow rejecting her husband's brother in marriage
is by loosing his shoe from off his foot ; and in Ruth
we find that "it was the custom in Israel concerning
changing that a man plucked off his shoe and
delivered it to his neighbour." It is customary, too,
in most places now-a-days, for showers of rice to be
thrown after the bride and bridegroom as they take
their departure from the bride's home, as this is
thought to promote their success and happiness in
their new life. A correspondent of 'Notes and

Queries' tells us that on coming out of a country
church on one occasion, after a wedding, he found a
sort of barrier erected at the churchyard gate, consisting of a large paving stone placed on its edge, and
supported by two smaller stones, and on either side a
rustic, who made the happy couple and everyone else
jump over it. On inquiry he was informed that it
was the "petting stone," over which the bride had to
jump, in case she should repent and refuse to follow
her husband. Hutchison, in his 'History of Durham,'
speaks of the "petting stone." Whenever a marriage,
he says, "is solemnized at the church, after the
ceremony the bride is to step upon it, and if she
cannot stride to the end thereof, it is said that the
marriage will prove unfortunate."

One of the most interesting antiquities of Jarrow
Church, Northumberland, is the chair of the Venerable
Bede. It is preserved in the vestry of the church,
whither all brides repair immediately the marriage
service is over, to seat themselves upon it. This act,
according to the general belief, will make them the
joyful mothers of children ; and the expectant mothers
would not consider the marriage ceremony complete
until they had been enthroned in the Venerable
Bede's chair. The chair, which is very rude and substantial, is made of oak ; is 4 feet 10 inches high ;
having an upright back, and sides that shape off for
the arms.* Formerly, too, on the lower declivity of

* See 'Antiquarian Repertory,' 1807, vol. i. p. 107.

Warton Crag, in the parish of Warton,* Lancashire, a seat called "the Bride's Chair" was resorted to on the day of the marriage by the brides of the village; and in this seat they were enthroned by their friends with due solemnity.

There is a couplet upon an unpopular bride :—

> " Joy go with her and a bottle of moss ;
> If she never comes back she'll be no great loss."

Bottle is equivalent to bundle, from the French boteler. "A bottle of straw" is a very popular phrase in Scotland, and was once common in England. A bottle of moss is a thing of no value. In Howell's ' English Proverbs' we have :—

> " A thousand pounds and a bottle of hay,
> Is all one thing at doom's day."

---

* Harland and Wilkinson's ' Lancashire Folk-Lore,' 1867, p. 265.

CHAPTER IX.

DEATH.

FEW subjects possess a wider or more extensive folk-lore than death, or are surrounded with a greater variety of mystic legends. We cannot be surprised that this is so, considering how all the nations of the world—learned or unlearned, ancient or modern—have believed in the animistic theory that the souls of men continue to survive after this life is over. Hence, the departure of the dead man's soul from the world of living beings here on earth, and its journey to the distant home of spirits, have become inter-woven with a network of superstitions varying more or less in every country and tribe ; the chief of which consist in the idea that, at death, the soul is free to do as it likes, either to wander on earth, to flit in the air, to linger near the tomb, or to travel at once to the world beyond the grave.* It is not our intention, however, to discuss these in the present pages, but to confine ourselves more especially to the superstitious notions respecting death as found in our own country, although occasionally we may deem it necessary to

* Tylor's ' Primitive Culture,' vol. i. p. 413.

refer to others of foreign nations when found to resemble those of our own.

In the first place, then, one of the most widespread beliefs, not, too, confined to this country, is that death generally announces its coming by some mysterious noise, such as a knocking at the wall or door, a rumbling in the floor ; or that dying persons themselves make known their decease in similar strange sounds. Thus, to quote Mr. Tylor's words, "Three loud and distinct knocks at the bed's head of a sick person, or at the bed's head or door of any of his relations, is an omen of his death." It is no exaggeration to say that there are very few families that are not in possession of anecdotes illustrative of this belief, and local histories supply countless details on the same subject. This superstition may be traced up to the time of the Romans, who believed that the genius of death announced his coming by some mysterious and supernatural noise. Grose informs us that besides general notices of death, many families have particular warnings ; some by the appearance of a bird, and others by the figure of a tall woman, dressed all in white, who goes shrieking about the house. This apparition is common in Ireland, and goes by the name of Benshea, and the Shrieking Woman. Pennant tells us how many of the great families in Scotland had their dæmon or genius, who gave them monitions of future events. In a note to the 'Lady of the Lake' there are some interesting particulars on this subject. A family is mentioned, the members of which received the solemn sign of approaching death by music, the sound of which floated from the family residence, and seemed to die in a neighbouring wood.

The most remarkable instance, however, we are informed, occurs in the MS. Memoirs of Lady Fanshaw. " Her husband, Sir Richard, and she, chanced, during their abode in Ireland, to visit a friend, who resided in his ancient baronial castle, surrounded with a moat.   At midnight she was awakened by a ghastly and supernatural scream, and looking out of bed, beheld, by the moonlight, a female face and part of the form, hovering at the window.   The face was that of a young and rather handsome woman, but pale ; and the hair, which was reddish, was loose and dishevelled.   This apparition continued to exhibit itself for some time, and then vanished with two shrieks, similar to that which had first excited Lady Fanshaw's attention.   In the morning, with infinite terror, she communicated to her host what had happened, and found him prepared not only to credit but to account for what had happened. 'A near relation of my family,' said he, ' expired last night in this castle.   Before such an event happens in this family and castle, the female spectre whom you have seen is always visible.   She is believed to be the spirit of a woman of inferior rank, whom one of my ancestors degraded himself by marrying, and whom afterwards, to expiate the dishonour done his family, he caused to be drowned in the castle moat.'"

Concerning the appearance of a bird which has been thought to augur approaching death, many curious anecdotes are on record. Mr. Fitz-Patrick, in his 'Life, Times, and Correspondence of Bishop Doyle' (vol. ii. p. 496), in his account of the death of Dr. Doyle, says :—"Considering that the season was midsummer, and not winter, the visit of two robin redbreasts to the sick-room may be noticed as interesting. They remained fluttering round, and sometimes perching on the uncurtained bed. The priests, struck by the novelty of the circumstance, made no effort to expel the little visitors ; and the robins hung lovingly over the bishop's head until death released him."

Lord Lyttelton, as is generally known, is said to have been forewarned of his death in a dream, in which the announcement was made by means of a bird. There are several versions of this remarkable occurrence, but the following, written by Lord Westcote, uncle of Lord Lyttelton, is the most trustworthy, and was published in 'Notes and Queries' (1862) :—

"On Thursday, the 25th of November, 1779, Thomas Lord Lyttelton, when he came to breakfast, declared to Mrs. Flood, wife of Frederick Flood, Esq., of the kingdom of Ireland, and to the three Miss Amphletts who were lodged in his house in Hill Street, London (where he then also was), that he had had an extra-ordinary dream the night before. He said he thought he was in a room which a bird flew into, which appearance was suddenly changed into that of a woman dressed in white, who bade him prepare to die; to which he answered, I hope not soon—not in two months. She replied, yes, in three days. He said he did not much regard it, because he could in some measure account for it; for that a few days before he had been with Mrs. Dawson, when a robin red-breast flew into his room. When he had dressed himself that day to go to the House of Lords,* he said he thought he did not look as if he was likely to die. In the evening of the following day, being Friday, he told the eldest Miss Amphlett that she looked melancholy; but, said he, you are foolish and fearful; I have lived two days, and, God willing, I will live out the third. On the morning of Saturday he told the same ladies that he was very well, and believed *he should bilk the ghost.*

"Some hours afterwards he went with them, Mr. Fortescue, and Captain Wolseley, to Pitt Place at Epsom, withdrew to his bed-chamber soon after eleven o'clock at night, talked cheerfully to his servant, and particularly inquired of him what care had been taken to provide good rolls for his breakfast the next morning; stepped into bed with his waistcoat on, and

* Parliament was opened on that day by George III. in person. Lord Lyttelton's name appears in the list of peers who were present.

as his servant was pulling it off, put his hand to his side, sunk back, and immediately expired without a groan. He ate a good dinner after his arrival at Pitt Place that day, took an egg for his supper, and did not seem to be at all out of order, except that while he was eating his soup at dinner he had a rising in his throat, a thing which had often happened to him before, and which obliged him to spit some of it out. His physician, Dr. Fothergill, told me Lord Lyttelton had in the summer preceding a bad pain in his side ; and he judged that some great vessel in the part where he had felt the pain, gave way, and to that he conjectured his death was owing."

In Devonshire the appearance of a white-breasted bird has from time immemorial been regarded as a certain omen of death. This superstition is said to have originated in a circumstance that happened to one of the Oxenham family in that county, and is related by Howell in his 'Familiar Epistles' : —

"I can tell you of a strange thing that I saw lately here, and I believe 'tis true. As I pass'd by St. Dunstan's, in Fleet Street, the last Saturday, I stepped into a lapidary or stone-cutter's shop, to treat with the master for a stone to be put upon my father's tomb ; and casting my eyes up and down, I might spie a huge marble with a large inscription, which was thus, to my best remembrance :—

"'Here lies John Oxenham, a goodly young man, in whose chamber, as he was struggling with the pangs of death, a bird with a white breast was seen fluttering about his bed, and so vanish'd.

"'Here lies also **Mary Oxenham,** the sister of the said John, who died **the next day,** and the same apparition was seen in the room.

"'Here lies, hard by, James Oxenham, the son of the said John, who dyed a child in his cradle a little after. And such a bird was seen fluttering about his head a little before he expir'd, which vanish'd afterwards.'

"At the bottom of the stone there is :—

"'Here lies Elizabeth Oxenham, the mother of the said John, who died **sixteen** years since, when such a bird with a white breast was seen about her bed before death.'

"To all these there be divers witnesses, both squires and ladies, whose names are engraven upon the stone."

There is a local ballad, says a correspondent of 'Book of Days' (vol. ii. p. 731), on this subject, which begins thus :—

> "Where lofty hills in grandeur meet,
>   And Taw meandering flows,
>   There is a sylvan, calm retreat,
>   Where erst a mansion rose.
>
> "There dwelt Sir James of Oxenham,
>   A brave and generous lord ;
>   Benighted travellers never came
>   Unwelcome to his board.
>
> "In early life his wife had died,
>   A son he ne'er had known,
>   And Margaret, his age's pride,
>   Was heir to him alone."

Margaret became affianced to a young knight, and their marriage day was fixed. On the evening preceding it, her father gave a banquet to his friends, who, of course, congratulated him on the approaching happy union. He stood up to thank them, and in alluding to the young knight, so soon to be his daughter's husband, he jestingly called him his son :—

> " But while the dear, unpractised word
>   Still lingered on his tongue,
>   He saw a silvery-breasted bird
>   Fly o'er the festive throng.
>
> " Swift as the lightning's flashes fleet
>   And lose their brilliant light,
>   Sir James sank back upon his seat,
>   Pale and entranced with fright."

He, however, managed to conceal the cause of his embarrassment, and the next day the wedding party assembled in the church, and the priest had begun the marriage service,—

> " When Margaret with terrific screams
>   Made all with horror start—
>   Good heavens ! her blood in torrents streams,
>   A dagger's in her heart."

The deed had been done by a discarded lover, who, by the aid of disguise, had stationed himself just behind her :—

> " ' Now marry me, proud maid,' he cried ;
>   ' Thy blood with mine shall wed ; '
>   He dashed the dagger in his side,
>   And at her feet fell dead.

> " Poor Margaret, too, grows cold with death,
>   And round her hovering flies
> The phantom bird for her last breath,
>   To bear it to the skies."

It was a belief formerly very prevalent, that in death the soul flew out of the mouth of the dying in the likeness of a bird. It is a common notion, too, that when death visits a home it frequently takes two members of a family away—a superstition current in Germany. In Longfellow's 'Golden Legend,' Ursula, lamenting the supposed loss of her daughter, says:—

> " Death never takes one alone, but two !
>   Whenever he enters in at a door,
> Under roof of gold or roof of thatch,
> He always leaves it upon the latch,
> And comes again ere the year is o'er ;
> Never one of a household only ! "

In West Sussex, there is a curious belief,* that when an infant dies, it announces the fact itself, by a visit, as if in the body, to some near relative.

The wraith, or spectral appearance, of a person shortly to die, is a given article of belief in Scotland, and even in our own country, and exists also abroad. Thus, in New Zealand, says Mr. Tylor,† " it is ominous to see the figure of an absent person, for if it be shadowy, and the face not visible, his death may ere long be expected ; but if the face be seen, he is already dead. A party of Maoris (one of whom told the story) were seated round a fire in the open

---

* ' Popular Antiquities,' vol. ii. p. 231.
† ' Primitive Culture,' vol. i. p. 405.

air, when there appeared, seen only by two of them, the figure of a relative, left ill at home ; they exclaimed, the figure vanished, and on the return of the party it appeared that the sick man had died about the time of the vision."

Folk-lore examples, says the same writer, abound in Silesia and the Tyrol, where the gift· of wraith-seeing still flourishes, with the customary details of funerals, churches, four cross roads, and headless phantoms, and an especial association with New Year's Eve. Heron, in his ' Journey through Part of Scotland' (1799, vol. ii. p. 227) tells us that "tales of ghosts, brownies, fairies, witches, are the frequent entertainments of a winter's evening among the native peasantry of Kirkcudbrightshire. It is common among them to fancy that they see the wraiths of persons dying, which will be visible to one and not others present with him." Dr. Jamieson, in his ' Etymological Dictionary of Scotland,' says, that "the wraith of a living person does not, as some have supposed, indicate that he shall die soon ; although in all cases viewed as a premonition of the disembodied state. The season in the natural day at which the spectre makes its appearance, is understood as a certain presage of the time of the person's departure. If seen early in the morning, it forebodes that he shall live long, and even arrive at old age ; if in the evening it indicates that his death is at hand."

It is a very popular fancy in Cornwall, says Hunt

('Popular Romances of the West of England,' 1871, p. 377), that "when a maiden, who has loved not wisely, but too well, dies forsaken and broken-hearted, she comes back to haunt her deceiver in the shape of a white hare. This phantom follows the false one everywhere, mostly invisible to all but him. It saves him sometimes from danger, but invariably the white hare causes the death of the betrayer in the end.

Watching in the church porch for death omens on the Eves of St. Mark and St. John, is a practice that in days gone by was much in use, especially amongst young people. The time observed was from eleven o'clock at night until one in the morning. In the same year, for this had to be done three times, it was supposed that the ghosts of all those who were to die the next year would pass into the church. Thus, when anyone was seriously ill who was supposed to have been seen in this manner, it was soon whispered abroad that he would not recover. Formerly this superstition was so prevalent and so readily believed, that if patients chanced to hear what was said about them, they at once began to despair of recovery, and many, indeed, are actually said to have died from the influence of their imaginations on this occasion. Montgomery has a pretty allusion to this superstitious custom :—

> " ' 'Tis now,' replied the village belle,
> ' St. Mark's mysterious Eve ;
> And all that old traditions tell,
> I tremblingly believe.

" ' How, when the midnight signal tolls,
 Along the churchyard green,
A mournful train of sentenced souls
 In winding-sheets are seen !

" ' The ghosts of all whom death shall doom
 Within the coming year,
In pale procession walk the gloom,
 Amid the silence drear.' "

In Ireland, **Camden** describes the looking through the blade-bone of a sheep, to try and discover a dark spot which foretells a death. **Drayton**, in his ' Polyolbion,' thus speaks of this act:—

" A divination strange the Dutch-made English have,
Appropriate to that place (as though some power it gave),
By th' shoulder of a ram from off the right side **par'd**,
Which usually they boile, the spade bone being **bar'd**,
Which when the wizard takes, and gazing thereupon,
Things long to come foreshowes, as things done long agone."

The practice thus described is called "reading the speal-bone." Mr. **Tylor**, in his ' Primitive Culture ' (vol. i. p. 113), quotes several interesting instances to show how it existed among the lower races. Thus the North American Indians, he tells us, would put in the fire a certain flat bone of a porcupine, and judge from its colour if the porcupine hunt would be successful.*

Fires and candles, says a writer in the ' Book of Days,' "afford presages of death ; coffins flying out of the former, and winding-sheets guttering down

* See Pennant's ' Tour to the Hebrides ' ; Brand's ' Popular Antiquities,' vol. iii. p. 339.

from the latter. A winding-sheet is produced from a candle, if, after it has guttered, the strip, which has run down, instead of being absorbed into the general tallow, remains unmelted; if, under these circumstances, it curls over away from the flame, it is a presage of death to the person in whose direction it points.

"Coffins out of the fire are hollow oblong cinders spirted from it, and are a sign of coming death in the family. I have seen cinders which have flown out from the fire, picked up and examined to see what they presaged; for coffins are not the only things that are thus produced. If the cinder instead of being oblong is *oval*, it is a cradle, and predicts the advent of a baby; while, if it is round, it is a purse, and means prosperity."

Gay, in his amusing fable of the 'Farmer's Wife and the Ravens,' ridiculing some of the common superstitions current in his day, alludes to the fire-coffins :—

> " ' Why are those tears? why droops your head?
> Is then your other husband dead?
> Or does a worse disgrace betide?
> Hath no one since his death applied?'
> ' Alas! you know the cause too well;
> The salt is spilt, to me it fell;
> Then, to contribute to my loss,
> My knife and fork were laid across,
> On Friday, too! the day I dread;
> Would I were safe at home in bed!
> Last night (I vow to Heav'n 'tis true)
> Bounce from the fire a coffin flew.
> Next post some fatal news shall tell.
> God send my Cornish friendsbe wel !"

In Cambridgeshire,* the peasants have a great objection to a child speaking of itself in the third person or giving itself a soubriquet, as it is considered a sign of its death in early youth.

"Few ears," says Sir Thomas Browne ('Vulgar Errors,' 1852, vol. ii. p. 210), "have escaped the noise of the death-watch, that is, the little clicking sound heard often in many rooms, somewhat resembling that of a watch; and this is conceived to be an evil omen or prediction of some person's death: wherein notwithstanding there is nothing of rational presage or just cause of terror. For this noise is made by a little sheath-winged, grey insect,† found often in wainscot benches and woodwork in the summer. We have often taken many thereof, and kept them in thin boxes, wherein I have seen and heard them work and knock with a little proboscis or trunk against the side of the box, like a *Picus martius*, or woodpecker against a tree. It worketh best in warm weather, and for the most part giveth not over under nine or eleven strokes at a time. He that could extinguish the terrifying apprehensions hereof, might prevent the passions of the heart, and many cold sweats in grandmothers and nurses, who, in the sickness of children, are so startled with these noises." It is curious that so many should, even now-a-days, regard the noise made by this little insect as an omen of death, considering how clearly the cause has been explained.

* 'Athenæum,' August 11th, 1849.
† *Anobium tessellatum.*

The witty Dean Swift has left us the following amusing charm to avert the fatal omen :—

> " A wood worm
> That lies in old wood, like a hare in her form ;
> With teeth or with claws it will bite, or will scratch,
> And chambermaids christen this worm a death-watch :
> Because, like a watch, it always cries click :
> Then woe be to those in the house who are sick ;
> For as sure as a gun they will give up the ghost,
> If the maggot cries click when it scratches the post.
> But a kettle of scalding hot water injected,
> Infallibly cures the timber affected ;
> The omen is broken, the danger is over,
> The maggot will die, and the sick will recover."

The superstition that the noise made by this insect is a death-omen is mentioned by Baxter, in his ' World of Spirits,' which, says Timbs,* obtained currency for its belief for upwards of a century.

It is a curious circumstance, says Harland (' Lancashire Folk-lore '), that in the district round Burnley, the real death-tick must only tick three times on each occasion.

It is a prevalent idea that the howling of a dog is an omen of death, which is ascribed by some to its keen sense of the odour of approaching mortal dissolution.   Be this, however, as it may, there can be no doubt that numerous remarkable coincidences have happened in which dogs by their piteous and restless whining have foretold coming death. Shakspeare says :

> " The owl shriek'd at thy birth ; an evil sign !
> The night crow cry'd, aboding luckless time ;
> Dogs howled, and hideous tempests shook down trees."

---

* ' Popular Errors,' p. 365.

Douce tells us that it was formerly believed that dogs saw the ghosts of deceased persons. In the 'Odyssey' (book xvi.), the dogs of Eumæus are described as terrified at the sight of Minerva, although she was then invisible to Telemachus. Capitolinus says that the dogs by their howling presaged the death of Maximinus. We are, it is evident, indebted to antiquity for this superstition, and it is one which has rooted itself most firmly in the feelings of many nations. Thus, "with quaint simplicity," says Tylor,[*] "the German cottager declares that if a dog howls looking downwards, it portends a death ; but, if upwards, then a recovery from sickness."

The same writer, too, quoting from Cranz's 'Grönland,' p. 267, tells us that the Greenlander believes that the seals and wild fowls are scared by spectres which no human eye but the sorcerer's can behold. The Jew[†] also, and Moslem, when they hear dogs howl, "believe that they have seen the Angel of Death come on his awful errand."

In Devonshire, a plentiful season for hazel nuts is believed to be unlucky ; hence the saying :—

> " Many nits (nuts),
> Many pits (graves)."

According to another version :—

> " Many slones (sloes), many groans ;
> Many nits, many pits."

---

[*] 'Primitive Culture,' vol. i. p. 107.
[†] Ibid., vol. ii. p. 179.

The presence of crickets in a house is generally believed to presage good luck, and hence they are most carefully preserved ; as their departure from a hearth which has long echoed with their cheerful chirp is thought to betoken approaching misfortune, and even death. It is said, too, to be very unlucky to kill a cricket, perhaps, says Grose, from its being a breach of hospitality ; this little insect generally taking refuge in houses. In White's 'Selborne' (1853, p. 174), the writer speaking of it, says, "it is the housewife's barometer, foretelling her when it will rain ; and is prognostic sometimes she thinks of ill or good luck, of the death of a near relation, or the approach of an absent lover. By being the constant companion of her solitary home, it naturally becomes the object of her superstition." Gay, in his 'Pastoral Dirge,' among the rural prognostications of death, gives the following :—

"And shrilling crickets in the chimney cry'd."

And in Dryden's 'Œdipus' occurs the subjoined :—

"Owls, ravens, crickets, seem the watch of death."

The Death's Head Moth (*Acherontia atropos*) has generally been the subject of no little alarm among the superstitious. In Germany it is very common, and is there called the "Death's Head Phantom," the "Wandering Death Bird," &c. "The markings on the back represent," says Timbs,* "to a fertile

* 'Popular Errors,' 1856, p. 364.

imagination, the head of a perfect skeleton, with the limb-bones crossed beneath ; its cry becomes the voice of anguish, the mourning of a child, the signal of grief. It is regarded as highly ominous when it flies into a room in the evening, oftentimes being supposed to foretell calamity or death.

Mice are said to portend death—a superstition not uncommon in Devonshire and Cornwall. In the former county, a poor woman one day speaking about the mice in her room, exclaimed, "I pray God at a night, when I hears them running about, to keep 'em down."

High spirits have been supposed to forebode evil, and to presage impending death. Thus Shakspeare (' Romeo and Juliet,' act v. sc. 8) says :—

> " How oft when men are at the point of death
> Have they been merry ; which their keepers call
> A lightning before death."

And, in the second part of ' King Henry IV.' (act iv. sc. 2) we find the following allusion :—

> " *Westmoreland.* Health to my lord and gentle cousin, Mowbray.
> *Mowbray.* You wish me health in very happy season ;
> For I am, on the sudden, something ill.
> *Archbishop of York.* Against ill chance, men are ever merry ;
> But heaviness foreruns the good event.
> *West.* Therefore, be merry, cos ; since sudden sorrow
> Serves to say thus—Some good thing comes to-morrow.
> *Archb.* Believe me, I am passing light in spirit.
> *Mow.* So much the worse, if your own rule be true."

And, to quote one more instance, from ' King Richard III.' (act iii. sc. 2), Hastings is represented as rising

in **the morning in** unusually high spirits. Stanley
says :—

> " The Lords at **Pomfret, when they rode** from London,
> Were **jocund, and suppos'd their states were sure,**
> And they, indeed, **had no cause to mistrust ;**
> And yet, **you** see, how soon the day o'ercast.
> **Before** dinner-time, Hastings is beheaded."

In ' Guy Mannering ' (chap. ix.) **we find the** following **allusion** to this superstition :—" ' **I think,' said
the old** gardener to one **of** the maids, ' **the gauger's**
fie,' **by** which expression the common people are
accustomed **to express those** violent spirits which
they look **upon as a presage** of death." In Miss
Benger's ' Memoirs **of** Elizabeth, **Queen** of Bohemia,'
we read :—" **It is by several writers** observed that
towards the **close of the ceremony, certain** corus-
cations of joy appeared **in Elizabeth's face,** which
were **afterwards supposed to be sinister** presages of
her **misfortunes."**

In some **parts** it is believed that if a corpse remains
warm longer than usual, it is a sign that there will
soon be another death in the house or family. As an
illustration of this we may quote the following story
recorded by a correspondent of ' Notes **and** Queries ':
" **T——** of P—— **was on his death-bed.** His wife
sat by his bed-side one night praying, when a light,
about the size of a penny candle, shone upon his
breast. The priest of Carham, Northumberland, said
it was a good sign, and that **he would go to** heaven ;

but my informant Jack didn't seem quite so sanguine
as the clergyman, for he uttered that truly Northum-
brian ejaculation, 'Dear kens!' in a highly interro-
gative manner."

Further, when they came to put T—— in his coffin,
he was not at all stiff, but was "as soople as a wullie".
(as flexible as a willow), and nearly doubled in two
when they placed him inside his wooden cell. The
old women of the neighbourhood said that some one
who should attend the funeral would die soon, owing
to the body not getting stiff, as it naturally ought to
have done. In less than three weeks, or at any rate
within a very short time, the prophetic old wives were
triumphant, as a man named R—— S——, one of the
" under-bearers " at the funeral, a " muckle strong,
sober fellow, who went wi' the cairts to the mill," took
unwell three days after the burial, and, after lingering
a few weeks, died. Another correspondent of the
same periodical says :—" I was told by an old woman
that if a corpse remained warm and 'limmack' (i. e.
flexible) longer than usual, it was a sign that there
would soon be another death in the house or family."
Sir Thomas Browne, too, in his ' Vulgar Errors' (1852,
vol. ii. p. 101), alludes to this superstition :—" If a child
dieth, and the neck becometh not stiff, but for many
hours remaineth lithe and flaccid, some other in the
same house will die not long after."

In Dorsetshire, if one of twins die, and the limbs
do not soon " stiffen rigidly," the funeral is delayed,

Q

from a notion that the dead one is "waiting for the
other;" and we are informed that the carelessness of
the relatives will sometimes verify the assertion, for
the dead one has not long to wait.* In some places,
too, it is said that if the eyes are difficult to close,
they are "looking after followers." Hence, as might
be naturally expected, at the very moment of death,
great care is taken that some one standing near shall
securely close the eyes of the deceased one.

If every remnant of Christmas decoration is not
removed out of church before Candlemas Day (February 2nd), it is believed by many that there will be
a death that same year in the family occupying the
pew where a leaf or berry is left. Hence, our forefathers have given minute directions for their removal.
An old lady, says a correspondent of 'Book of
Days' (vol. ii. p. 53), whom I knew, was so per-
suaded of the truth of this superstition, "that she would
not be contented to leave the clearing of her pew to
the constituted authorities, but used to send her servant on Candlemas Eve to see that her own seat, at
any rate, was thoroughly freed from danger." Herrick,
in his 'Hesperides,' alludes to this superstition :—

> " Down with the rosemary, and so
> Down with the baies and mistleto :
> Down with the holly, ivie, all
> Wherewith ye dress the Christmas hall ;

---

* 'Notes and Queries,' 5th series, vol. vi. p. 364.

That so the superstitious find
Not one least branch there left behind :
For look, how many leaves there be
Neglected there (maids, trust to me),
So many goblins you shall see."

In Sussex it is, here and there, believed that if the church clock strikes twelve while a hymn is being sung in the morning service, a death will most surely follow in the course of the week. This ridiculous superstition is most firmly believed in by many, and great importance is therefore attached to its occurrence. In the counties of Leicester and Northampton there is a very prevalent idea that the removal or exhumation of a body after interment bodes either death or some misfortune to the surviving members of the deceased's family. Turner, in his 'History of Remarkable Providences' (1677, p. 77), speaks of this curious belief:—"Thomas Fludd, of Kent, told me that it is an old observation which was pressed earnestly to King James I., that he should not remove the Queen of Scots' body from Northamptonshire, where she was beheaded and interred; for that it always bodes ill to the family when bodies are removed from their graves; for some of the family will die shortly after, as did Prince Henry, and, I think, Queen Anne." In some counties, as, for example, Norfolk,* Berkshire, &c., agricultural labourers generally believe that if a drill go from one end of a field to the other without depositing any seed—an accident

* See 'Notes and Queries,' 1st series, vol. vii. p. 353.

which may result from the tubes and coulters clogging with earth—some person connected with the farm will die before the year is out, or before the crop then sown is reaped. In illustration of this superstition, a correspondent of 'Notes and Queries' tells us that some twenty years ago an old gentleman died in Berkshire, a near relative of his own ; and on going down to his house, he was informed by a farm overseer that he was certain some of his lordship's family would die that season, as, in the last sowing, he had missed putting the seed in one row which he sowed! "Who could disbelieve it now?" quoth the old man.

In some parts death is said to be delayed until the ebb of the tide ; and in cases of sickness many thus pretend to foretell the hour of the soul's departure.*

George Macdonald, in his 'England's Antiphon,' says : "It was at one time a common belief, and the notion has not yet, I think, altogether vanished, that the dying are held back from repose by the love that is unwilling to yield them up." This notion is still prevalent in the North of Fife, and perhaps elsewhere ; but with it is coupled a remarkable superstition, that if the beloved one is withheld from dying by being "cried back," as the prayers for their recovery are called, the person so called back will be deprived of one or more faculties, as a punishment to the

* See Couch's ' History of Polperro,' 1871, p. 168.

parent or other relation who would **not** acquiesce in the Divine will. A correspondent of 'Notes and Queries,' speaking **of** this superstition, tells **us** the following occurrence which happened to **him** :—" I said to Mrs. B., ' Poor little H. lingered a long time ; I thought when **I** saw **him,** that he must have died the same day, but he lingered **on !'** 'Yes,' **said** Mrs. B., ' **it was a great** shame of his mother. **He** wanted to **die, and** she would not let him die ; she couldn't **part** with him. There she stood, fretting over him, and couldn't give him up ; and so we said to her, " He'll never die till you give him up !" And then she gave him up ; and he died quite **peace-** ably.' "

In many places it is supposed that the departure of life is delayed so long as any locks or bolts **in the** house are fastened, as they are believed **to** hinder the soul in taking its leave of the body. It is a very common practice, therefore, when a person is **appa-** rently at the **point of** death, to open every door in the house, so that **the** struggle between life and **death** may not be **painfully** prolonged, but the soul allowed at once to accomplish its exit from this world without the slightest impediment. A correspondent of ' Notes and Queries ' mentions the following incident, which is illustrative of this curious **superstition.** He tells us **that** he had for a long time visited **a** poor man who **was** dying **of a** very painful disease, **and was daily** expecting his death. Upon calling **one** morning to see his poor friend, the wife informed him that she thought he would **have died during** the night, and, consequently, she and her friends unfastened every lock in the house. On inquiring the reason, he was informed that any bolt or lock fastened was supposed to cause uneasiness to, and hinder the departure of, the soul. This superstition is said to be founded on the idea that the minister of purgatorial pains takes the **soul** as it escapes from the body, and, flattening it against some closed door (which alone can serve the purpose), crams it into the hinges and hinge openings. Thus the soul in torment is likely to be miserably pinched and squeezed by the movement, on any casual occasion, of **such door or lid.** An opening or swinging door frustrates **this ; and the** fiends have to try some other **locality. The** friends, too, of the departed have the consolation that they are not made the unconscious instruments of torturing them in their daily occupations. A reference to this notion may be found **in 'Guy** Mannering' (chap. xxvii.) :—"The popular belief that the protracted struggle between life and death is painfully prolonged by keeping the door of the apartment shut, was received as certain **by the su**perstitious eld of Scotland." This superstition is very common, too, in France ;* and is found even among the Chinese, who make a hole **in** the roof to let out the departing soul. To **this** day, says Tylor,† "it

---

* Monnier, 'Traditions Populaires,' p. 142.
† 'Primitive Culture,' vol. i. p. 410.

remains a German peasant saying that it is wrong to slam a door, lest one should pinch a soul in it." The same writer also informs us how the Congo negroes abstained for a whole year after a death from sweeping the house, lest the dust should injure the delicate substance of the ghost.

Church dust brought to the bed of a dying person is supposed to shorten and ease a lingering and painful death.

In days gone by, and up to the close of the last century, it appears to have been a common practice to shut up rooms in which members of the family had died. In one of Addison's papers on Sir Roger de Coverley, in the 'Spectator' (No. 110, July, 1711), we have this amusing passage bearing on the subject :—

"My friend, Sir Roger, has often told me, with a good deal of truth, that, at his first coming to his estate, he found three parts of his house altogether useless ; that the best room in it had the reputation of being haunted, and by that means was locked up ; that noises had been heard in his long gallery, so that he could not get a servant to enter it after eight o'clock at night ; that the door of one of his chambers was nailed up, because there went a story in the family that a butler had formerly hanged himself in it ; and that his mother, who lived to a great age, had shut up half the rooms in the house, in which either her husband, a son, or a daughter, had lived. The knight, seeing his habitation reduced to so small a compass, and himself in a manner shut out of his own house, upon the death of his mother, ordered all the apartments to be flung open, and exorcised by his chaplain, who lay in every room, one after another, and by that means dissipated the fears which had so long reigned in the family." It is most curious to find this custom existing among savage tribes, although, however, from different causes—the general one being either the utter abnegation of all things belonging to the dead,* or their simple surrender to the ghost. Thus the Hottentots left the dead person's abode for fear of coming in contact with the spirit, who, it was thought, might still linger within. And in Old Calabar, the child let his father's house go to decay for two years, and then rebuilt it,—the spirit by this time being supposed to have taken his departure.

Another piece of folk-lore connected with death is, that demons or evil spirits hover about the chamber of the dying, seeking to take possession of their souls as soon as they leave the body. In one of Latimer's Sermons on the Epistle for the Twenty-first Sunday after Trinity, we find the following curious practice mentioned :—" I was once called to one of my kins-folk : it was at that time when I had taken degree at Cambridge, and was made Master of Arts. I was called, I say, to one of my kinsfolk which was very sick, and died immediately after my coming. Now there was an old cousin of mine, which, after the man

* ' Primitive Culture,' vol. ii. p. 23.

was dead, gave me a wax candle in my hand, and commanded me to make certain crosses over him that was dead, for she thought the devil should run away by-and-by. Now, I took the candle, but I could not cross him as she would have me to do, for I had never seen it before. Now she, perceiving that I could not do it, with a great anger took the candle out of my hand, saying, 'It is a pity that my father spendeth so much money upon thee!' And she took the candle and crossed and blessed him, so that he was sure enough—no doubt she thought—that the devil could have no power against him."

CHAPTER X.

DAYS OF THE WEEK.

THE influence of superstition has never, perhaps, been more clearly seen than in the widespread regard paid in all ages and countries to certain days, as being either good or evil, lucky or unlucky. Indeed, it may be truly said, there is not a tribe to be found which has not its particular days for beginning, or abstaining from, anything of importance. Going back for a moment to past times, we would note that this phase of superstition was very general among the Greeks, who received it from the Egyptians, and they again from the Chaldæans. Hesiod, in his 'Days,' asserts how—

"Some days, like surly stepdames, adverse prove,
 Thwart our intentions, cross whate'er we love ;
 Others more fortunate and lucky shine,
 And, as a tender mother, bless what we design."

This notion was common among other nations, and particularly among the Romans, who had their *Dies Atri,* or unlucky days ; and was held, too, by the early Christians. Thus, St. Paul reproves the Galatians (chap. **iv. 10**) for observing days, and months, and years ; a passage upon which St. Augustine in his comment has the following remarks :—" The persons whom the Apostle blames are those who say, ' I will not set forward on my journey, because it is the next day after such a time, or because the moon is so ;' or, ' I will set forward that I may have luck, because such is just now the position of the stars.' ' I will not traffic this month, because such a star presides,' or, ' I will, because it does not.' ' I shall plant no vine this year, because it is leap year.'" Those who may be inclined to follow up this subject more fully, will find a good essay on " Day Fatality " in John Aubrey's ' Miscellanies,' and some interesting information in the ' Book of Knowledge' (book i. p. 19), as also in that excellent book, Brand's ' Popular Antiquities' (1849, vol. i. pp. 44–51). In the present chapter we would confine ourselves more especially to the folk-lore of the days of the week, briefly enumerating a few of the many superstitions and sayings connected with them. Commencing, then, with Sunday, we find it considered highly unlucky in many places to cut the nails on this day, and according to the Devonshire rhyme,—

> " Who on the Sabbath pairs his horn,
> 'Twere better for him he had ne'er been born."

Some, too, connect this superstition with a Friday, as will be seen from another rhyme, which, by-the-bye, includes each day of the week in this piece of folk-lore :—

> " A man had better ne'er been born,
>   Than have his nails on a Sunday shorn.
>   Cut them on Monday, cut them for health ;
>   Cut them on Tuesday, cut them for wealth ;
>   Cut them on Wednesday, cut them for news ;
>   Cut them on Thursday for a pair of new shoes ;
>   Cut them on Friday, cut them for sorrow ;
>   Cut them on Saturday, see your sweetheart to-morrow."

There are various versions of this rhyme, differing somewhat in detail, as, for example, in Hertford-shire :—

> " Cut your nails on a Monday, cut them for news ;
>   Cut them on Tuesday, a pair of new shoes ;
>   Cut them on Wednesday, cut them for health ;
>   Cut them on Thursday, cut them for wealth ;
>   Cut them on Friday, cut them for woe ;
>   Cut them the next day a journey to go ;
>   Cut them on Sunday, you cut them for evil ;
>   For all the next week you'll be ruled by the devil."

Sir Thomas Browne, in his 'Vulgar Errors,' commenting on this foolish custom, says :—" The set and statutory times of paring nails and cutting hair is thought by many a point of consideration, which is, perhaps, but the continuance of an ancient superstition. To the Romans it was peculiar to pare their nails upon the Nundinæ, observed every ninth day ; and was also feared by others in certain days of the week." The Jews, however, superstitiously, says Mr. Addison, in his 'Present State' of that people, pare their nails on a Friday. In some parts, again, it is considered unlucky to cut the hair on Friday, or shave the beard on Sunday; hence the following couplet:—

> " Friday cut and Sunday shorn,
> Better never have been born."

Sunday is not without its share of weather-lore, and scattered through the country are sundry proverbial sayings, of which we quote one or two as specimens. Thus, in Norfolk, it is commonly said:—

> " Rain afore chutch (church),
> Rain all the week,
> Little or much."

And in Fifeshire:—

> " If it rains on the Sunday before mess (mass),
> It will rain all the week more or less."

In the North it is said that,—

> " To-morrow come never,
> When two Sundays come together."

" This is sometimes addressed," says Halliwell, " to one who promises something ' to-morrow,' but who is often in the habit of making similar engagements, and not remembering them."

In the West of England we find some curious sayings which profess to predict the characters of children born on certain days of the week. Thus, beginning with **Sunday, in Cornwall** we are **told that,—**

> " Sunday's **child is full of grace,**
> Monday's **child is full in the face,**
> Tuesday's **child is solemn and sad,**
> Wednesday's child is merry and glad,
> Thursday's child is inclined to thieving,
> **Friday's child is free** in giving,
> Saturday's child works hard for his living."

The Devonshire rhyme is very much the same :—

> " Sunday, gentleman,
> Monday, fair in face,
> **Tuesday, full** of grace,
> Wednesday, sour and grum,   ·
> **Thursday, welcome home,**
> **Friday, free in giving,**
> **Saturday, work hard for your living."**

In Gloucestershire **it is a prevalent idea** that after an open grave on a **Sunday, a death is** sure to take place within a month. **This, says a** correspondent of Chambers's ' Book of Days ' (vol. ii. p. 52), is a **very narrowly limited** superstition, as Sunday is generally **a favourite day for** funerals among the poor. " I have, however," he says, " met with it in **one parish, where Sunday** funerals are the exception, **as I** recollect one instance in particular. **A woman** coming down from church, and observing **an** open grave, remarked, ' Ah, there will be somebody else wanting a grave before the week **is out !** ' Strangely enough (the population of the **place** was then under a thousand), **her words came true,** and the grave was dug for her."

In Devonshire it is considered **highly** unlucky to

turn a feather bed on a Sunday, as, in the opinion of many, death is sure to follow.

In Sinclair's 'Statistical Account of Scotland' (1793, vol. v. p. 82), the minister of Logierait, Perthshire, speaking of the superstitious practices in the parish, says:—" In fevers the illness is expected to be more severe on Sunday than on the other days of the week ; if easier on Sunday, a relapse is feared."

In some places great notice is taken as to the time and the day one sneezes. Thus, in Devonshire, it is said that if you—

> " Sneeze on Sunday morning fasting,
> You'll enjoy your own true love to everlasting."

This superstition differs in different localities. A common rhyme, much quoted by poor people, especially too in Devonshire, is as follows :—

> " To sneeze on Monday hastens anger ;
> To sneeze on Tuesday, kiss a stranger ;
> To sneeze on Wednesday,
> To sneeze on Thursday,
> To sneeze on Friday, give a gift ;
> To sneeze on Saturday, receive a gift ;
> To sneeze on Sunday before you break your fast,
> You'll see your true love before a week's past."

Another version of this rhyme, once common in Hertfordshire, is as follows :—

> " If you sneeze on Monday, you sneeze for danger ;
> Sneeze on a Tuesday, kiss a stranger ;
> Sneeze on a Wednesday, sneeze for a letter ;
> Sneeze on a Thursday, something better ;
> Sneeze on a Friday, sneeze for sorrow ;
> Sneeze on a Saturday, see your sweetheart to-morrow ;
> Sneeze on a Sunday, and the devil will have dominion over you all the week."

If you sneeze **any** morning before breakfast, it is a sign that **you** will **have** a present before the week is out.

Another saying is, that **"if you** sneeze on a Saturday night after the candle is put out, **you** will next day see a stranger you never saw before ; " and a piece of East Anglian folk-lore on this subject is :—

> " Sneeze on Monday, and you will
> Have a present ere the week is out."

Of course, the above rhymes are not intended to apply to sneezing produced either by cold or snuff-taking. · The mere mention of Monday, says Hampson, in the North of Scotland, in company for the first time, is lucky or unlucky, according to the sex of the person by whom it is named; and in Ireland, Monday is a very auspicious day for the commencement of any undertaking.

In ' Divers Crab-tree Lectures ' (1639, p. 126), we find the following amusing and homely rhymes upon the several days of the week, commencing with Monday :—

> " You know that Monday is Sunday's brother ;
> Tuesday is such another ;
> Wednesday you must go to church and pray ;
> Thursday is half-holiday ;
> On Friday it is too late to begin to spin ;
> The Saturday is half-holiday agen."

In Devonshire, Tuesdays and Wednesdays are regarded as lucky days, and generally chosen for the performance of any important duty. The following curious extract is quoted by Brand from a rare tract called the 'Animal Parliament,' 1707 ; and, apart from its incidental allusion to certain days of the week, is extremely quaint:—"That none must be thought good lawyers and docters, but those which will take great fees. That all duty and submission belongs to power, not to vertue. That all must have ill-luck after much mirth. That all those that marry on Tuesdays and Thursdays shall be happy. That a man's fortune can be told in the palme of his hande. That the falling of salt portends misfortune. Those that begin journeys on a Wednesday shall run through much danger. That the houling of a dog, or croaking of ravens foretell a friend's death."

Thursday is said to have one lucky hour, namely, the hour before sunrise. Stow informs us that it was noted as a fatal day to Henry VIII. and his posterity. Working people are wont to say :—

> " Thursday come,
> The week's gone."

Friday, perhaps, has more superstition and folk-lore attached to it than any other day in the week, and this, no doubt, originates from the fact of its being the day on which our Saviour Christ was crucified In many places it is considered unlucky for a child to be born, on account of its being a day of ill-omen. For the same cause, too, marriages seldom take place,

R

and persons are often found to dislike commencing any
new work. Sailors, especially, object to go to sea,
and absolutely refuse to do so until the Saturday
morning. "A respectable merchant of the City of
London informed me," says Brand, "that no person
there will begin any business, i.e., open his shop for
the first time, on a Friday." Lord Byron partook of
the superstition about Friday, and if anything of the
slightest importance, in which he was concerned, were
commenced on a Friday he was seriously disconcerted.
Curious to say, among the Brahmins of India this
same feeling prevails, for "on this day no business
must be commenced." The Spaniards look on Friday
as a very unlucky day; and among the firms those
who begin any business must expect but little success.
There are numerous rhymes and proverbs connected
with Friday, and of which the following are specimens :—

> "Friday's always the best or the worst day in the week."

Another common one is :—

> "As the Friday so the Sunday,
> As the Sunday so the week."

This relates more especially to the weather, for
according to a piece of weather-lore—

> "A rainy Friday, a rainy Sunday;
> A fair Friday, a fair Sunday."

In Devonshire it is said that—

> "Fridays in the week
> Are never aleek."

In Lancashire,* a man must never "go a courting" on Friday. If an unlucky fellow is caught with his lady love on that day he is followed home by a band of musicians, playing on pokers, tongs, pan-lids, &c.; unless he can escape from his tormentors by giving them money for drink.

A rhyming proverb informs us how "Friday's moon, come when it will, comes too soon." Sir Thomas Overbury, in his charming 'Character of a Milk-maid,' mentions a superstition alluding to dreams on Friday :—"Lastly her dreams are so chaste that she dare tell them, only a Friday's dream is all her superstition ; that she conceals for fear of anger."

In Lancashire there is a rhyme to the following effect :—

> " Friday night's dream,
> On the Saturday told,
> Is sure to come true,
> Be it never so old."

Lastly, Saturday has been regarded as partly an inauspicious, and partly a lucky day. Henry VII., we are told, looked upon it as ominous. " He entered the citie," says Lord Bacon, "upon a Saturday, as he had also obtained a victorie upon a Saturday, which day of the weeke, first upon observation, and after upon memorie and fancie, he accounted and chose as a day prosperous unto him."

In Ireland, it is said that a Saturday's rainbow

---

* Harland and Wilkinson, 'Lancashire Folk-Lore,' p. 155.

is sure to be followed **by** a week of rainy, or as they term it, "rotten weather." With respect to the new **moon,** there is in Norfolk the following rhyme :—

> " Saturday new, and Sunday **full,**
> Was never fine, nor never wull."

—a superstition which may be **found** here and there in **England,** as well **as in** Scotland, **varying, of.** course, according to the locality. **Thus** another version is :—

> " **A** Saturday moon,
> **If it comes once in seven** years,
> **Comes once too soon."**

A piece of Northamptonshire **folk-lore** informs us that the sun shines, **if only for a minute,** on every **Saturday throughout the year.** The Spaniards have a similar **notion.***

Saturday and Sunday are **considered unlucky days for servants to go to** their **places;** hence **the** saying † :—

> " Saturday servants never stay,
> Sunday servants run away."

Bourne observes that, in **his** time, **it was** usual in country villages **to** pay a greater **deference** to Satur- day afternoon **than to** any other **of** the working days of the week. The first **idea,** says Brand, of this **cessation** from labour at **that time** was, that everyone

---

* See Southey's ' Doctor,' vol. iii. p. 165.
† Sternberg's ' Northamptonshire Glossary,' 1851, p. 169.

might attend evening prayers as a kind of preparation for the ensuing Sabbath. In Jacob's 'History of Faversham' (p. 172), in 'Articles for the Sexton of Faversham' (22 Henry VIII.), we find: "Item, the said Sexton, or his deputy, every Saturday, Saint's Even, and principal feasts, shall ring noon with as many bells as shall be convenient to the Saturday, Saint's Even, and principal feasts," &c.

In old books we sometimes fall across the expression "Saturday's Stop" (or "Setterday's Stopp"), an expression signifying a space of time from Saturday evening until sunrise on Monday, when it was unlawful to take salmon in Scotland and the northern parts of England. In some extracts published from Saxon manuscripts by Dr. Hicks, we find the following:—"If on the entering year the first thunder happen on a Sunday, then it denotes mortality in royal families; if it thunder on a Saturday, then it will be mortality of judges and governors."

"The English nurse," says Mr. Tylor,* "who tells a fretful child, 'you got out of bed wrong foot foremost this morning,' seldom or never knows the meaning of her saying, but this is still plain in the German folklore rule, that to get out of bed left foot first will bring a bad day—one of the many examples of that simple association of ideas which connect right and left with good and bad respectively."

---

* 'Primitive Culture.'

In the north it will be seen from the following that attention is paid to the day washing is done:—

> " They that wash on Monday
>   Have a whole week to dry ;
> They that wash on Tuesday
>   Are not so much arye ;
> They that wash on Wednesday
>   May get their clothes clean ;
> They that wash on Thursday
>   Are not so much to mean ;
> They that wash on Friday
>   Wash for their need ;
> But they that wash on Saturday
>   Are clarty-paps indeed."

Clarty-paps is equivalent to dirty sluts. In Lancashire it is commonly said that—

> " As the days grow longer,
>   The storms grow stronger ;
>   As the days lengthen,
>   So the storms strengthen."

We might easily mention many other curious instances of superstition connected with the days of the week, but those we have already referred to show how very prevalent these are. It is worthy, too, of note that this portion of folk-lore still, as in former. times, retains its firm hold on the minds of our uneducated and credulous countrymen.

CHAPTER XI.

THE MONTHS AND THEIR WEATHER-LORE.

CONNECTED with each of the months, we find a great deal of curious weather-lore prevalent, not only in this country, but equally abroad. To attempt to give even a tenth part of this would occupy a volume, so in the present chapter we must content ourselves with simply noting some of the chief and most important superstitions attached to the months.

According, then, to old lore, if the weather in January be warm or windy, March and May will be chilly :—

> " March in Janiveer,
> Janiveer in March, I fear."

And

> " A warm January, a cold May."

Another rhyme informs us that a fine day on the first of January is not to be wished for, as—

> " If January kalends be summerly gay,
> 'Twill be winterly weather to the kalends of May."

Many consider that a dry and cold January is far better than a mild and wet one, the latter doing more harm than good. Hence the proverb—

> " If the grass grow in Janiveer,
> It grows the worse for it all the year."

An exception, however, to this rule is recorded by Ray, who says that "in the year 1667 the winter was so mild that the pastures were very green in January; yet was there scarcely ever known a more plentiful crop of hay than the summer following."

There are numerous rhymes descriptive of this month, as, for example :—

> " Jack Frost in Janiveer,
> Nips the nose of the nascent year."

And again :—

> " The blackest month in all the year,
> Is the month of Janiveer."

It must not be forgotten that nearly all the old weather sayings and superstitions have reference to the days of the month according to the old style of reckoning; hence, if we would test, the accuracy of the weather wisdom of our ancestors, we must take into account the change of style. Thus, for instance, sayings connected with Christmas and New Year's Day, should be placed under January 6th and 13th respectively, and the same rule, of course, applies to all other days.

January 6th, then, which answers to Christmas of the old style, was formerly looked upon as a great day among weather prophets; and, scattered here and there throughout the country, we find many curious proverbs associated with this day, of which the following are specimens :—

" If the **sun** shine through **the** apple-tree on Christmas Day there will **be** an abundant **crop in the** following year."

In Rutlandshire, it **is said** that "a green **Christmas** brings a heavy harvest." A full moon **about** Christmas Day was not considered **a good sign, hence it was** said—

> " Light **Christmas, light** wheatsheaf ;
> Dark **Christmas, heavy** wheatsheaf."

A **windy Christmas and a calm** Candlemas were held **as signs of a good year.** And rain during the twelve days **after Christmas was said to prognosticate** a wet **year.**

St. **Paul's Day (January 25th), or according to the** old style, February the **6th, was** looked **upon as** ominous :—

> " If Saint Paul's day **be** faire and **cleare,**
> It doth betide a happy yeare ;
> But if by chance it then should rain,
> It will make **deare** all kinds of graine ;
> And if ye **clouds make** dark ye skie,
> Then neats and fowles this year shall die ;
> If blustering winds do blow aloft,
> Then wars shall trouble ye realm full oft."

Bourne observes, upon St. **Paul's Day, "How it** came to **have this** particular knack of foretelling **the** good or ill-fortune of the following **year, is no** easy matter to find out. **The** monks, who undoubtedly were the first who made this wonderful observation, **have** taken care it should be handed **down to posterity,** but **why or for** what reason this observation **was to** stand good they have taken care to conceal. St. Paul did indeed labour more abundantly than all the Apostles ; but never, that I heard, in the science of astrology. And why his day therefore should be a standing almanack to the world, rather than the day of any other saint, will be pretty hard to find out."

Wind on St. Paul's Day, too, foretold wars, mist, famine, and pestilence. The weather of the whole year thus depending, says a writer in 'Whitaker's Journal' (1876, p. 77), on the humour in which St. Paul might chance to be on his feast day, the people made no scruple of showing their resentment if, by his wearing cloudy looks at such a time, he disappointed their hopes for the season. In many parts of Germany they dragged his statue down to the river on these occasions, and soused it well. In Alsace there is a common belief that on the evening of this day a fierce contest prevails among the winds, and the wind which proves victorious at midnight— the devil's dancing hour, by the way—will be the prevailing wind throughout the year. Gay, in his 'Trivia,' thus humorously speaks of St. Paul's Day :—

> " All Superstition from thy breast repel ;
> Let cred'lous boys and prattling nurses tell
> How, if the Festival of Paul be clear,
> Plenty from liberal horn shall strow the year ;
> When the dark skies dissolve in snow or rain,
> The lab'ring hind shall yoke the steer in vain ;
> But if the threat'ning winds in tempests roar,
> Then War shall bathe her wasteful sword in gore.'

Our ancestors generally regarded a wet February as the forerunner of a fine summer, and rain therefore during this month was looked upon as desirable :—

> " If February give much snow,
> A fine summer it doth foreshow."

According to another saying :—

> " All the months in the year,
> Curse a fair Februeer."

And again, "When gnats dance in February the husbandman becomes a beggar."

"Upon the whole," says Chambers ('Popular Rhymes of Scotland,' p. 365), "there is a prejudice against February in the Scottish mind." The pastoral people of Peeblesshire and Selkirkshire, say :—

> " Leap year
> Was never a good sheep year."

Ray tells us how—

> " The Welshman would rather see his dam on her bier,
> Than see a fair Februeer."

Candlemas day is rich in weather-lore, there being more proverbs relating to this day than to any other in the year. It is agreed on all sides that it must on no account be fine, for—

> " If Candlemas Day be fair and clear,
> There'll be twa winters in the year."

And the old Latin rhyme asserts :—

> " Si sol splendescat Maria purificante,
> Major erit glacies post festam, quam fuit ante."

In Scotland there are numerous rhymes much to the same purport :—

> " After Candlemas Day the frost will be more keen,
> If the sun then shines bright, than before it has been."

And once more :—

> " If Candlemas Day be dry and fair,
> The half o' winter's to come and mair ;
> If Candlemas Day be wet and foul,
> The half o' winter gane at Yule."

Shrove Tuesday, which falls sometimes in February, sometimes in March, according to the date of Easter, is not without its weather lore. Thus, when it thunders on this day, "it foretelleth wind, store of fruit, and plenty." Brand, quoting from a MS. miscellany, dated 1691, tells us that if the wind blows on this night it betokens " a death amongst them that are learned, and much fish shall die in following summer." An old proverb, too, informs us that "so much as the sun shines on Shrove Tuesday, the like will shine on every day in Lent."

It was commonly said that " Wherever the wind lies on Ash Wednesday, it will continue in that quarter during all Lent."

A wet March has been regarded as a bad omen, for, says the proverb—

> " A wet March makes a sad harvest."

Whereas—

> " A dry and cold March never begs its bread."

According to an old superstition, the weather at the end of March is always the exact opposite of that at the beginning, hence the familiar saying, " March comes in like a lion, and goes out like a lamb," which is sometimes transposed to suit the season. The Scotch form is, " March comes in with an adder's head, but goes out with a peacock's tail." Old St. Matthew's Day, the 8th of this month, is supposed to influence the weather. " St. Matthew breaks the ice ; if he finds none, he will make it."

The last three days of March are called the " Borrowing Days," said to have been a loan from April to March. The most common rhyme on the subject is the following :—

> " March borrows of April
> Three days, and they are ill ;
> April borrows of March again
> Three days of wind and rain.

> " March borrowed from April
> Three days, and they were ill ;
> The first was frost, the second was snaw,
> The third was cauld as ever't could blaw.

> " The first day was wind and weet ;
> The second day was hail and sleet ;
> The third day was birly banes,
> And knocked the wee birds' nibs agin the stanes."

There are various versions of this story. In north Ireland, says a writer in the 'Leisure Hour' (1876, p. 158), it is said that March had a spite against an old woman, and wished to kill her cow ; failing to do so in his own month, he borrowed three days of

April to enable him to complete the task, but whether he succeeded does not appear. In Scotland, the story varies by supposing he had a grudge against three pigs instead of a cow. In this case the result of all his attacks on them was that "the little pigs came hirpling hame." Sir Walter Scott, in a note to his 'Heart of Midlothian,' says, the three last days of March (old style) are called the borrowing days, for, as they are remarked to be unusually stormy, it is feigned that March had borrowed them from April to extend the sphere of his rougher sway. In an ancient Romish calendar quoted by Brand ('Popular Antiquities,' 1849, vol. ii. p. 41) there is an obscure allusion to the borrowing days. It is to the following effect:—"A rustic fable concerning the nature of the month; the rustic names of six days which shall follow in April, or may be the last of March."

Aubrey tells us that the vulgar in the West of England "do call the month of March, *Lide*," and quotes an old rhyme:—

> "Eat leekes in Lide, and Ramsins * in May,
> And all the year after Physitians may play."

A cold April was regarded by our forefathers as lucky for farming operations. Hence, the following rhymes:—

> "A cold April
> The barn will fill."

---

* Garlic.

And saying :—

> " Cold April gives bread and wine."

Thunder on All Fools' Day was held welcome :—

> " If it thunders on All Fools' Day,
> It brings good crops of corn and hay."

If the first three days of April be foggy, it prognosticates that there will be a flood in June. Easter Day is not without its superstitions. Thus :—

> " A rainy Easter betokens a good harvest."

Again :—

> "If the sun shine on Easter Day, it shines on Whitsunday likewise."

No reliance, however, can be placed on these prognostications, owing to the fact that the time of Easter varies so much.

We must not omit the following distich so well known, and one of the most familiar of our household words :—

> " March winds and April showers
> Bring forth May flowers."

In the north of England the agriculturists, making use of a different version, are wont to say :—

> " March dust, and May sun,
> Make corn white, and maidens dun."

The explanation is, says Chambers ('Popular Rhymes') that water in the month of March is supposed to be of a more cleansing quality than in any other month, as expressed in the proverb :—" March water is worth May soap."

May, from the uncertainty of the weather, has given rise to various proverbs :—

> " May, come she early or come she late,
> She'll make the cow to quake."

A common saying tells us :—

> " Till May be out
> Change not a clout."

That is, change not your winter clothing till the close of May. A good maxim, if we are to follow the advice of the great father of modern medicine, Boerhaave, who, on being consulted as to the proper time for putting off flannel, is said to have replied, "On Midsummer night, and put it on again next morning." There are various predictions respecting rain in this month. "Water in May is bread all the year." In Scotland it is said that :—

> " A leaky May and a dry June,
> Keeps the puir man's head abune."

This is also prevalent in England, under a slightly different form :—

> " A leaky May, and a warm June,
> Bring on the harvest very soon."

A warm May is considered unhealthy :—

> " A hot May makes a fat churchyard."

It has already been mentioned in a former chapter*
that it is supposed to be unlucky to marry in May,
and according to an old proverb :—

> " To wed in May is to wed poverty."

In the year 1857 there were fewer marriages in
Scotland in May than in any other month of the
year.

According to an old saying, "If it rains on Midsummer Eve, the filberts will be spoilt." Rain in
this month is considered lucky :—

> "A good leak in June
> Sets all in tune."

July is noted chiefly for the superstition attaching
to St. Swithin's Day — one which is most firmly
believed in, not only by common people, but by those
who lay claim to a fair amount of education :—

> " St. Swithin's Day, if thou dost rain,
> For forty days it will remain :
> St. Swithin's Day, if thou be fair,
> For forty days 'twill rain nae mair."

With respect to this superstition, Mr. Howard, the
meteorologist, observes : — "The notion commonly
entertained on this subject, if put strictly to the test
of experience of any one station in this part of the
island (London), will be found fallacious. To do
justice to popular observation, I may now state, that in
the majority of our summers a showery period, which,

---

* Marriage-lore.

with some latitude as to time and circumstances, may be admitted to constitute daily rain for forty days, does come on about the time indicated by this tradition ; not that any long space before is often so dry as to mark distinctly its commencement."

There is a quaint saying, to the effect that when it rains on St. Swithin's Day, it is the Saint christening the apples.

August has but little weather-lore. A common saying, which is self-obvious, remarks that :—

> "Dry August and warm,
> Doth harvest no harm."

August the 24th is St. Bartholomew's Day, and according to the following couplet :—

> "St. Bartholomew,
> Bringst the cold dew."

There are several rhymes connected with this day, which point it out as having a certain reputation among weather prophets :—

> "All the tears that St. Swithin can cry,
> St. Bartlemy's mantle wipes them dry."

Again :—

> "If the twenty-fourth of August be fair and clear,
> Then hope for a prosperous autumn that year."

The shepherd of Banbury alludes to the sudden storms that often prevail during August, and gives certain signs by which they may be prognosticated.

In harvest, when the **wind has been south** for two or three days, and it grows very hot, and you see clouds arise with great white tops, like towers, **as if one** were upon the top of another, **and** joined together with black on the nether side, there **will be thunder and** rain suddenly. If two such **clouds arise, one on either** hand, it is time **to make** haste to shelter.

Holy Rood **Day,** September 26th, is an important day in **Scotland, where it is** said to have the same influence **on succeeding weather as** St. Swithin's Day is supposed **to have with us.** Hence there is a popular **rhyme :—**

> " If dry be the buck's horn
>   On Holyrood morn,
>   'Tis worth a kist of gold ;
>   But if wet it be seen,
>   Ere Holyrood e'en,
>   Bad harvest is foretold."

The poor are also accustomed to say that " if the hart and the hind meet dry and part dry on Rood Day fair, for six weeks there'll be nae mair."

St. Matthew's **Day is said to bring** " the cold rain and dew," and—

> " The Michaelmas moon
>   Rises nine nights alike soon."

St. Simon and St. Jude's Feast (October 28th) was considered rainy by our ancestors, as well as that of St. Swithin. In an old play occurs the following passage :—" I know it as well as I know 'twill rain on Simon and Jude's Day." In another old play, too, we read, "Now a continued Simeon and Jude's rain beat all your feathers as flat down as pancakes." Holinshed curiously tells us that in the year 1536, when a battle was appointed to have been fought upon this day between the king's troops and the rebels in Yorkshire, so great a quantity of rain fell upon the eve thereof as to prevent the battle from taking place. October the 30th, old St. Luke's Day, often brings with it fine sunny weather, and consequently has received the name of "St. Luke's little summer." About this season the wild fruits come to their perfection, and beautify the landscape, now variegated with the rich hues of autumn. Weather prophets have, therefore, turned these to good account in their prognostications :—

> " Many haws,
> Many snaws ;
> Many sloes,
> Many cold toes."

"If the oak bear much mast (acorns) it foreshows a long and hard winter."

Ice and cold in November predict warm weather about Christmas. Hence the proverb, "If the ice bear a man before Christmas, it will not bear a mouse after." And again :—

> "If there's ice in November that will bear a duck,
> There'll be nothing after but sludge and muck."

There is a similar saying attached to Hallowe'en or
All Saints' Eve (October 31st) :—

> " If ducks do slide at Hollantide,
>   At Christmas they will swim ;
>   If ducks do swim at Hollantide,
>   At Christmas they will slide."

In the North of England, there is a curious rhyme
descriptive of the value of rain in the latter part of
the year :—

> " 'Tween Martinmas and Yule,
>   Water's wine in every pool."

Thunder in December prognosticates fine weather.
In some parts there is an old adage :—

> " Winter thunder,
>   Rich man's food and poor man's hunger."

It is a popular notion that a mild winter is less
healthy than a cold one.   Hence the saying :—

> " A green Christmas makes a fat churchyard."

The returns of the registrar-general, however, prove
that it is quite the contrary ; the mortality of the
winter months being always in proportion to the
intensity of the cold.*

From the foregoing pages, it will be seen how rich
in folk-lore our months are ; but, as Mr. Chambers

---

* Kelly's ' Proverbs of All Nations,' 1870, p. 215.

remarks in his ' Popular Rhymes of Scotland,' "the most sensible, after all, perhaps, of the meteorological rhymes is the following, which may be given as a wind up:—

> " To talk of the weather, it's nothing but folly,
>   For when it's rain on the hill, it may be sun in the valley."

CHAPTER XII.

BELLS.

AMONG our ancestors bells were a great object of superstition, and were supposed to possess many important virtues. Warner, in his 'Topographical Remarks on the S.W. Parts of Hampshire' (vol. ii. p. 162), enumerates some of these, citing from an old monkish rhyme :—

> " Men's death I tell
> By doleful knell.
> Lightning and thunder
> I break asunder.
> On Sabbath all
> To church I call.
> The sleepy head
> I raise from bed.
> The winds so fierce
> I doe disperse.
> Men's cruel rage
> I doe assuage."

Aubrey, in his 'Miscellanies,' tells us that it was once customary, whenever it thundered and lightened to ring St. Adhelm's Bell at Malmesbury Abbey. Lord Bacon, in his 'Natural History' (1635), refers to this olden superstition :—" It has anciently been reported, and is still received, that extreme applauses and

shouting of people, assembled in multitudes, have so
rarefied and broken the air, that birds flying over have
fallen down, the air not being able to support them ;
and it is believed by some, that great ringing of bells
in populous cities hath charmed away thunder, and
also dissipated pestilent airs. All which may be also
from the concussion of the air, and not from the
sound." Wynkin de Worde tells us that bells are
rung during thunderstorms, to the end that fiends and
wicked spirits should be abashed, and flee and cease
the moving of the tempest.

Bells are not without their legends. On the eve of
the feast of Corpus Christi, to this day, says a correspondent of Chambers's ' Book of Days ' (vol. ii.
p. 49), the choristers of Durham Cathedral ascend
the tower, and in their fluttering white robes sing the
Te Deum. This ceremony is in commemoration of
the miraculous extinguishing of a conflagration on
that night, A.D. 1429. The monks were at midnight
prayer when the belfry was struck by lightning and
set on fire ; but although the fire raged all that night
and until the middle of the next day, the tower
escaped serious damage, and the bells remained
uninjured ; an escape that was attributed to the
special influence of the incorruptible St. Cuthbert,
enshrined in the cathedral.

In some country villages it is customary to ring the
church bell while the congregation are leaving church.
The reason assigned for doing so, is to inform the

parishioners who have been unable to attend in the morning, that divine service will be celebrated in the afternoon. In scattered villages, or where a single clergyman had to perform the duties of more than one church, this was in days gone by quite requisite. It is sometimes called the "Pudding-bell," and according to some is rung in order to warn the cooks that dinner time is near at hand.*

In the old church at Ravenstonedale, Westmoreland, a small bell, called the "Saints'-bell," was formerly rung after the Nicene Creed, to call in the dissenters to the sermon.†

In the injunctions of Edward VI., quoted from Sparrow's Collection in Cranmer's Letters by Parker Society (p. 498), we find mention made of the "Sermon-bell":—"All ringing of bells shall be utterly foreborne at that time (Litany, Mass, &c.), except one bell in convenient time to be rung or knolled before the sermon."

The ringing of bells at marriages, as a sign of rejoicing, is common everywhere. At Kendal church, Westmoreland, there is the following inscription on the fifth bell :—

> " In wedlock bands
> All ye who join with hands,
>   Your hearts unite ;
> So shall our tuneful tongues combine
>   To laud the nuptial rite."

* See 'Notes and Queries,' 1st series, vol. ix. pp. 311, 567.
† Nicholson and Burn, 'History of Westmoreland,' 1777, vol. i. p. 524.

Bells were formerly baptized. Pennant, speaking of St. Winefride's Well, in Flintshire, tells us:—"A bell belonging to the church was also christened in honour of her. They laid hold of the rope; bestowed a name on the bell; and the priest sprinkling it with holy water baptized it in the name of the Holy Trinity; he then clothed it with a fine garment. Thus blessed, it was endowed with great powers, decayed all storms, diverted the thunderbolt, and drove away evil spirits."

In many places the pancake-bell was formerly— and still is—rung on Shrove Tuesday, to call the people together to confess their sins, or to be "shriven," or, as some have supposed, merely as a signal for people to commence frying their pancakes. At Daventry, Northamptonshire, it goes by the name of the "Pan-burn bell"; and at All Saints, Maidstone, it is known as the "Fritter-bell."

In Poor Robin's Almanack for 1684, we read:—

> "But hark, I hear the Pancake-bell,
> And Fritters make a gallant spell."

The origin and purpose of the Curfew-bell is too well known to need repetition. If we may believe the reporters, it was as important to ghosts as to living men;* it was their signal for walking, and their furlough lasted till the first cock. Fairies and others

* Nares' 'Glossary,' edited by Halliwell and Wright, 1872, vol. i. p. 216.

were under the same regulations ; hence Prospero says
of his elves, that they—

> " Rejoice
> To hear the solemn curfew."

The passing-bell, called also " the melancholy warning of the death crier," was formerly tolled for a person
who was dying. The custom is of very great antiquity, being alluded to by Bede :—

> " When the bell begins to toll,
> Lord, have mercy on the soul."

Douce thinks it was originally intended to drive away
the evil spirit that might be hovering about in
readiness to seize the soul of the deceased,* hence
it was called the " Soul-bell." Shakspeare, in his
' Henry IV.,' part ii., alludes to the practice :—

> " And his tongue
> Sounds ever as a sullen bell,
> Remember'd knolling a departed friend."

And Ray has the following couplet :—

> " When thou dost hear a toll or knell,
> Then think upon thy passing-bell."

Pennant tells us that in his time the peal after a
funeral was " a merry peal, rung at the request of the
relations ; as if, Scythian like, they rejoiced at the
escape of the departed out of this troublesome world."
Grose says that the passing-bell was anciently rung

* See chapter on Death.

for two purposes: one, to bespeak the prayers of all good Christians for a soul just passing away from life; the other to chase and drive away the evil spirits that stood round the bed to frighten and scare the soul in its passage. Bishop Hall, alluding to the reason for calling it the soul-bell, remarks:— "We call it the soul-bell because it signifies the departure of the soul, not because it helps the passage of the soul."

In some parts, on Holy Innocents' Day the church bells ring a half-muffled peal. This custom prevails in Somersetshire and Staffordshire. On the last night of the year the muffled peal is rung in various places, which is exchanged for a merry one as soon as the striking of the clock heralds in the new year.

Of what may be called * "the local ghosts of bells," many stories might be told. "Where the churches are said to have been swallowed up either by earthquake or ravages of the sea," says Mr. Glyde,† "the old church bells are said to ring, deep, deep in the earth, every Christmas morning, and people go forth and put their ears to the ground, hoping to catch the music of the mysterious chimes in the subterranean temple." Near Raleigh, in Nottinghamshire, there is a valley said to have been caused by an earthquake several hundred years ago, which swallowed up a

---

* Harland and Wilkinson, 'Lancashire Folk-Lore,' p. 44. See 'British Popular Customs,' p. 476.

† 'The Norfolk Garland,' 1872, p. 67.

whole village, together with the church. It was formerly customary for the inhabitants to assemble in this valley every Christmas Day to listen to the ringing of the church bells beneath them ; which, it was said, might be distinctly heard.

On the sands near Blackpool, out at sea, once stood the church and cemetery of Kilgrimal, long ago submerged. Wanderers near this spot are said, from time to time, to have been terrified by the " dismal chimes of the bells pealing over the murmuring sea."

CHAPTER XIII.

MISCELLANEOUS FOLK-LORE.

THE magical uses of pins are very curious, and not confined to our own country. Indeed Mr. Peacock informs us,* alluding to this subject, " that there is no class of superstition more widely spread—none that is to this hour more firmly rooted in the minds of our more ignorant poor." In some parts we find a curious rhyme :—

> " See a pin and pick it up,
> All the day you'll have good luck ;
> See a pin and let it be,
> All the day you'll have to cry."

Borlase, in his 'Natural History of Cornwall,' speaking of Madron Well, tells us :—" Here people who labour under pains, aches, and stiffness of limbs, come and wash, and many cures are said to have been performed. Hither also, upon much less justifiable errands, come the uneasy, impatient and superstitious, and by dropping pins or pebbles into the water, and by shaking the ground round the spring, so as to raise bubbles from the bottom, at a certain time of the year, moon, and day, endeavour to settle such doubts and inquiries as will not let the idle and anxious rest."

* 'Notes and Queries.'

At Derby, on July 15th, 1873, Benjamin Hudson was found guilty of having murdered his wife, and was sentenced to be hanged. In the murdered woman's pocket a purse was found which contained some pins and a piece of paper, on which the deceased had written :—

> " It is not these pins I mean to burn,
> But Ben Hudson's heart I mean to turn ;
> Let him neither eat, speak, drink, nor comfort find,
> Till he comes to me and speaks his mind."

Despite their quarrels and jealousies, says Cuthbert Bede (' Notes and Queries,' 4th series, vol. xii. p. 184), it would seem they had a certain strong affection for each other, and the " charm " was no doubt to regain her husband's love. In some counties a similar charm is often made use of by some unmarried person to compel the love of another, "to turn the heart" of the indifferent one.

The following extract from the ' Western Times ' (April 28th, 1877) describes a curious case of counteracting witchcraft by pin-sticking :—" Mr. Chown, cooper, of the parish of Honiton Clyst, owns some houses ; and a tenant of one of them having left, certain repairs were found necessary to prepare for the next. In carrying out the work the chimney had to be explored, and in the course of the operation there was found secreted a pig's heart stuck all over with thorn-prickles. This is said to be the third curiosity of the kind found here. It is supposed to have been done by direction of some 'white witch,' as a method of taking revenge on the witch to whose incantations the party considered some mischief due, in the belief that the heart of the ill-wisher would be pierced in like manner until it became as pulseless as that of the pig."

It is said to be extremely unlucky when soap slips out of a person's hand; and this superstition is widely spread. A correspondent of 'Notes and Queries' relates the following anecdote illustrative of this notion :—A woman in the Highlands, named Kate Elshender, *Anglicè* Alexander, went to a quarry-hole to wash her clothes. As she passed the village shop she went in and bought half a pound of soap, and proceeded to wash ; the soap slipped out of her hands, and she went back and bought another half pound. The shopkeeper warned her to be careful, remembering the old superstition, but she laughed, and went off again. It slipped again from her hands, and she returned for a third half pound of soap. This time the old woman in the shop was thoroughly frightened, and begged and prayed her not to go back again ; but she would go, in spite of everything that could be said to her. Shortly after, the old woman, being quite unable to rest in the shop, went away to the quarry. She found no one there, and the clothes lying on the side of the hole. She gave the alarm, and, on search being made, the said Kate Elshender was discovered, drowned, at the bottom of the quarry-hole.

"Cuthbert Bede," to whom the thanks of all those interested in folk-lore are due for the many valuable scraps of information he has recorded in that excellent periodical 'Notes and Queries,' tells us that he was told by a person in Rutlandshire that if you wash your hands in the same water in which another person has washed his hands, you should first make the sign of the cross over the water. If you neglect to do so, you will quarrel with that other person. This notion exists also in Devonshire, where an extra remedy is in use, i. e. spitting in the water. It is believed, too, in this county that if the palms of a baby's hands are washed before a certain age, the child will never have money.* In Cornwall, if the left palm of the hand itches, the person will have to pay money; if the right, to receive it.

There are a good many odd bits of folk-lore connected with salt. In the North it is considered unlucky to put it on another person's plate. Hence the saying :—

> " Help me to salt,
> Help me to sorrow."

The ill-luck is averted by a second help. Salt falling towards a person is said to be a bad omen. Mr. Pennant, in his 'Journey from Chester to London,' says :—" The dread of spilling salt is a known superstition among us and the Germans, being reckoned a presage of some future calamity, and particularly that

* See ' Report of Devonshire Association,' 1877, vol. ix. p. 90.

T

it forebodes domestic feuds ; to avert which it is customary to fling some **salt over the** shoulder into the fire, in a manner truly classical :—

> " Mollivit aversos Penates,
>   Farre pio, saliente mica." *

Grose, **alluding to this subject, says :—**"To scatter salt, **by overturning the vessel in** which it is contained, is **very unlucky, and portends** quarrelling with a friend, or **fracture of a** bone, sprain, **or** other bodily misfortune. **This** may in **some** measure be averted by throwing a small quantity **of it over one's** head." In the ' British Apollo ' **(1708), there are** some amusing lines :—

> " We'll tell you **the reason,**
>   **Why** spilling **of salt**
>   Is esteemed **such** a fault :
> **Because** it doth ev'rything **season.**
>   The antiques did opine
>   'Twas of friendship a sign,
> So serv'd it to **guests in decorum ;**
>   **And** thought love decay'd
>   When the negligent maid
> **Let** the salt-cellar tumble before them."

Leonardo **da Vinci, in his picture of** the Last Supper, has represented **Judas Iscariot** overturning the salt—a dark foreshadowing **of the** betrayal of our Blessed Lord.

If you wish to **see your lover, throw salt on** the fire

* Horat. lib. iii. Od. 23.

every morning for nine days, and repeat the subjoined rhyme :—

> " It is not salt I mean to burn,
>   But my true lover's heart I mean to turn,
>   Wishing him neither joy nor sleep,
>   Till he come back to me and speak."

This charm, if carefully attended to, is believed seldom to fail.

Eating salt was formerly said to excite anger, or to cause melancholy. Waldron, in his 'Description of the Isle of Man,' mentions a curious superstition. He says :—" No one will go out on any important business without taking salt in the pocket, much less remove from one house to another. Many will not put out a child, or take one to nurse, without salt being mutually interchanged; nay, although a poor creature be almost famished in the streets, he will not accept any food you may give him unless you join salt to the rest of your benevolence." " The reason," says Brand,* " ascribed by the inhabitants for this, is the account given by a pilgrim of the dissolution of an enchanted palace on the island occasioned by salt spilled on the ground."

A piece of superstition, that is perhaps almost more common than any, is that it is unlucky for thirteen to sit down together to dinner. This notion is prevalent on the Continent—in Russia and Italy. Moore, in his 'Diary' (vol. ii. p. 206), tells us that on one occasion

* ' Popular Antiquities,' vol. iii. p. 164.

when there were **thirteen at a dinner** party given by Madame Catalani, **a French countess,** who lived with her upstairs, was **sent for to remedy** the grievance.

Quetelet, on the 'Calculation of Probabilities,' has **shown the folly of this** superstition : **"For,"** says he, "if **the probability** be required, **that out of** thirteen persons of different ages, one of them at least shall die within **a year, it** will be found that the chances **are** about **one to one** that death at least will occur. This calculation, **by** means **of a** false interpretation, **has** given rise to **the** prejudice, no less ridiculous, that the danger will **be** avoided **by** inviting a greater number **of guests,** which can only have the effect **of** augmenting the probability of **the** event so **much** apprehended." In the 'Gentleman's Magazine' **(1796,** vol. lxvi. p. 573) **is an account of a** dinner party consisting of thirteen, **and of a** maiden lady's observation that, as none of her **married** friends were likely to make an addition to the number, she was sure that one of the company would die within the twelvemonth.

Poor people **in many parts** of the country consider it **highly unlucky** to leave, either lying about, or to throw **away, the** smallest piece of human hair, for fear birds should build their nests with it—a fatal thing **for** him or her from **whose** head it may have chanced **to fall.** If a magpie should **use it** for such a purpose, the person's death **"within year** and day" is sure. Some consider it ominous **when the** hair comes out in any large **quantities** as prognosticating misfortune of some kind **or** other. It is by no means an

uncommon notion—one, too, not confined to the uneducated classes—that a person's hair will turn gray
upon a "sudden and violent fright"; an allusion to
which is made by Shakspeare, in a speech of Falstaff
to Prince Henry :—

> "Thy father's beard is turned white with the news."

It is considered by some most unlucky to break a
looking-glass—the notion being that it prognosticates
a death in the family, especially that of the master.
In Cornwall, breaking a looking-glass is said to ensure
seven years of misfortune. Most of our readers are,
no doubt, acquainted with Bonaparte's superstition on
this point. During one of his campaigns in Italy, he
broke the glass over Josephine's portrait. So disturbed was he at this, as he thought, ominous occurrence, that he never rested until the return of the
courier, whom he forthwith despatched to convince
himself of her safety, so strong was the impression of
her death upon his mind.

Candles are not without their omens. "A collection
of tallow," says Grose, "rising up against the wick of
a candle, is called a winding-sheet, and regarded as
an omen of death in the family. A bright spark on
the candle wick indicates that a letter is coming to
the house, and that the person towards whom it
comes will be the one to receive it." "The time
of its arrival," says Hunt,* "is ascertained by striking
the bottom of the candlestick upon the table. If the

* 'Popular Romances of the West of England.'

spark comes off on the first blow, the letter will be received to-morrow, if two blows are required, the next day, and so on."

Dr. Goldsmith, in his 'Vicar of Wakefield,' speaking of the waking dreams of his hero's daughters, says :—
" The girls had their omens too, they saw rings in the candles."

The hands and finger nails have from the earliest times been the subject of superstition. Thus, Shakspeare, in ' Macbeth,' says :—

> " By the pricking of my thumbs,
> Something wicked this way comes."

A moist hand is vulgarly accounted * a sign of an amorous constitution ; whereas a dry hand is said to be one of the characteristics of old age. In West Cornwall, white specks on the nails are considered to foretell the arrival of presents, which may be looked for after the nail has grown sufficiently to admit of the speck being cut off. There is a popular rhyme in allusion to this piece of folk-lore :—

> " A gift on the finger
> Is sure to linger ;
> A gift on the thumb
> Is sure to come."

It is considered unlucky to cut a baby's nails until it is a year old ; consequently they are frequently

* Brand's ' Popular Antiquities,' vol. iii. p. 179.

bitten off. The reason assigned by some for this practice is, that if cut before a year old, the child will grow up a thief. The same notion exists in Germany, but a different cause is assigned, viz. lest the children should grow up to stammer.

The tingling of the ears is supposed by many to signify that some one is speaking of them, a belief which is very old indeed, dating as far back as the time of Pliny—the tingling of the right ear denoting that a friend is speaking, the tingling of the left an enemy. In Shakspeare's 'Much Ado about Nothing,' Beatrice says, "What fire is in mine ears," which Warburton explains as alluding to this superstition. Herrick, too, in his 'Hesperides,' has the following :—

"On Himselfe :

"One eare tingles ; some there be
That are snarling now at me ;
Be they those that Homer bit,
I will give them thanks for it."

In France, this superstition differs somewhat from ours, for the tingling of the left ear denotes the friend, and the tingling of the right ear the enemy.

In Cornwall, if the cheek burns, then some one is talking scandal of you. These lines are frequently made use of on such an occasion :—

" Right cheek !—left cheek !—why do you burn ?
Cursed be she that doth me any harm :
If she be a maid, let her be a slaid ;
If she be a widow, long let her mourn ;
But if it be my own true love—burn, cheek, burn."

One more instance of a wide-spread superstition, and our chapter shall close. A belief was formerly current throughout the country in the significance of moles on the human body. When one of these appeared on the upper side of the right temple above the eye, to a woman it signified good and happy fortune by marriage. This superstition was especially believed in in Nottinghamshire, as we learn from the following lines, which, says Mr. Briscoe,* were often repeated by a poor girl at Bunny :—

> " I have a mole above my right eye,
>   And shall be a lady before I die.
>   As things may happen, as things may fall,
>   Who knows but that I may be lady of Bunny Hall ? "

The poor girl's hopes, it is stated, were ultimately realized, and she became " Lady of Bunny Hall."

* 'Nottinghamshire Facts and Fictions.'

INDEX.

U

LONDON : PRINTED BY WM. CLOWES AND SONS, STAMFORD STREET & CHARING CROSS.